THE WHISPER HOUSE

C.S. Green is a bestselling author of psychological thrillers and an award-winning writer of fiction for young people under the name Caroline Green. Written under the name Cass Green, her first novel for adults, *The Woman Next Door*, was a No.1 ebook bestseller, while the follow-up, *In a Cottage in a Wood*, was a *USA Today* bestseller and a *Sunday Times* top ten bestseller. She is the writer in residence at East Barnet School and teaches courses for City University and Writers and Artists. She lives in London with her family. *The Whisper House* is the second volume in a new series featuring the UCIT.

🐦 @carolinesgreen

C S GREEN

THE WHISPER HOUSE

HarperCollins*Publishers*

HarperCollins*Publishers*
1 London Bridge Street,
London SE1 9GF

www.harpercollins.co.uk

HarperCollins*Publishers*
Macken House, 39/40 Mayor Street Upper,
Dublin 1, D01 C9W8, Ireland

This paperback edition 2023

1

Published by HarperCollins*Publishers* Ltd 2022

A catalogue copy of this book is available from the British Library.

ISBN: 9780008390853 (PB)

This novel is entirely a work of fiction.
The names, characters and incidents portrayed in it are
the work of the author's imagination. Any resemblance to
actual persons, living or dead, events or localities is
entirely coincidental.

Typeset in Meridien by Palimpsest Book Production Limited, Falkirk, Stirlingshire

Printed and Bound in the UK using
100% Renewable Electricity at CPI Group (UK) Ltd

MIX
Paper | Supporting
responsible forestry
FSC™ C007454

This book is produced from independently certified FSC™ paper
to ensure responsible forest management.

For more information visit: www.harpercollins.co.uk/green

"It watches," he added suddenly. "The house. It watches every move you make."
The Haunting of Hill House by Shirley Jackson

Prologue

He can't ignore the furious buzzing for a second longer. Throwing back the blanket, the boy crosses on bare feet to the windowsill, where he pauses to stare.

The bumblebee seems monstrously big against the smeared pane of glass that's causing its noisy frustration. The furry body looks so soft, he almost wants to stroke its back like it is a kitten rather than an insect, which he associates with spiders, even though he knows they are something else again. The bee is getting weaker now and it drops to the windowsill and crawls sluggishly, looking for an escape. It won't sting him, he thinks, but as he bends down to get a closer look, the bee emits a loud, angry buzz and his heart rate spikes thrillingly.

For a minute, there's only him and the bee in the whole world. All he has to do is open the window and let it fly free or give it some sugary water. He read that somewhere.

Moving ever so slowly, so as not to startle the little creature, he reaches into his pocket for the handkerchief that is balled up there and begins to wrap it around his hand. Tying it into a knot, he examines it until he's satisfied.

The action itself is fast, a slamming down of his whole palm so he feels the slight resistance, like the breaking of tiny bones, even though – of course – there are no bones to break.

1

Peeking underneath, he's surprised the bee is not as flat as he might have expected.

But it's definitely dead.

The warm satisfaction is like the aftermath of drinking hot cocoa, not that he's had that for some time now. It's a temporary distraction from the resentment that constantly burns inside him anyway. A moment of being the one in control.

Taking off the handkerchief, he adjusts his focus from this tiny drama and stares down from the attic window to the garden below.

There he is. The object of a hatred so intense, it scares him sometimes.

Lifting his thumb, the boy places it so it completely obscures the man below.

He presses until his nail floods bright with blood. It's easy to imagine the satisfying 'squish' of bone and flesh beneath his thumb.

1

The roadworks outside hadn't seemed that bothersome first thing. But over the course of this morning, the pneumatic drills have moved across the roundabout, through the car park, into the building, and directly into Detective Constable Rose Gifford's brain.

At least, that's how it feels.

Squinting against the headache that squeezes her temples, she notes the time on the large railway clock on one wall and sighs. Can it really be so early?

Rose gazes over at Scarlett, the division's civilian admin officer whose bright blonde head is currently bent over her desk as she writes something down. Her other colleague, DC Adam Lacey, is also hard at work. He seems to spend most of his time trawling through records and researching the kind of crimes they investigate here at UCIT, the Uncharted Crimes Investigation Unit.

Such a sensible sort of word, 'uncharted'. Rose much prefers it to anything less euphemistic – more direct – like, for example, 'supernatural'. That's a concept she fought hard to deny all her life until the end of last year, when she could no longer pretend that there weren't more things in heaven and earth. And more importantly, that some of them were out to cause crimes and hurt the public.

Not for the first time this week, or even today, Rose finds herself wondering what she would be doing right now if she were back in her old job with the Murder Investigation Team at Angel Street police station. She wouldn't have time for all this *thinking*, that's for sure.

Picturing her old sergeant, DS Colin Mackie, slowly typing with two fingers, brow furrowed in concentration, she feels a little ache in her sternum.

Mack was her mentor, the provider of quiet wisdom and, most of all, her mate. Rose has never known her father but Mack is probably the closest thing she has ever had to one. She hasn't seen him for months and it's not through a lack of trying on his part. He keeps inviting her over for dinner, but she has made a whole series of excuses about being too busy. Lies, really. It's not that she doesn't want to see him. It's simply that she knows what he would say. 'So how is the ghost-busting going, kiddo?'

Well-meant, of course. But that joke ran its course within about ten seconds of her accepting the job here at UCIT, which runs out of an old Water Board building on the farthest northern outskirts of London. But he'll also be able to see, with that annoying Dad-radar or whatever it is, that she isn't that happy in her new role.

It's only Mack from her old office who knows the true nature of her job now. As far as the others are concerned, she's moved into a department that deals with the highly dry business of compliance training.

Some of her friends and colleagues probably think this was a self-imposed demotion, a stepping back into a quiet, unthreatening job after a serial killer called Dr James Oakley kidnapped and then murdered her. For three and a half minutes, anyway, until she was revived by ambulance staff.

Rose is knocked out of her contemplation by another distinctive vibration in the air outside. It's the sound of her boss, Detective Sergeant Sheila Moony, arriving on her motorbike in the car park.

Nice of her to grace us with her presence, Rose thinks.

When she accepted this job, a few months ago, she'd felt that while Moony was a little hard to like, she seemed like someone Rose could really learn from. But the truth is that she's barely ever here.

Her thoughts are interrupted by Moony bursting into the office, cheeks rosy and her small dark eyes bright with the promise of . . . something. The leathers that enclose her short, stocky frame creak slightly as she hurries across the office.

'Gather up, people,' she says, walking to her desk and beginning to peel off the leather jacket. She fans her face. 'Christ,' she says, 'thought I'd put hot flushes behind me, but I'm bloody sloshing in here.'

Rose can't help comparing this sort of earthy talk with that of her old boss, the always cool and restrained DCI Stella Rowland. Judging by the atmosphere when the two women briefly crossed paths last year, there was no love lost between them.

Moony goes to the small briefing area, which is on the far side of the large office, and waits for Rose, Adam and Scarlett to come over.

'Okay,' she says, when everyone is assembled. 'I've been contacted by Kentish Town CID about something that may or may not be for us.'

'The suspense is killing me,' says Adam with a yawn. Rose suppresses a laugh when she sees the expression on Moony's face. For all her earthy tell-it-like-it-is approach, she doesn't have much of a sense of humour.

'All right, all right,' she says, 'I know we've had slim pickings lately, but that's how it is sometimes. Let's focus on this.'

She writes, '*42 Wyndham Terrace*', on the whiteboard in her messy, slanting handwriting and turns back to the small, assembled group. 'So, a family of three living at this address have been reporting neighbour harassment on and off for the last year to the local force. They have investigated and repeatedly attempted to find any evidence of criminal behaviour but have managed to turn up nothing.'

'What sort of harassment are we talking about?' says Rose.

'Noise, mainly,' says Moony. 'The family say there's constant banging on the walls at all hours. Really loud banging. But there was something about rubbish on the front steps too.'

'Sounds like half of London could complain about that kind of thing,' says Adam.

'Well,' says Moony, 'the neighbours deny everything.'

'Right,' says Rose. 'So far, so standard. What does this have to do with UCIT?'

Moony gives a small smile and raises her eyebrows. 'That's the thing,' she says. 'The mother thinks it might be a poltergeist.'

There's a pause before Adam breaks the silence.

'And we think they aren't nutters because . . .?'

Moony appears deflated at the lack of enthusiasm she is witnessing from her colleagues and her expression turns stony.

'Well, we don't know!' she says. 'They might be. But there's a twelve-year-old kid. Social services have nothing much on the family, but we might be able to ascertain exactly what's going on there if we go in and have a nosy.'

'At the very least,' says Rose, 'I guess we can make sure the kid is okay.'

'Gold star to DC Gifford,' says Moony. 'Knew there was a reason I hired you.' She grins, revealing the snaggle tooth at the front of her mouth, then continues. 'Anyway, they've just been in touch with Kentish Town again – something about the garden this time – who've handed it over. Lucky us, eh?'

Rose practically runs to the door with her car keys in her hand, such is her relief at getting out on a job. Adam is right behind her. Moony says something vague about a 'funding meeting'.

How a department like UCIT can exist in a time when most forces, including the Met, have been slashed to the bone had been a source of puzzlement to Rose when she first heard of its existence. She has since learned from Scarlett that the reason it exists at all is because it is mostly funded by a bequest from an individual who was the chief superintendent of a Cheshire police force with an independent income. The man, Henry Tolhurst, had been passionately interested in new approaches to assessing crime after his wife and child seemed to disappear into thin air one night when he was sleeping in the house.

There had been no suggestion of his involvement and a thorough investigation had revealed absolutely no promising leads. Tolhurst had become obsessed with solving the case and when he died at his own hand, he had left instructions for his inheritance to be invested in a police department that would investigate esoteric and 'off-grid' crimes. But funding rules meant that some part of the salaries of Moony, Adam and Rose come from the public purse and so Moony still has to take part in the usual budgetary meetings. There seem to be a lot of these lately.

As Rose pulls out of the car park, they are almost immediately stopped at a temporary traffic light, courtesy of the roadworks that have been making her morning hellish.

She drums her fingers on the steering wheel as she waits for the lights to change, conscious that she hasn't been on a car journey with Adam before. His right thigh is disconcertingly close to her hand resting on the handbrake and for a fraction of a second she pictures herself leaning over and placing her palm there, feeling the swell of his muscle, honed from a good deal of running when he isn't at work or wrangling kids.

The image is so vivid, she almost snatches her hand away. Rose turns her head to hide the creep of fire up her cheeks.

Rose's blush-inducing, groin-twanging crush on her colleague is one of the many parts of her life she would dearly like to change. Adam is a single father and she works in close proximity with him. There is literally nothing that screams 'good idea' about imagining something could happen outside of the office. Not that there's any reason to think he sees her as anything other than a slightly grumpy new workmate anyway.

'Right,' says Adam, scrolling through on his phone. 'Let's see what we have on this property from colleagues at Kentish Town.'

He runs through the family details. Anton and Gwen Fuller, parents of twelve-year-old Gregory. Anton Fuller is a teacher and Gwen Fuller is down as 'housewife and mother'.

The first call to the police came six months ago, when they claimed neighbours wouldn't stop banging on the walls. Local officers had a word with the family living on that side in the relevant flat, but any misdemeanours were strenuously denied. Three similar calls followed over the next month, then the complaint came in about the rubbish being tipped in the back garden. The latest call-out was about supposed banging on the walls again.

Adam puts down his phone. 'I'm not convinced this is going to be anything other than the usual sort of toxic neighbour nonsense,' he says, 'but if the boss insists . . .'

He lets the rest of the sentence die out.

'Do you know that area much?' Rose says.

'Kentish Town?' Adam frowns. 'I've been to gigs at the Forum over the years.' He pauses. 'And my ex grew up in Highgate, which isn't far. So yeah, spent a fair bit of time there in my youth, I guess.'

Rose snatches a glance in his direction. She knows Adam is divorced and has two girls, Tandi and Kea, whom he worships. She's longing to ask more about the ex, but how to pull off casual interest, that's the tricky part.

But she doesn't get a chance.

'So how are you finding the wonderful world of UCIT then?' says Adam. 'Haven't really had the chance to check in with you properly since you started.'

Rose pretends to be concentrating on the road, as the traffic on the North Circular slows and comes to a stop. It's a bright, sunny day in March and spring is in the air, but the light is merely an assault to Rose's eyes. She seems to sleep in snatches of three hours at a time these days and never properly feels rested. Sometimes she thinks she never will again.

'Oh, well,' she says with a vague laugh, 'I'm still settling in, I guess.'

Adam shakes his hand as though he's touched something too hot.

'Ouch!' he says. 'Is that you being all diplomatic?'

Rose laughs again, despite herself. 'Well, do you want me to be honest?'

'Always.' She looks across and his brown eyes are trained on her, with a softness in them that makes her quickly look away again.

She blows air out slowly through her lips. 'Okay, well you asked,' she mutters, then: 'I don't really know whether it's for me. I'm used to working MIT and it's a bit of a culture shock to be somewhere so . . .' she hesitates '. . . dead. No pun intended.'

Adam winds the window down a little, letting in a blast of cool, traffic-fumy air. 'Yeah,' he says, 'can't argue with you there. But . . .' He abruptly stops, prompting Rose to glance over again.

'What?'

'I don't know,' he says, 'something's going on with Moony at the moment. She's not normally so distant.'

'What do you think it is?'

'I've got no idea,' says Adam, 'but she's had some very mysterious phone calls and been a bit snappy when I've tried to probe.'

Rose is silent for a moment. 'Well,' she says, 'if it's something juicy, I hope to God she lets us in on it.'

Adam is fiddling with his phone now.

'Yeah,' he says, distracted. 'And maybe this so-called poltergeist thing will give us something to be working on.'

She smiles at him. 'You said "poltergeist" like it was an effort.'

He laughs. 'Yeah, I did, didn't I?'

'That doesn't seem like a very UCIT-y attitude?' says Rose. This is possibly the most 'real' conversation she has had since she started.

'Put it this way,' says Adam, 'I originally wanted to be a scientist. If there is a rational, real-world explanation for something, then we are going to make damn sure we find that.'

'No lazy assumptions, in other words?' says Rose, feeling a tug of intense gratitude towards the man next to her. This sounds like real police work in a new and confusing world and it's the thing she's been craving.

'No lazy assumptions,' he says and holds up a fist. Rose bumps her own knuckles to his with a laugh, then turns away to hide the flush brought on by the touch of his skin.

2

It is one of those parts of North London where two very different worlds live shoulder to shoulder within the same narrow post-code. At one end of the long, curving road that is Wyndham Terrace, there are Porsches and BMWs, the houses freshly painted, with bright spring flowers in neat iron window boxes. But as they get to the other end, a distinct air of shabbiness takes over.

Some houses have grubby blankets across the windows, or flags, both the English variety and from countries Rose can't identify. The small front gardens are filled with rubbish in several properties, including one that has an entire upended sofa, ripped open like some massive roadkill, metal guts splayed.

Number 42 is in better condition but has a neglected air nevertheless, its off-white window frames peeling. All the houses here are four storeys high. Adam whistles as he looks up.

'This would cost you a couple of million, whatever state it's in on the inside,' he says.

Before Rose can reply, the door of number 42 opens and a young woman hurries out, holding a woolly scarf over the lower part of her face. She's barely in her twenties, with a pale blue bobble hat pulled over long fair hair. Her pretty, wide-eyed face is clearly creased through the effort of trying not to cry. The door has been closed forcefully behind her.

She glares at them as she hurries down the stairs and almost pushes past.

'Everything okay?' says Rose, stepping to one side.

The woman looks back at her and lets out a torrent of what is clearly French. Rose's own GCSE grade C isn't up to the task, beyond the word '*enculè!*', which wasn't on the curriculum, but Rose is fairly sure means 'arsehole'.

The young woman is still muttering as she stomps away, pulling a mobile out of her pocket and stabbing furiously at the screen.

They exchange amused, slightly curious glances, and are about to climb the stairs when there's a sudden movement at the window. Someone had been looking out and has abruptly pulled the net curtain shut again.

Rose presses the old-fashioned circular doorbell and waits.

After a few moments, the door opens. A tall, thickset woman with a ruddy complexion and short, thin, greyish hair regards them warily. She looks in her mid-forties but could be older; it's hard to tell. Judging by the redness around her eyes, she has either been crying, or is close to doing so.

'If you're collecting for something, then it's really not . . .'

Adam holds up his ID, and her eyes widen.

'We're helping colleagues at Kentish Town station, who I believe you've been in contact with recently?'

The woman's shoulders drop and she runs a hand across her face. 'Oh,' she says. 'You'd better come in then.'

They walk into a gloomy hallway that's lined with a dark mustard wallpaper. The walls are hung with small, framed prints of birds and landscapes in washed-out colours.

Rose feels a cold fluttering in her stomach. Glancing around, she notices a pale face peering at her through the banister at the top of the stairs. It's a boy, his eyes like saucers behind unfashionable glasses, and it reminds her of herself, doing exactly this as a child, looking down on the adult drama below. It's a disquieting feeling.

They follow the woman down the hallway, easing past a bright blue bicycle with a jaunty basket on the front. She is wearing a patterned shapeless dress and her cracked heels slip-slop in large Birkenstock sandals as she leads them through a kitchen-diner and to a back door.

Rose absent-mindedly rubs the inside of her arm, which has begun to itch intensely. It's an unwanted quirk, the way her skin responds to unusual atmospheres, or anywhere there is great stress. Unfortunately, since she'd had to draw blood there while trying to escape from James Oakley last year, the skin never seems to be fully healed now.

'I suppose you know I'm Gwen Fuller,' the woman says, turning to look back at them. Rose and Adam introduce themselves. 'I'd better introduce you to my husband.'

They follow her out into the back garden, where a tall, imposing man with a dark beard and glasses is staring down the garden.

'Darling?' says Gwen in a high, bright voice. 'The police are here.'

He turns, glowering. 'Another visit from the pointless squad, is it?' he says. 'Or are you finally going to do something?'

Gwen Fuller's cheeks go a little pinker. 'Darling . . .' she says again but it's not really a warning and she trails off.

The man gives a theatrical sigh. 'Anton Fuller,' he says. 'And you are?'

'I'm DC Rose Gifford and this is my colleague DC Adam Lacey. Colleagues from Kentish Town asked us to pop by. Can you tell us what's been going on here?'

Anton makes a sound of impatience and passes his hand through his thick, dark brown hair, which is swept high off his forehead. Dressed in a green sleeveless jumper over a checked shirt and a knitted red tie, he exudes pomposity. And judging by the way his dark brown eyes behind their wire-framed glasses rove up and down Rose's body, he's a bit of a creep too.

'Well, have a look for yourselves,' he says.

It's only now that Rose properly takes in the garden. It's long and narrow, with a wall on one side and a slatted wooden fence on the other.

It's like many other urban gardens.

But something is . . . off, which she doesn't immediately identify.

The first thing she notices is that the long flowerbed along the right-hand side of the garden is filled with some sort of thick green plant, all neatly cut at the same height. But that's when her eye is drawn to the bright splash of yellow at the far end of the garden.

The daffodil heads are in a big circular pile, very evenly spaced, like some sort of flower arrangement on the ground. Like a funeral wreath, she realizes with a jolt of shock.

She looks at Adam, who wears the same puzzled expression as her own and they both turn to Fuller. Angry energy burns off him.

'Oh for God's sake!' he explodes. 'Can't you see? You surely don't think I did this myself!'

'What exactly has happened, Mr Fuller?' says Adam. 'With the flowers?'

Fuller runs a hand through his thick hair in frustration. 'Someone has cut all the heads off my daffodils,' he says, 'if it really needs spelling out! And laid them in that rather disturbing way!'

Adam goes to the edge of the flowerbed and crouches down, peering intently. He gets a small black device out of his pocket and fiddles with it, still looking carefully at the damaged plants.

Getting back up he says, 'They've been cut incredibly neatly.'

Fuller's eyes are almost popping out of his head now. 'If you're suggesting I got my Flymo out and butchered my own plants then I don't know why you bothered coming!'

'No one is saying that,' says Rose. 'We're just trying to understand what happened.'

'Then there's the swing!' says Fuller, as if she hasn't spoken. 'What do you make of that bit of mischief?'

Rose and Adam look to the far corner of the garden, near a shed, where they see a child's swing that's twisted and appears out of use.

'Take a closer look,' says Fuller. 'Go on.'

They walk down the garden and stop in front of it. It takes a moment to see what he was referring to. And it's very odd indeed.

She remembers as a kid twisting a swing round and round until the chains were bunched and tight, then letting go in a euphoric spin.

But this is like someone with great strength has twisted the chains together, impossibly tightly, and somehow got them to remain static. The blue plastic seat is tipped at an angle. The air around the swing has a feeling of stillness, as though someone has pressed pause on a recording.

'Has this been glued in position or something?' says Adam, gently touching the bunched metal with an outstretched finger. It doesn't budge.

'You tell me,' says Fuller. 'But it's clearly some sort of practical joke by that idiot next door.'

'Are you referring to a Mr Eric Quinn at number 40?' says Adam, looking at his phone then glancing over at that property. The fence is low enough that climbing over would be possible but tricky, especially as there is a rickety trellis with climbing plants along one side.

'That's him,' says Fuller, mouth turned down, as though the thought literally tastes bad.

'Your garden looks relatively secure though,' says Adam. 'How do you propose he got back here?'

'Well, *I* don't know, do I?' says Fuller. 'Isn't that your job?'

There's a moment of silence.

'Could it have been anyone who's been in the house?' says Rose.

Fuller clears his throat. 'Well . . .' He falters. 'I did . . . well, I did wonder if it was my son's French tutor. But on reflection I think that's unlikely.'

Gwen, silent during this whole exchange, stares down at her own feet as if there is something fascinating between her long, pale toes.

'Was that the woman we saw leaving just now?' says Rose.

Anton Fuller doesn't respond straight away and for a moment his expression is utterly desolate. He looks exhausted. 'Probably,' he says, quieter now. 'We had a little . . . falling-out. It may not, in retrospect, have been my finest hour. But we're all getting a bit ragged, you see?'

'What about that shed?' says Adam. 'Have you looked in there?'

'Of course I have,' says Fuller. 'There's no one hiding in there if that's what you're thinking.'

'Mind if we take a look anyway?' says Adam.

'I suppose not,' says Fuller. 'Get the key, will you, Gwen.'

Gwen scurries off and there's silence until she returns a few moments later.

'Here it is.' She hands a key to her husband, who strides off to open the shed.

Inside it is neat and tidy, with the usual things inside: a lawn mower, a work table with tools on the top. Various boxes.

'No obvious sign that anyone has been hanging out in here,' says Adam quietly.

'Exactly,' says Fuller. 'Just as I said.'

'Look,' says Gwen, chafing her arms although it isn't an especially cold day. 'Shall we go inside and have some tea? I think we need it.'

Rose is about to reply when a gentle creaking sound behind makes them turn back.

The swing violently jerks into life, spinning so fast they simply watch, mutely. Finally, it slows, then gently sways one way and the other, before coming to a total stop. It's like someone has a hand placed, just *so*, to prevent further movement, even though it's a breezy day. It's hard to know what's more disconcerting: the unexplained movement, or the utter stillness that follows behind.

'Maybe you dislodged it when you touched it?' says Fuller, but he sounds doubtful.

'Maybe,' says Adam, clearly not convinced either.

Gwen makes a small sound in her throat, and then manages

to squeak out the word, 'Tea!' before marching back towards the house.

'Excuse me for a moment,' says Anton when they are inside again. 'I need to remind our son about something. I'll be right back.'

He heads off up a flight of stairs. There's no sign of the boy now.

Rose and Adam are directed down the hallway to a dining room. It is decorated with dark burgundy wallpaper. A large piano sits near some French windows and they are invited to sit at a mahogany, oval dining table. All the furniture feels too big for the space it occupies, like it came from a much bigger and older property. The sound of someone haltingly playing a violin – presumably the child – drifts from somewhere upstairs.

They both look around the room. The mantelpiece is lined with pictures of the boy, from when he was a tiny, red-faced bundle in a white blanket, held by a beaming and much younger-looking Gwen, through toddlerhood in a series of poses, to gap-toothed smiles in karate gear and holding up a variety of medals. The most recent is a school picture in which the boy isn't smiling.

One of the photos catches Rose's eye and she takes a closer look. Shock jolts through her. The picture is of Gwen, a man who might be Anton, and the boy. Gwen is sitting on a beach and shading her eyes while looking into the camera with a smile, while the same small boy grins up from a sandcastle. But the man in the photo has had his eyes removed with two perfect circular holes.

'Adam,' murmurs Rose. 'Take a look . . .'

He comes to her side and bends to look at the picture. 'Bloody hell—' he murmurs and goes to say something else but Gwen comes into the room then with a rattling tray. She's already halfway through a sentence.

'. . . it's lapsang souchong. I hope that's all right. It's not to everyone's taste but it's Anton's favourite.'

Catching sight of the framed photo in Rose's hand, she looks puzzled, glancing between her and Adam.

'Everything all right?' she says, placing the tray on the table. Rose falters.

Frowning, Gwen reaches for the picture, then she lets out a small cry and almost drops it. 'Oh my God,' she says and flaps a hand around her face as though physically waving away potential tears. This isn't entirely successful. Her nose reddens and she has to sink her face into a large handkerchief she pulls from a pocket in her dress. 'That's horrible. I mean, honestly. I can't take much more.'

'Why don't we sit down,' says Adam gently. 'We can have some of that tea and chat further about all this.'

'Yes, yes, of course,' she says, clearly fighting tears as she sinks into a chair opposite them. The tray contains a proper teapot with Chinese art on it and delicate cups and saucers. A plate with some kind of plain biscuits is balanced next to a sugar bowl and a proper milk jug. All this effort for one simple cuppa.

'What do you think happened to the photo?' says Rose as Gwen pours tea with slightly shaking hands.

'I have no idea,' says Gwen. 'I haven't looked at it for a while, so I don't know how long it's been like that. But I,' she falters, 'I suspect that it's all just part of the same . . . harassment. I mean, you saw what happened outside.'

Adam takes the offered cup of tea and pours – in Rose's opinion – enough milk that it should be a criminal offence. She takes her own and adds a tiny dash before settling her gaze on the woman opposite.

The violin caterwauls on, then comes to an abrupt stop.

'But how can your neighbours possibly have done this?' says Rose. 'Do they have access to the house?'

'No. I mean, I don't know,' says Gwen, then lowers her voice even further. 'I'm not really sure it's anything to do with them, but Anton hates me saying that.' Her eyes dart about. 'It's all a little . . . hard to explain.'

'I want to assure you that our division is all about the—' Adam hesitates '—harder-to-explain cases. You really can tell us anything, however unusual it may sound.'

Gwen shoots him a suspicious look, brows knitted.

'Can you go right back to the beginning?' says Adam, his tone kind. 'When did what you call the "harassment" begin?'

Gwen takes a miserable sip of her tea, her eyes and mouth downcast. She's evidently still struggling with control as she reaches for a biscuit, takes a bite, and then puts it down on her saucer with a precise neatness, despite her large fingers. It strikes Rose that she has had to learn this delicacy.

'About six months ago,' she says. 'It started with the banging. I say banging, but it's so loud. Almost like the wall is going to come down. You can actually see it bowing with the strain. I don't even know how they could physically do that! We had a word with our neighbours and they denied they'd done anything. They claimed it was *us* who was making all the noise! Things got—' she bites off the end of her sentence, before swallowing and continuing '—a little tense. My husband, he, well he has a *very* important job and it was making him ill.'

'What does he do?' says Rose.

Gwen seems to sit up a little straighter. 'He is the head of Year Ten at Beamishes,' she says with obvious pride.

'The Beamish School?' says Adam. Rose has never heard of it, but Adam looks a little impressed.

Gwen nods. 'He has been there for twenty years and is one of the most senior teachers,' she says, then repeats, 'He works very hard. Gregory is in Year Seven.'

'Okay . . .' says Rose, hoping to move on from how important and impressive Anton Fuller is and back to the issue at hand. 'When you say things got tense with the neighbours, what exactly do you mean?'

Gwen fusses with a thin gold cross at her throat, where the skin grows pinker by the moment. As a fellow blusher, Rose can almost sense the rising heat from the other side of the table.

'Well . . .' Gwen pauses again. 'There was a little bit of an altercation one evening between Anton and Eric at number 40. Things got a little . . . physical.'

'They had a fight?' says Adam.

'Well, it wasn't a big thing,' says Gwen, eyes widening, 'only a scuffle. You know how men can get when they're defending their property!'

Neither of them respond. Rose feels a lick of satisfaction that Adam is on the same page with this interview. The working telepathy she had with Mack is one of the things she has been missing most. She senses that Gwen will close up if she has to focus too much on the fight, which they can easily verify later. But she makes a mental note to look for any police reports from that incident, and to speak to the neighbours.

She focuses again as Adam asks Gwen what happened next.

'There was an upturned rubbish bag in the garden,' she says, 'which we were pretty certain was down to that lot next door. More and more of the terrible banging. All this should be in your notes.' She pauses and chews on her bottom lip before continuing. 'But then some other things began happening and it all got a little more, well, strange.' She gives an embarrassed laugh and twists the cross the other way. The tips of her fingers whiten as she presses hard on the thin metal shape. It's a wonder she doesn't break it.

'In what way, strange?' says Adam.

Gwen lets out a shaky sigh. 'Gregory, our son, he was the one affected at first. Bad dreams, you know, but we dismissed that. He's a very highly strung and intelligent boy – in all the top sets – and he can be prone to . . .' she pauses '. . . imaginative episodes.' She takes a long sip of her tea, bobbing her head almost in apology as she does so. Rose lifts her own cup to her lips and the strange fishy whiff rising up is enough to make her lower it again.

'So Gregory kept saying someone was yanking his bedclothes off him at night. We thought this was just a nightmare. I mean, people can imagine all sorts of strange things when they're half asleep, can't they? Things that seem terrifying are only dreams, really.'

It takes every drop of effort in Rose's body not to look at Adam at these words.

Oh, Gwen, she thinks, *if only you knew.*

Not only did Rose almost die at the hands of Oakley, who had been haunting women with sleep disorders by astrally projecting into their nightmares before killing them, but Rose had been putting up with a range of night-time visitations from her own dead mother for quite some time.

'But then,' Gwen goes on, her speech coming faster now. 'Then there was the door-knocker going crazy, with no one there. We even put CCTV in and could see that it was happening with not a soul around. There have been other things too, but Anton thinks that it's all—'

As the large, hulking presence of Anton Fuller enters the room again, they all seem to tense at once.

'For God's sake, woman, you're not on that nonsense again?'

'Oh, Anton,' she says in a disappointed tone, and begins fussing about, pouring tea. 'I just thought it might—'

'If I hear one more word about ghosts—' snaps Anton, leaving the rest of the sentence dangling. But it sounded worryingly like a threat.

Rose meets his gaze.

'How do you explain what's been happening?' she says. 'I take it you don't agree with your wife about the cause?'

Anton Fuller hitches his trousers at the knees then sits at the table.

'It's very clear to me,' he says, with a grimace. 'I think you lot should do your jobs and charge our neighbours with harassment, as I have been saying for six months.'

'Mr Fuller,' says Adam patiently. 'You should be aware that this has been quite thoroughly investigated by our colleagues and they could find no criminal activity on the part of your neighbours. I don't even see how they could have got in to do that to your swing, or to cause damage inside the house.'

Anton looks at Adam for what might be the first time now. Rose senses a moment, so fleeting she almost isn't sure if it was there, of distaste flashing across his face like a shadow. *Wow,* she thinks, *a pompous slimeball and racist too.*

'What damage?' he says.

'This,' says Gwen and gets up to pass behind where Rose and Adam are sitting.

She lifts the butchered photo and holds it up for him to see. His expression doesn't change. The only tells of how he is feeling are a flaring of his nostrils and the fact that he squeezes both his palms momentarily into fists, before letting them go again.

'Gregory!' The sudden bark makes everyone flinch.

'Darling, I really don't think . . .' says Gwen but doesn't finish her sentence.

The boy from the stairs appears at the door so fast, it's clear he was lurking outside for the whole conversation.

'Yes, Daddy?' he says in a fluting voice. He looks younger than twelve, with thin, hunched shoulders and a pointed, serious face. He sniffs ripely, then fumbles in his pocket and produces a crumpled hankie: the old-fashioned cloth kind.

'Did you do this?' Anton holds the picture aloft. The boy peers at it then blanches. One of his hands flies to his mouth and he begins to nibble on his nails.

'Nails, darling!' says Gwen in a breezy tone that's entirely out of place in the general atmosphere.

Rose and Adam exchange looks.

'I didn't do it, Daddy,' says the boy, then, in a tinier voice again. 'It's the house that's doing it all – I told you.'

'Don't start that "house" nonsense,' says Anton. 'You're as bad as your mother. I've told you about this before. And stop lingering outside doorways when adults are speaking. Go and get on with that violin practice. I shall be wanting to hear your progress later.'

The child pauses, then exits the room quickly. They hear another bout of wet sniffing then the thump-thump-thump of feet ascending stairs.

'We're all a bit exhausted, as I said,' says Anton again. 'It's the noise. It's affecting us all.'

Adam gets to his feet and Rose follows his lead.

'We'll have another word with the neighbours for you, okay?' he says.

'That would be most welcome,' says Anton, lips drawn back in another non-smile. 'It's about time we put all this to bed. Gregory has a very important time coming up and this isn't helping at all.'

As Gwen begins to usher them out, Rose says, 'What's happening for Gregory that's so important?'

'He's got exams in May,' says Gwen with a tight smile.

'Yeah, but didn't you say he's only in Year Seven?' says Rose.

Gwen's expression closes down so fast, it's like someone has physically wounded her. 'You clearly don't understand what kind of school it is,' she says with a sniff. 'It's never too early to work hard at Beamishes.'

It's only as Rose glances back at the house that she sees the pale face of the boy peering down at them from a window at the very top of the house.

He's smiling.

An involuntary swoop of something icy encircles her insides as if she has drunk chilled water too fast.

3

'That told you, didn't it?' says Adam with a snigger, then, more seriously: 'What do you think, though?'

'I'm not sure,' says Rose. 'Can't say I'd blame the neighbours for not inviting them over for barbecues and drinks. But seriously . . . that thing with the swing? And the flowers?'

Adam makes a face. 'Gave me the bloody creeps – I'm not going to lie. And I'll tell you what else.' He pauses.

'Go on.'

'I measured those daffodil stalks with a digital spirit level and the precision of the cut was quite extraordinary,' he says. 'Every single one was cut exactly at the same height, to the *millimetre*. I don't see how even a machine could have done it so precisely.'

Rose stares back at him. 'What are you saying?'

'I don't know what I'm saying really,' he says. 'It would have to be technically possible if you had proper time and access.' He pauses. 'There is one obvious theory. That kid. I reckon he's behind everything that's going on in a bid for attention that doesn't involve a test at the end of it.'

'Yeah,' says Rose. 'He looks like an unhappy child. But I don't think he'd have the strength to do that to the swing.'

'True,' says Adam. They are silent for a moment, thinking

about this. Then Adam does a decisive pat on both of his thighs.

'Come on then,' he says, 'let's see if the notorious Mr Quinn is at home.'

Quinn and family live in the top flat and the occupants below are a couple in their sixties called Jemima and Grant Osei.

Rose presses on the doorbell for the top flat.

Nothing.

They try again and wait for a few moments. But it's clear no one is in so they try the bottom buzzer.

The door opens.

'Yes?' The woman has light brown skin and grey dreadlocks piled high and tied with a turquoise wrap. A sleeping toddler is awkwardly held in her arms, his small mouth squashed open on her shoulder. The material of her cream T-shirt is wet from drool.

'Mrs Osei?'

She nods, suspicion stealing across her face.

'I'm sorry to bother you,' says Rose, 'but I'm DC Rose Gifford, and this is my colleague DC Adam Lacey. Would you have a few minutes spare to talk to us?'

Rose has struggled with introductions since her move to UCIT. In her old job, she would simply say she was from Silverton Street police station. Now, she's reluctant to say she is from UCIT, in case anyone wants chapter and verse on what it is. She could say 'Reservoir Road' station, but it isn't one, technically; at least, not in the sense that a member of the public could come in to report a crime. So far she has got away with not saying anything other than her name and rank. She hopes this woman will assume she is from the same station as previous visitors.

'Oh for goodness' sake,' says Jemima Osei, sotto voce. 'What've we done now?'

Adam gives her a sympathetic smile.

'We really are sorry to bother you,' he says, lowering his own voice to match. 'The Fullers have experienced some damage to their back garden. We're just trying to work out what has been going on and wondered if you could give us a little background? From your own perspective?'

Adam's careful phrasing seems to do the trick. She lets out a sigh of resignation and opens the door wider.

'Come in, then,' she says. 'But this is the very last time I'm doing this. I mean it.'

They step into the hall and the woman beckons for them to walk down to a kitchen at the back of the house. It's painted bright yellow and the sun has come out, bathing it in buttery light. Frothy plants spill down off high shelves, giving the room the feel of a pleasant conservatory, despite the broken kitchen fittings and cracked glass of the big window. There's a delicious spicy smell of cooking coming from the stove.

'That smells like jollof,' says Adam easily, as Jemima Osei comes back into the room. 'Nigerian or Ghanaian?'

She casts a sharp look at him, then lets out a small, grudging 'humph'. 'The one true kind,' she says. 'Ghanaian.'

'My mum would agree,' says Adam with a grin.

She 'humphs' again, but her manner has softened a little.

'So go on then,' she says, gesturing for them to sit at a wooden table surrounded by four rickety chairs. 'What's happened now?'

'Someone has damaged flowers in the garden and . . .' Rose flails '. . . messed about with their swing.'

Jemima Osei gives her a sharp look. 'I'm looking after my grandson,' she says, 'and I have two dodgy knees. Grant has been on disability for his back since 2009. How exactly did we get into that garden?'

'Okay,' says Rose in a conciliatory tone. 'Can you tell us a bit about the family? How this whole dispute developed originally?' She opens her notepad.

Jemima kisses her teeth. 'They are crazy people,' she says. 'They bang and crash about in there like you would not believe,

26

then they have the cheek to pretend it's us making all that noise.'

'What kind of noises do you hear?' says Adam.

Jemima looks into the middle distance, frowning. 'Like I say, banging, crashing . . . Sometimes there's a scraping sound, like someone is moving heavy furniture across the floor. It must be very loud for Eric and Emma upstairs if I can hear it down here.' She pauses. 'There's a lot of shouting and arguing too. Not that I've ever called the police on *them*.'

'About the arguing,' says Rose. 'Can you hear details?'

'Sometimes,' says Jemima, nodding and reaching for one of the grapes in the fruit bowl in front of her, which she pops into her mouth. 'I think it's often about the child – Gregory. If you ask me,' she says, heated now, 'that's one unhappy little boy.'

As Jemima goes into more detail, Rose writes down all the key points.

Seems Gregory spends every waking hour being coached in something, from piano to violin, Chinese to French. He's been spotted sitting in a tree at the bottom of the garden and simply staring at the house for periods of time in a way that Jemima calls 'creepy as anything'.

'If you ask me,' she says, 'and let's face it, that's exactly what you're doing, I think the father is a bully. I hear his loud voice all the time, booming away. I think he thinks he's the lord and master and no one better argue with him.'

They get up a few minutes later. As they are leaving, Jemima and Adam exchange a few more words about the food she's making. This includes a lively discussion about Jamie Oliver, which makes Rose lift a questioning eyebrow once outside.

'Trust, me,' he says with a grin, catching her expression. 'Jollof is a serious business. You have no idea.'

'I'll take your word for it,' says Rose. 'So . . . we might as well speak to people on the other side, number 44?'

Adam looks at his notes. 'Bottom flat is a couple called Jacobs:

Gerald and Margot. But it looks like Margot died earlier this year and Gerald has just gone into a home.' Adam keeps reading. 'Couple of junior doctors on top.'

'Come on then,' says Rose and begins to climb the stairs. 'Let's see if they're in.'

They ring the top doorbell several times before they hear the sound of someone coming down the stairs.

A man in his early twenties opens the door. He's dressed in a crumpled T-shirt and black jacket. His dark eyes look a bit glazed and Rose concludes he has either been out on the lash, or he's newly back from a shift.

'Can I help you?' he says.

Adam looks at the notebook, 'Are you Arif Rohan?'

The man nods, hesitantly. 'Is something wrong?'

'Not at all,' says Rose. 'We're police officers and we're just investigating some problems the family at number 42 have been experiencing.'

'Oh God, not this again,' says Rohan with the weariest of sighs. 'I've told you lot before. I really wish I had the energy to bang on the walls at 3 a.m., but if I'm not busting my arse at work, I'm sleeping like a man in a coma. They have repeatedly woken me from what I can assure you is very well-earned sleep to complain.' He rubs a hand across his face. 'I'm really sick of this now.'

'Can we come inside for a minute?'

Rohan stands a little straighter. 'Look,' he says, 'I'm sorry, but I've just worked a long shift that included dealing with a fourteen-year-old who'd been stabbed to death. I'm not in the mood for this. If you really want to know, then yes, *maybe* someone from this house chucked a bit of rubbish onto their front step one night when they were a bit pissed. But that was the start and the end of it. We don't bang on walls. We're too knackered to do that. And if you want to speak to me, you're going to have to arrest me and force me to go down to the station.'

There's a moment when Adam and Rose both regard him silently.

When Adam speaks, Rose is relieved his words match her own conclusions. This is clearly a waste of time.

'That won't be necessary for now, Mr Rohan,' he says, removing a card from his jacket. 'But please take my number and get in touch if there's anything you'd like to discuss at a later date, okay?'

Rohan looks at the card and then takes it.

'And let's not have any more incidents with rubbish, or we really will have a problem, okay?'

Rohan's eyes narrow but he nods.

'Thank you,' says Rose and they both go to leave.

The door closes behind them, a little more firmly than necessary.

Rose and Adam take a moment on the pavement.

'It's starting to sound as though it's the Fullers who're the difficult neighbours in this scenario, isn't it?' says Adam quietly. 'I mean, apart from the rubbish thing, which he's admitted.'

'Hmm,' says Rose. 'Short of us sitting there all evening and witnessing it for ourselves, I'm not sure what we're meant to do about the garden.'

Adam nods. 'We can't rule out these neighbours are lying. But they seem genuinely sick of all this, don't they? And no one so far seems the type to be deliberately malicious in that way.'

As they get back into the parked car across from number 42, a blue van pulls up on the other side of the road. A middle-aged man with a pink face and a bald head jumps to the kerb. He's dressed in a straining black T-shirt covered with paint and saggy-arsed jeans. He goes round to the other side and helps down a tiny old woman, who grips his arm with a small, claw-like hand. They slowly cross the road, him murmuring to her the whole time, and head towards number 40.

Rose and Adam simultaneously get out of the car and hurry back across the road.

'Mr Eric Quinn?' says Rose and the man turns. He has a doughy face with small eyes, and thick eyebrows that immediately meet in a suspicious frown. There's a smudge of something on his cheek. Dirt? Paint? Perhaps a tattoo.

'Jesus Christ,' he says. He seems to immediately understand they are police, which is interesting in itself.

She introduces herself and Adam. Then: 'We're not going to take much of your time, Mr Quinn, but we've been talking to the Fullers at number—'

But she doesn't get to finish her sentence. Quinn has taken a fast step closer to her, which makes her instinctively want to take one back. She resists.

'I've just about had my fill of that dickhead,' he says in a low voice. 'I don't want my mum hearing this and getting all upset. He's a fucking psycho, that man. They're all nuts in that house. I've never done *nothing* to him, not one thing. *They're* the bad neighbours.' He stabs a meaty finger towards number 40 for emphasis.

'Look,' says Rose, 'we're not trying to waste anyone's time here. We're simply trying to get to the bottom of why this family feel they are being harassed.'

The old woman, who has been peering at them with a scrunched brow throughout this exchange suddenly speaks in a quavering voice. 'Is it about that lot next door?' she says. 'It's a rotten place – I told you that, Bobby. I don't want to live here. I keep telling you but you don't listen.' Her eyes fill with tears and her son closes his own for a moment as though trying to will infinite patience.

'Come on, Mum,' he says in a tired but surprisingly gentle voice. 'You know I'm not Dad, um, Bobby. I'm Eric. And we've talked about this. You have to come and be with us now. You know it's the best thing.'

'What do you mean about it being rotten?' says Rose, but the old lady's eyes are shut and she is muttering too quietly for them to hear, small pink tongue darting across her lips.

Quinn looks at Rose, his pale blue eyes as cold as glass.

'If they're saying we're bashing the walls again, they can, quite frankly, go and do one,' he says. 'I'd love to have the

30

spare time to even think about doing DIY or winding up that tosser next door.' He's breathing heavily.

'So you haven't been in their garden?' says Adam.

Quinn lets out a mirthless hoot of laughter. 'Garden? How would I get into their garden? Do you think I can climb like Spider-Man or something? Now if you'll excuse me, I'm going to get my eighty-seven-year-old mum a cup of tea.'

'We'll leave you alone, but please take this,' says Rose and thrusts a card at him, which he takes, begrudgingly. 'If anything concerns you regarding the property next door, you can give us a call directly and we'll try to help straighten this out.'

Rose and Adam get into the car. Rose pauses before starting the engine.

'I don't know about you,' she says, 'but my feeling is that none of those neighbours has even got the time to harass the Fullers, even if they had the inclination.'

Something is bugging her though and she can't quite reach for it. Adam gets there at almost the exact moment she does.

'That facial tattoo,' he says. 'Did you notice?'

'Yes! I wasn't sure if it was a smudge of dirt or . . .'

'Teardrop?'

'So he's probably been inside then,' says Rose, thinking about teardrop tattoos on the face and how they're a signifier in the criminal underworld of several things, including having served time in prison.

'Let's check him out when we get back,' says Adam. 'But there's definitely a strange vibe about it all. What do you think the old lady meant about it being a bad place?'

'Not sure,' says Rose, starting the engine. 'You'd think Kentish Town would have mentioned if there was a history there, wouldn't you?'

'You would,' says Adam, looking down at his phone screen and beginning to tap out a message. 'I reckon this is all a bit of a waste of time. I think it's an unhappy family in there but if social services aren't concerned, then what can you do? We can see if the kid has had any involvement from CAMHS.' He glances over at her. 'I wouldn't be surprised. I mean, would you want to live with that guy?'

Rose grimaces. 'I guess anyone would act out a bit,' she says. The very notion of fathers has long been a source of fascination for Rose, who grew up without one and with no information on who he may have been. Any kind of normal family interests her, really. Although she's not sure she would ever have wanted the kind of 'normality' to be found at the Fullers' house either.

That swing . . . and the banging no one seems able to explain. Her arms are prickling uncomfortably again.

It's her own peculiar form of time travel, taking her back to a place she has no wish to go again.

It's fair to say she didn't have a conventional childhood.

Rose called Adele Gifford 'Mother' (never 'Mum'. This was one of the woman's affectations). But Rose knew from a young age that Adele was really her grandmother.

Kelly Gifford was a drug addict who died when Rose was a toddler, leaving Adele to bring up the child alone. Adele made her living by scamming bereaved people into 'readings' from their deceased loved ones in the stuffy, incense-thick living toom of the semi in Barnet that Rose still, reluctantly, calls home. Rose suspects now that this business was a front for a money-laundering operation. A man only known as Mr Big – some type of minor gangster probably – used to turn up and collect wads of cash once a month. She has never tried to find out more because, well, why would she? But Adele Gifford was never short of business, and there was a constant stream of people trooping through the house, eyes clouded with grief, but with a chink of hope there too.

How ironic, then, that it was Rose who occasionally glimpsed movement in the shadowy corners of the house or heard whispering when no one was there. She learned to ignore this unwanted 'gift', mainly because it gave her pleasure to deny

Adele something she would have dearly coveted, had she ever known about it. And would have exploited, no doubt.

Over the years Rose was able to tune out these feelings but there are moments when she has that same sense.

Of something dead that's still somehow active.

And she's pretty sure she felt it at number 42 Wyndham Terrace.

4

Coming through the front door that evening, Rose pauses in the hallway. She waits for a moment then takes a tentative look into the living room. No one there. Then she walks into the kitchen. All clear. Letting out a breath, she feels her shoulders dropping a little bit. To be really sure, she would need to check the rest of the house, but it *feels* as though she is alone.

It's a thing she does so often it's almost normal now when actually it is about as far from that as it's possible to be.

Rose isn't exactly sure when Adele Gifford first began to appear, despite having been dead for twelve years, but it got much worse last winter when she was working on the Oakley case. Her mother would simply be there, perhaps at the kitchen table, or hunched in an armchair in the living room, wearing her ratty old fur coat, and looking back at Rose with an almost defiant expression. *See, you thought you'd got rid of me.*

Not that she ever spoke.

Lately she has been absent but Rose isn't under any illusions that she has gone for good. She assumed that once before after a quiet period and had begun feeling a little more settled. A little more normal. She was so confident that, when things took an exciting change of direction with her colleague and friend Sam Malik, she brought him back to the house to spend the night.

But Adele had appeared right by the bed at 2 a.m., staring down with disapproval on the sleepy, entwined bodies. Rose had screamed the house down. Yes, she could have said it was a nightmare, but it all felt too complicated. Too much. Rose essentially pushed Sam away the next day and their friendship never really recovered.

Adele is a burden she can't ever share and one of the reasons Rose is tied to this grim little house in East Barnet.

But her home has become even less appealing since the events of last year.

The time it took for her to wake up – in total blackness – and to be knocked unconscious by James Oakley probably lasted about three minutes in total. But in her mind, particularly at bedtime, that sensation of utter, paralysing terror and helplessness plays on an endless loop. It's why she can only sleep in catnaps, and never in the bedroom where it happened. So she is either on the lumpy old sofa or in the single bed of her childhood room, which is stuffed with rubbish.

Rose is, frankly, knackered.

She diverts her mind from thoughts of bedtime now by starting to prep her dinner.

This has been one of the resolutions since the night she almost died: to stop living like a student and to look after herself a bit more.

Once she has a neat pile of chopped onions and carrots in front of her, she regards them, not completely sure what she was going to do with them. Then she goes to the fridge to get out a bottle of wine. No intentions of giving that up yet. If she can stay lightly oiled in this house, she can cope with the dark terror that comes sweeping in, bombarding her senses with horror.

Sitting down at the kitchen table with her drink, she flicks through Instagram.

The latest update from Sam causes a jolt in her stomach. It's him and his girlfriend Lucy, heads together on an evening out. Sam's eyes are hazy enough for Rose to know that he's pissed, and Lucy has a proprietorial gleam in hers that makes Rose grimace.

Got to let that go.

Sam was one of Rose's best friends at Silverton Street station and it all went wrong after they slept together. And now he's engaged and off limits. But she still misses him. She misses his company, but part of it is an ache for what Might Have Been.

She lets out a slightly tragic sigh. Admitting how deep her loneliness goes, even to herself, is horrible. It seems that having lustful thoughts about Adam, who is totally out of bounds, is not enough to fill the gaping hole in her life.

With a sudden hot burst of determination, Rose picks up her phone. For the next few minutes, her fingers are a blur as she taps at the screen.

Then she sits back, heart racing as if from exertion.

It was about time she got on a dating app. About time she got out there and behaved like a normal, young person.

Her phone startles her when it rings. The display says Unknown Caller.

'DC Rose Gifford,' she says, a little wary.

Silence.

'Hello?'

Someone's there. She can hear them breathing on the other end.

'Wow, that's quite old-school, isn't it?' she says but then another sound makes her stop dead.

It's a wet, bubbly sniff. The very one she heard earlier today.

'Gregory?' she says, quietly. 'Is that you?'

Silence, then more sniffing. Is he crying?

'Gregory—' she's more focused now '—is your mum or dad there? Can you put them on? Is everything all right?'

He, or whoever it is, has hung up.

Rose thinks about the business card she left with Gwen Fuller earlier. The kid is probably just being curious or something. She thinks of that little smile he gave at the window. It could be that he's enjoying all this attention. It could be that he is *causing* all this attention. But what if it's some kind of cry for help?

She dials the number the call came from but it rings out. Next she tries Adam.

Adam takes a few minutes to reply and there's the sound of laughter and music in the background.

'What's up?' he says, then: 'Hang on, got my girls here. I'm just going into another room where it's a bit less shrieky.'

There's a pause, then he comes back.

'Yup?'

'So I just had a really strange phone call from a landline,' says Rose, 'and I'd bet my last Cheesy Wotsit that it was Gregory Fuller on the phone.'

'Oh yeah? What did he say?'

'Nothing,' says Rose. 'That's the thing. It was all a bit weird. But do you have numbers for the parents?'

'I do,' says Adam. 'I'll send them over. Hey, let me know once you've spoken to them, okay?'

Rose tries Gwen Fuller first, but it goes straight to a generic voicemail. She calls Anton Fuller. This time there's a personalized message.

This is Anton Fuller. If your call relates to the Beamish School, please call 0208 333 2098 instead. Otherwise, leave a message after the tone.

What a pompous git he is. Even his disembodied voice winds Rose up.

She leaves a message for him and then stands in the middle of the kitchen, racked with indecision. Eyeing the sad pile of chopped vegetables, she moves over to the table and then back to the sink where she washes her hands, even though she doesn't need to. The phone remains mute on the table.

Rose works out she's only had about two sips of that wine. It's probably nothing. He's a weird kid and his parents are likely playing the harp and reciting poetry; too busy to do anything as lowbrow as look at their phones in the evening.

But something is niggling at her and she knows she won't be able to let it go. Briefly, she contemplates ringing Adam back. But she can't pull him from an evening with his kids for a stupid 'feeling'. No, she'll just drive down there to be sure. Then she'll come back and get on with what's left of her own evening.

It's bound to be nothing. If she's quick, she could be drinking that glass of wine within an hour and a half.

5

Rose has to drive past number 42 to the other end of the road to look for a parking space. But, as she passes the property, it's clear something's going on outside.

Finding a space at the far end of the road, she hurries back.

Anton Fuller is outside the front of the house, cradling his left arm and shouting up at the house next door. Gwen stands in the doorway, watching. The woman is literally wringing her large, red-knuckled hands together.

'Are you trying to kill me? Is that it?' yells Fuller, apparently at no one.

'What's going on here?' says Rose. Fuller doesn't seem especially surprised to see her. Gwen, on the other hand, attempts a weak, apologetic smile.

'Oh golly, you shouldn't have bothered coming out,' she says. 'Anton, don't you think we should get you checked over?'

But Fuller is having none of her attempts to placate him. If anything, his face seems to be getting redder by the moment. Rose pictures his skin bursting like an overripe tomato.

'I climbed up my ladder to take a look at the guttering,' he says. 'The ladder that was *in my front garden*, I should add, and I almost bloody broke my neck! Take a look at this!'

Obviously in pain from the way he's holding his arm, he

kicks an old wooden ladder that's lying at an angle on the ground and then winces. In Rose's opinion it should have been thrown away years ago, but one of the struts is clearly broken in the middle.

'Go on!' he says to Rose, eyes bulging. 'Look at it!'

'I am looking at it, Mr Fuller,' says Rose patiently, 'and I can see that it's damaged. Are you suggesting someone did this deliberately?'

'Of course I bloody am!' he yells. 'That bloody chav next door did it!

At this the door to number 40 opens suddenly and Eric Quinn comes charging down the steps.

'Did you just call me a chav, you stuck-up piece of shit?'

As he starts to come through the gate into 42, Rose blocks him with one hand raised.

'I suggest you calm down, Mr Quinn,' she says, sorely wishing she had Adam here. But Quinn stops, even though he has a very unpleasant look on his face that doesn't seem only meant for Fuller.

'Right,' she says, 'kindly step back over to your own property, Mr Quinn, while we try and sort this out.'

Quinn hesitates then does as she says, muttering something under his breath that sounds very much like 'filth' but Rose can't be sure.

'Okay,' she says. 'Now do I need to call for back-up and get the two of you down to the station? Or can we all behave like adults?'

Both men remain silent, looking like large, sulky boys.

'Are you alleging that Mr Quinn deliberately tampered with your ladder?' says Rose.

'Well, who else would have done it?' says Fuller.

'For fuck's sake!' says Quinn. 'I've been inside my house for the entire evening trying to get my old mum settled. My wife and daughter are at her school play, which I have had to miss. Why would I even do something like that?'

Fuller merely barks a sarcastic laugh in response.

The old lady, Quinn's mum, comes shuffling to the front door at 40 now.

'Eric?' she says in a querulous voice. 'I can't find any of my things.'

Quinn rubs his face with his hands in a manner of extreme irritation. 'Please go inside, Mum,' he says. 'I'll be with you in a tick. You'll catch your death out here.'

'Anton?' pleads Gwen. 'Come in and let me look at your arm. You might need to go to A&E. And please, all this shouting in the street . . . Think of our boy upstairs.'

The old lady turns to look towards Gwen, an expression of what appears to be fear on her face.

'That boy?' she says. 'He's a wicked, wicked lad! Don't think I don't know about the things he gets up to!'

Gwen blanches and lifts her hand to her mouth.

'Mum!' Quinn looks horrified. 'Go inside, I said!'

The old lady glares at him and, after a pause, shuffles off back inside, muttering to herself.

Everyone seems a little cowed by her words. Gwen still has her hand across her mouth, her eyes wide and shocked.

'You mustn't pay any mind to Mum,' says Quinn. It might have been an apologetic tone, if it weren't for the thunderous expression on his face. 'She's not . . .' He pauses. 'You mustn't mind what she says.'

'I'll tell you what I'm going to do,' says Rose, 'I'm going to take that ladder away and get it forensically tested to see if it's been tampered with. And we can check for Mr Quinn's fingerprints too.' She allows a small pause, meeting Quinn's stare directly. She doesn't need to say his prints will be on the database. He gets it, all right.

'Meanwhile,' she continues, 'everyone is going to go inside and calm down, or arrests *will* be made for breaching the peace. Got it?'

'Loud and clear,' says Fuller sullenly. Quinn doesn't say anything before going back into the house, closing the door softly behind him.

Rose would very much like to get the hell away from here as soon as possible. But she isn't done yet.

'Can I come in for a minute before I head off?' she says.

'Oh,' says Gwen. 'Well . . .'

'Thank you,' says Rose, not giving her the chance to refuse. 'You lead the way.'

Once inside the hallway, Anton disappears off towards the kitchen. Gwen and Rose pause at the bottom of the stairs. Rose is about to speak when Gwen cuts across her.

'I'm sorry you were called out by that horrid man,' she says. 'There was no need to come. Really.'

'It wasn't Mr Quinn, actually,' says Rose. 'That's what I was about to ask you.'

'Oh?' says Gwen, a frown pinching the space between her eyebrows. 'Then who . . .?'

'I had a call from your number,' says Rose. 'No one spoke but I think Gregory was on the other end. I thought I'd better come over.'

Gwen's expression does that closing-down thing again. Rose gets the impression that she's adept at switching between masks she thinks are socially acceptable. *Maybe we all are,* she muses. But with Gwen Fuller it's very hard to know what's artifice and what's the real her.

'Well, I apologize. That was naughty of him,' says Gwen, lips a thin line. 'But there's no need for you to hang around.'

'Nonetheless,' says Rose, meeting her eyes directly, 'I'd like to see him before I go.'

Gwen's expression switches from being appalled to annoyed and offended in one smooth sequence.

'I don't know what you're suggesting.'

'I'm not suggesting anything,' says Rose. 'Can you call him for me?'

There's a moment's standoff and then Gwen calls Gregory's name. Again, he appears at the top of the stairs suspiciously quickly.

'Yeah?' he says, then: 'Oh hello,' in an unsurprised way at the sight of Rose.

'Don't say "yeah",' says Gwen. 'Say "yes". Now did you ring this busy police officer?'

Gregory shifts on the spot. He's wearing a fleecy dressing gown over pyjamas.

'It was a mistake,' he says. 'I didn't mean to ring. Sorry. I was fiddling with the phone.'

It's not a very likely story. But he seems fine, which is the most important thing.

'It's okay,' says Rose with a smile. 'Everything all right though?'

'Yes,' says Gregory. 'Can I go back to my book now?'

'Of course,' says Rose and he pads back up the stairs. 'I'll be off,' she says to Gwen, 'but can I use the toilet before I go?'

Gwen hesitates before replying, 'Upstairs, third door on the left.'

At that moment there's a shout from the kitchen.

'Gwen! Where's the ibuprofen? This medicine box is a bloody mess! I can't find anything useful in it at all!'

With an apologetic wince Gwen hurries down the hall.

Rose climbs the stairs, which are covered in a dark burgundy carpet that's shiny with wear. It's a steep staircase and there's a sensation of the space narrowing as she gets to the top, like the air is somehow becoming thinner.

Probably low blood sugar, she thinks.

At the end of the corridor there's another short staircase, presumably leading to an attic room. It is totally silent up there but she knows, somehow, that someone is present at the top, listening and still. *Gregory?*

She hurries to the toilet.

After she's finished, she notices one of the doors on the landing is now wide open when it wasn't before. A flickering light spills out and there's an unusual clicking sound, like crickets, or when a tiny piece of paper has become trapped in the blades of a fan.

Rose pauses, listening intently. From downstairs she can make

out Anton's loud voice honking away, with Gwen's softer conciliatory words in an undertone. They're not listening out for her
so she walks to the room and steps inside, curious to see what's
going on in there.

It appears to be an office and spare bedroom in one, with a
large oak desk with neat files and paperwork in a pile, and an
old orange futon in the other corner.

But what grabs her attention are the images dancing across
the wall. It's like someone is projecting an old film onto it, with
the clickety, whirring sound to match. Rose looks around the
room for the sort of old-time projector she has seen in films
but there's nothing like that here. It seems to be coming from
the wall itself but she can't see how.

She walks over and peers more closely. At first, the effect is
like watching pigment drops spreading and swirling in water
but then the colours – muted orange and browns – begin to
take shape. A picture forms. Two women are dancing together,
slim arms outstretched, palms together, hips swaying. One of
the women has short dark hair and a thin face. She's mouthing
words, perhaps singing, and gazing intently at the other woman,
who is startlingly pretty, with thick blonde hair down her back
and a flower crown on her head. Her eyes are closed, her lips
parted.

A tall, slim man with a handlebar moustache comes into the
frame. He's dressed in a close-fitting shirt and flared, tight
trousers. It looks like this is the Sixties, Seventies maybe? The
man grins as he turns to the camera and he puts his arms
around the two women, drawing them both into his chest. But
something is happening to his face now. A hole with black edges
appears in the centre of his forehead and begins to grow, like
fire devouring him from the inside. It spreads and spreads and
then the image is gone – the wall blank again, so fast it makes
Rose flinch.

She's still staring at the wall in confusion when she feels a
shivery sort of tickle on her left breast, quickly followed by
a sharp pain. Frantically stretching open her top, Rose pulls

the elastic of her bra away from her skin and looks for the insect, or whatever it is that has bitten her. The skin near her nipple is red and sore-looking but there's no insect and no tell-tale pinprick of blood.

An insect bite in March? Inside?

If she didn't know better, it would have felt exactly like a pinch from cold, mean fingers.

Heart hammering and skin crawling, Rose hurries out of the room.

Just in time, as it happens.

'Are you all right up there?' Gwen sounds as though she is having to make a major effort not to be impatient.

'Yes, yes, all fine,' says Rose as she comes quickly down the stairs to see the other woman waiting for her by the door.

'I heard a noise and popped my head into one of the rooms,' she says as casually as she can. 'I think it was your study? And there was some sort of film playing on the wall.'

'Film?' says Gwen blankly. 'I don't know what you mean. What sort of film?'

She's only half paying attention because Anton calls her name again from the kitchen. Her head turns and it's like he's literally tugging a string to reel her back into his orbit. It's clear she has no idea what Rose is talking about.

'No worries,' says Rose after a beat. 'You get back to your evening.'

As she gets into her car a few minutes later, her hands are trembling. There's something very wrong at 42 Wyndham Terrace.

And bad neighbour relations are the least of it.

6

Listen to her down there, pandering and fawning over *him*. She'd walk over burning coals if that man asked her to. It's like a disease infecting her brain, robbing her of the capacity to see what's right in front of her face. She's meant to be an intelligent woman in her own right. Isn't that the sort of thing she goes on about? But it stands for nothing when *he* is in the room. A big dirty magpie who steals all the shiny things.

The boy grabs the pillow, musty with his own smell, and silently screams his frustration into it. He doesn't want to give them the satisfaction of hearing his rage and hatred. Better to keep it under control. Remaining blank-faced at the small humiliations is the only weapon he has. It pleases him to look as though he isn't paying attention when in his mind he is imagining all the ways *he* might suffer.

He read about quicksand the other day for the first time. There was a thrilling horror in picturing it all; first the realization that you couldn't quite move your feet, then the cold, wetness sucking you down, down, covering your shoulders, then your chin. You'd close your lips tightly, resisting its deathly kiss but in a second it would be creeping inside your nostrils, stoppering your breath. You wouldn't even be able to scream . . .

Yeah, that would do nicely.

It occasionally troubles him, how much time he spends picturing horrible deaths in graphic detail. Sometimes he's not sure this is entirely normal.

Sometimes he worries about what he might do.

7

'Well, that's a turn-up for the books.'

Adam has come off the phone the following morning after a long call.

'What?' says Rose, looking up from her computer. She's been checking whether Gregory has had any social services intervention. So far, nothing. Rose has also spent a ridiculous amount of time this morning organizing for the Fullers' ladder to be picked up and tested for fingerprints. It's not going to be happening any time soon, but at least she's done what she said she'd do.

'I had a word with the family's GP,' says Adam, getting up and coming over to Rose's desk. 'And I'm relieved to say that Gregory hasn't been in A&E any more than any other kid. He went after falling off a bicycle and spraining a wrist when he was four, and once more for a bad bout of croup at about the same age.'

'That's a relief,' says Rose, feeling something loosen a little inside.

'But,' says Adam with the relish of someone who has news to impart, 'someone *else* in the family has had more than their fair share of accidents.'

'Oh no,' she says. 'Please tell me all my instincts about that horrible man were wrong.'

Adam smiles. 'All your instincts about that horrible man were wrong.' Then: 'Possibly, anyway. Because it's *him* who has been extremely accident-prone over the last few years. Anton Fuller.'

'Him?' Rose can't keep the squeak of surprise out of her voice. 'That great big bully? Has she been beating him up or something?'

'Stranger things have happened, I guess. Look,' says Adam, 'I've been on to the Royal Free and made a list.'

He comes to stand at her desk, placing his notebook on the table in front of her. He smells so unbelievably good – a mix of citrus aftershave, fresh fabric conditioner and his own warm skin – that Rose's treacherous cheeks begin to prickle with incipient heat. And it's not just her cheeks.

She coughs and forces her brain to the task at hand.

It's quite a list, spanning a period of eight months.

Twisted ankle after slipping on rug. Burned wrist from faulty hot tap. Cut head, requiring three stitches, after decorative plate fell from above doorway. Cut foot, stitches required, after mirror broken.

Rose is about to comment when the door to the office opens and Moony comes in, her face scrunched into a grumpy expression.

She normally comes into the office clad in motorcycle leathers, a somewhat unusual choice for a woman in her late fifties who is about five foot tall. But her Harley is her pride and joy and primary means of transport. Today, though, she has on a charcoal grey suit, a bit wrinkled, but even with Rose's limited fashion knowledge she knows it's expensive. She is a mass of contradictions, this woman. She wears virtually no make-up, yet her hands are never without a veritable knuckle-duster of knobbly rings, and she often dresses in leathers but carries incredibly expensive handbags. Sometimes she will wear a slash of dark red lipstick that only makes her different-coloured eyes – one brown, one blue – seem even smaller.

Adam mutters, 'Uh-oh,' under his breath as she stomps over.

'Where are you at on this supposed poltergeist thing?' she says without preamble.

Adam and Rose exchange looks.

'We're just doing some background checking into the family,' says Rose. 'And it seems the dad – Anton – has been in and out of hospital after various accidents. All looks a bit off.'

'Hmm,' says Moony distractedly. 'What did you glean from going over there?'

'Well,' says Adam, 'there have been some very unusual things going on in that house, but it's not out of the question that the boy, Gregory, is behind some of this stuff. He seems pretty unhappy from what we've seen.'

'Right,' says Moony. 'Rose, what's your impression of it all?'

Rose hesitates, thinking about the weird film on the wall and the pinch, or whatever it was. There's no bruise today. *Was it really only the bite of a rogue insect?*

'I was over there last night as it happens,' she says and then fills in Moony on the events of the previous evening. She had already told Adam the full story first thing.

'Hmm, that sounds unpleasant,' says Moony, grimacing. 'Do you think there's something supernatural in the house?'

Rose hesitates. 'Yes, maybe,' she says, after a moment. There is an odd sort of relief in saying this out loud, here in this room with a couple of no-nonsense detectives. For the first time, she experiences a feeling that she is in the right place.

Adam's phone rings and he goes to answer it, apologizing for the quick interruption.

His face is immediately alight with bright interest.

'Thank you,' he says to the person on the other end, 'I appreciate that you thought to do this.'

After hanging up he blows air out through his lips.

'Wow,' he says. 'That was the Royal Free. Seems our Mr Fuller is back. This time in an ambulance with suspected poisoning.'

8

Anton Fuller is still being assessed when they get to the hospital. A doctor tells them they're doing a full toxicology screen to try to work out what has caused this reaction and that Anton appears to have had severe vomiting before passing out. He is conscious now but seems 'confused' and weak.

They find Gwen sitting in the waiting area with her head in her hands. She looks up at them with bleary eyes, puffy from crying. No sign of Gregory.

'Have they told *you* anything else?' she says by way of greeting, seemingly unsurprised by their presence.

Rose and Adam sit down on either side of her.

'We've been told exactly what you have,' says Rose. 'Look, shall we get you a coffee or something?'

Gwen shakes her head vaguely.

'Mrs Fuller,' says Adam gently, 'can you explain what happened?'

Gwen swipes at her reddened nose with her hand and gives a sort of hopeless shrug. 'This is it,' she says. 'I don't really know. Anton had come back from a cycle, is all I can say. He and Gregory were downstairs in the kitchen. The next thing I knew, Gregory was shouting that his daddy—' her voice cracks on the word '—was very unwell and that I had to come straight away.' She sobs. 'I thought,' she says, 'I thought he was dying when I first came into the kitchen.'

They give her a moment to cry.

'The doctor said this looks like suspected poisoning,' says Rose. 'I have to ask you first of all if Mr Fuller could have accidentally eaten or drunk something that harmed him?'

Gwen shakes her head vigorously. 'No, no, no,' she says. 'It's actually something Anton has a bit of a . . .' she pauses '. . . thing about. He ate some poisonous berries when he was a little boy – thankfully not enough to be lethal – but he was very sick indeed. It's one of his earliest memories, being in that hospital and seeing the awful fear on his parents' faces. He's someone who checks the instructions on medication very carefully and things like that. He would never make that sort of mistake. Not Anton.'

Rose and Adam momentarily meet eyes.

'Has anyone new been in your house since we last saw you?' says Adam.

A sharp look now. 'Like whom?' she says. 'We don't socialise much. We keep ourselves to ourselves.' Then she stops abruptly. 'But I wouldn't put anything past that Quinn man.'

'That's a serious allegation,' says Rose. 'And we need to wait and see exactly what's wrong with your husband before taking that any further.'

Gwen's lips purse and she gives a loud sniff.

'As it's half-term,' says Adam, 'I'm guessing Gregory's at home?'

Gwen's eyes slide away and her hands come together in her lap. 'Yes,' she says.

'Is someone with him?' says Adam.

'He'll be fine,' says Gwen with a defensive tilt of the chin. 'I said he could watch television until I came back.'

Rose makes a face at Adam over her head.

'Must have been upsetting? Seeing his dad going off in an ambulance?' says Adam.

'It's not ideal,' says Gwen, tightly. 'But I wasn't exactly thinking straight.' There's an awkward silence, then Gwen attempts a watery smile. 'Look,' she says, 'I know this is a bit unorthodox . . .' She seems to wrestle with the words before they come. 'Maybe I could ask you the most *enormous* favour? Is there any way you could drop round and . . . bring him here? Because,' she says hurriedly, 'you're right. He is quite young and I would never forgive myself if anything happened to him too.'

'We just got well and truly played there,' says Rose when they're back in the car and heading towards Kentish Town again. 'She leaves the poor kid all alone after witnessing something that must have been bloody traumatic, then guilt-trips *us* into going to get him.'

'Yep,' says Adam. 'They're a right pair, aren't they? We shouldn't pick up Gregory without an appropriate adult but she's basically just appointed us as that very thing.'

'Oh well,' says Rose. 'At least we can get the measure of him a little bit. So far we haven't had much chance of that.'

By the time they get to the house, ice-cold rain is hammering down from a leaden sky. They hurry up the steps to ring the doorbell. Music thumps from a house nearby and there's a low hum of traffic from the main road in the background.

A woman they haven't seen before is climbing the steps to number 40. She's in her forties and harried-looking, with unwashed hair roughly pulled into a ponytail.

Tired eyes immediately slide away from them. Her movements become jerky as she attempts to get her key in the lock. But evidently her hands are shaking because she drops it. Cursing under her breath, she picks up the key and has more success, practically throwing herself through the front door, then closing it firmly behind her.

Adam and Rose exchange amused looks.

'Wow,' says Rose. 'Something we said?'

'Hmm,' says Adam. 'Guilty conscience about anything? Let's pop round after we check on Gregory.'

No one answers when he rings the doorbell a couple of times.

The lace curtains on the ground-floor bay window shift and Gregory's pale face peers out at them. Rose gives a little wave and what she hopes is a reassuring smile.

After a few moments there's a sound of scraping on the other side, presumably a bolt being drawn back. The door opens wide enough for a slice of Gregory to appear.

'Hi,' says Rose. 'Do you remember me? We're the police officers from the other day? Your mum asked us to come and pick you up.'

'Why?' says Gregory.

What a strange thing to ask. Rose looks at Adam.

'Well,' says Adam. 'Because she wants you with her. Is it okay if we come in?'

A pause seems to stretch for an uncomfortably long time.

'I suppose,' says Gregory, 'that it's essential police officers are DBS checked?'

Rose avoids glancing at her colleague, knowing it would be hard to hide her amusement. Gregory has probably heard his father talk about criminal records checks – the sort anyone working with the young must go through. But it's more like he's wanting to show off his knowledge than actually asking.

'We definitely are,' says Adam with a smile. 'All up to date on that front.'

Gregory opens the door wider and beckons them in.

Inside, a window must be open because there's a sudden cool touch of air on her face. Goose pimples creep up her arms. It happens again, quick and sharp and Rose looks around, startled. For a moment, it felt exactly like someone blowing on her neck. Teasing . . . somehow sexual.

She shivers involuntarily.

Then she sees that Gregory's eyes are fixed on her, his mouth slightly open. He *knows* something about what just happened. Did he cause it? Surely not. Not least because she can't imagine how, but there was something more adult about that . . . touch, or whatever it was. She forces herself to greet Gregory's goggle-eyed gaze with a cool and professional smile.

'So, Gregory,' she says. 'I'm sorry your dad isn't well.'

Gregory makes the smallest movement with his head, a slight dip of the chin. His owlish eyes don't seem to have blinked for several moments, as if he's scared to take them off Rose.

'Do you want to get ready to go to the hospital?' says Adam in a gentle voice and Gregory's gaze finally leaves Rose. 'Get anything you might want to have while you're waiting?'

The hallway feels overcrowded with the three of them standing there but Gregory makes no sign of moving. He turns one socked foot slowly on top of the other one; his small shoulders, in what looks like a hand-knitted jumper, rounding as though a great weight is pressing down on him. He could easily pass for two years younger than he is.

'Do I *have* to come?' he says. 'I mean, can you stay here with me instead?'

Adam shoots a surprised look at Rose and emits a small laugh. 'I think you do, buddy, yes,' he says.

'Don't you want to go, Gregory?' says Rose and he looks down at his feet, biting his lips, which look a little dry and chapped.

Gregory mutters something so quietly they can't hear and then turns suddenly and walks down the corridor to the kitchen. The two police officers follow him.

On the kitchen table there's a large bag of Butterkist popcorn, some of the contents spilling out, an iPad and a cheap, Nokia telephone, which Gregory snatches up and places in his pocket. Then he flicks a guilty look towards them.

'Been having a chat with a mate?' says Adam.

'No,' says Gregory, blinking rapidly. 'I haven't been speaking to anyone.'

What a funny little kid he is, thinks Rose.

She glances over at the sink where there has been a messy attempt at washing up. Soapsuds are all around the sides and there is a little puddle of water on the floor. The rack contains a jug, a bowl, and a pint glass, along with the end piece of a hand blender.

Gregory watches Rose take this in, his eyes wide. He's almost quivering with some kind of internal anguish.

'Daddy won't die,' he blurts out. 'He only thinks he's been poisoned. The smoothie was perfectly okay really.'

Rose and Adam sharply meet eyes and then look back at the boy.

'Poisoned?' says Rose, keenly aware of how carefully they need to tread. 'What do you mean, Gregory?'

'He *wasn't* though,' says Gregory impatiently. 'You're not listening. There wasn't any of the black bryony actually in it. He only thought there was.'

Rose is aware that she and Adam have gone quite still.

'Right,' says Adam carefully. 'What is black bryony, exactly? And why did he think he'd taken it?' His tone is light.

'It's a highly poisonous berry from our garden,' says Gregory. 'It's also known as *Tamus communis*. I picked some of the berries and put them next to the blueberries and the acai berries he uses in his Power Smoothie.' He pauses. 'He *thought* he'd used them, you see.'

Rose's heart begins to beat faster.

'Gregory,' says Adam, taking a step closer to the boy. 'Now this is very important. Think carefully. Is there any chance *at all* that your dad did eat those berries?'

'You're really not listening,' he says. 'I only *wanted* him to think so. I already said they were next to the ones he was using, not mixed in.'

Adam turns to Rose, expression grave. 'I'll call the Royal Free,' he says quietly.

Rose turns back to Gregory, who has picked up the popcorn bag and is shovelling the contents into his mouth.

'Gregory,' says Rose. 'I'm going to call your mum now, okay? We're going to go down to the police station and make a record of everything that happened today.'

The boy's face instantly transforms into something hopeful.

'Really?' he says, excitedly. 'Do I get to go in a real police car?'

9

'It's going to have to be a formal interview,' says Moony, tapping her beringed fingers against her leg. 'You're going to have to caution him, although I don't think there's any need to arrest him first.'

They are crammed into a huddle near the entrance to the office.

Rose glances over to where Gregory is currently sitting with Scarlett and a woman called Mrs MacDonald, who has been appointed as the Appropriate Adult for the interview.

Rose is still boiling about Gwen Fuller, who hadn't really reacted at all to the news that Gregory had perhaps pretended to poison her husband. She'd gone totally silent and then merely replied, 'Thank you for telling me.' Worse, she'd said she couldn't possibly leave Anton's side to accompany her own son to a formal police interview. So calls had been made and a legally appointed Appropriate Adult had turned up – the thin, anxious-looking Mrs MacDonald with pinkish-grey curly hair.

Thank God for Scarlett, who has made tea and offered biscuits while they waited for her arrival and for Moony to brief Rose and Adam.

Gregory hadn't seemed especially surprised that his mother wasn't coming, which Rose found a bit heart-breaking in itself. Scarlett has magicked up a pack of cards and Gregory has been shouting, *'Snap!'* gleefully at the game, quite as though he was on a pleasant trip away from home. Maybe this counted for a day out in his schedule-packed life. Did he understand the gravity of attempted murder? At twelve, there would have to be something very wrong with the child if he didn't.

He had been animated in the car, asking questions about where they were going and why they couldn't put the siren on. The fact that it had been an ordinary unmarked Honda and not a police car had been a source of disappointment.

The news from the hospital was that Anton Fuller's toxicology screen had come back negative for the poisoned berries, and for anything else, but they were continuing to monitor him because he was still exhibiting signs of a severe gastrointestinal reaction and shock.

Moony listened attentively to the description of what had taken place at Wyndham Terrace since the last briefing.

They all look over at Gregory, who is now spinning the office chair first in one direction and then the other. When it comes to a stop, he does an exaggerated dizzy wobble with his head and arms.

'Just remember at all times that he is a little boy,' says Moony, 'even if he has just tried to bump off his own father.'

It's the first time Rose has been inside the interview room at the UCIT building, which is down the long, low-ceilinged corridor from the main office.

The stone walls are painted yellowish white and there's a modern desk in front of a large, domed window with wobbly, aged glass. The rest of the building is empty and Rose seems to sense the weight of it, all around. Gregory, too, has become still now, his expression serious at last.

Mrs MacDonald, shivering, clutches her coat around her as all take their seats.

Adam turns on the recorder. It's one of the strange aspects of this crumbling old building that the UCIT technology is largely the most up-to-date, and this digital recorder is much newer than she was used to at Angel Street nick.

Rose smiles, with what she hopes is encouraging warmth. He's a strange kid but it can't be easy being here in these circumstances. He isn't exactly overburdened with love at home and that's something she can very much identify with from her own joyless childhood.

'Who won at Snap?' she says. Gregory grins, small teeth revealed in a flash of white.

'I did,' he says. 'Scarlett is enthusiastic but has a very poor technique.'

Rose smiles and Adam lets out a little laugh.

'So, Gregory,' she says, 'I hope you're not finding any of this too alarming but we want to chat with you about what happened at home today and because we want to follow all the right rules and look after you properly, that means we have to do something called a caution first. Is that okay?'

Gregory nods and begins to chew at his nail.

While Rose recites the caution, his eyes flit between her, Adam, and Mrs MacDonald.

'Am I under arrest?' he says in a hoarse little whisper. He's nervous, but Rose is sure she detects something else there too. Excitement?

'No,' says Adam gently, 'but we need to find out why your dad got so sick and why he thought that he was eating something poisonous. He's going to be fine, but it can't have been very nice for him if he thought he had eaten poisoned berries, can it? Would you be able to talk us through what happened?'

Gregory opens his mouth to speak then closes it again.

'Can I have another biscuit first?' he says.

Rose dutifully stops the recording and goes to collect the packet from Scarlett, who raises one of her perfectly sculpted eyebrows.

'You'd think he'd never seen a Hobnob before, the way he went at them,' she grumbles, handing them over with a tiny bit of reluctance.

'I don't think he has,' Rose replies. 'I reckon he's one of those kids who gets extra kale as a special treat.'

Back in the interview room, Gregory stuffs down a biscuit and says something through a mouthful of crumbs that's impossible to catch.

'What was that, Gregory?' says Rose, leaning forward a bit.

The boy swallows and then takes a drink from his glass of water. His eyes remain lowered when he speaks again.

'It's all to do with the nocebo effect, you see,' he says. 'Do you know what that is?'

'No,' says Rose. 'Why don't you tell us?'

'Okay.' Animated now, his air that of a teacher explaining something to a child. 'You know what the placebo effect is, right?' he says. 'Where people take a sugar pill but because it looks like medicine, they get better anyway?'

'Yes,' says Rose, 'I've heard of that.'

'Okay,' he says again. 'The nocebo effect has been called the placebo effect's *evil twin*.' His eyes are bright and he shuffles forward a bit on his seat. 'I think that's quite cool, don't you?'

Adam takes over.

'I think I read something in *New Scientist* about this,' he says and Gregory nods with great enthusiasm.

'Yes, yes, me too!' he says. 'That's where I got the idea!'

There's a pause.

'What idea would that be?' says Adam in the same easy tone.

For the first time, Gregory looks upset. His eyes dart from Rose to Adam and back again.

Mrs MacDonald has remained silent throughout this exchange, her head going back and forth as though watching a tennis match.

'Gregory,' she says gently, 'try and answer the policeman if you can.'

'You take your time, buddy,' says Adam. 'But what did you mean then about the idea?'

Gregory stares down at his lap, cheeks reddening. 'I only

wanted to keep Daddy out of the house, without there being anything *really* wrong with him,' he says. 'It felt like the best thing because he would *seem* sick, but wouldn't really *be* sick, do you see?'

When he raises his head, his eyes shine with unshed tears.

'Why did you want him out of the house, Gregory?' says Rose. A sick, heavy feeling settles in her stomach. *Is that what this is all about? Abuse?* She shouldn't be surprised but hadn't really expected it. 'Does your dad ever . . . hurt you in any way?'

Gregory's silence seems to expand to fill the room.

Mrs MacDonald fusses with a hanky in her lap.

The boy's shoulders shake, and he breaks into loud sobs, hands covering his face.

'I knew you wouldn't understand!' he says in an angry voice that comes as a shock. 'No one does! It's not my dad hurting *me*. My dad is the one *in danger*!'

'Why is he in danger?' says Rose, leaning forwards. 'Who wants to hurt him?'

Gregory is sobbing now and doesn't answer.

'I think we need to stop for a while,' says Mrs MacDonald. 'Give the lad a little break.'

'I agree,' says Rose, despite the disappointment washing over her. You can't push a child in interview the way you would an adult. They have to stop now, even if they were getting to something important.

Gregory stops crying after a few moments. Rose hands him a tissue, which he drags savagely across his eyes and nose.

'It's the boy, you see,' he says finally.

'The boy?' Adam's voice is whisper-soft. 'Which boy?'

Gregory looks very directly at him and then fixes his eyes on Rose.

'The one who lives in the wall. The one who wants to kill my dad.'

10

It's been a long day.

After Gregory dropped his bombshell about a murderous ghost in his bedroom wall, he became tight-lipped and distressed, so Rose brought the meeting to a close.

His words prompted action anyway, and various calls had to be made under the umbrella of the Multi Agency Safeguarding Hub, which is involved whenever there is a potential crime involving a child. He was to be seen by the GP and social services might be involved. It was an unusual set of circumstances. After much discussion about whether he was in any actual danger, it was decided that Gregory would be allowed to go home to his mother. While he may be having harmful delusions, he wasn't himself at risk.

As for Anton Fuller, he was going to be kept in overnight for further observation and hopefully released in the morning.

'We need a bloody drink,' Moony had said once everything was done for the day. There was no nearby pub at Reservoir Road, but to Rose's surprise, Moony suggested that everyone come over to hers for dinner and drinks. Scarlett had plans – she and her wife were going to their Lindy Hop class. Rose had expected Adam to decline, but he'd said he was child-free and that he'd love to. The hopeful look on his face as they waited for Rose to reply had propelled the words, 'Oh, okay then, thanks,' out of her mouth before she could stop herself.

Rose drove home to drop off the car and spent half an hour putting on make-up and then wiping it off again. She didn't want to look like she was trying to impress anyone. Not that she was. Trying to impress anyone.

Now, she sits in Moony's North Finchley home, looking around at her surroundings. She's not sure what she expected but it was definitely something a little more eclectic and colourful. They are sitting in a room decorated in various shades of pale grey. Apart from a huge painting over the fireplace – an abstract series of splashes that Rose finally realizes is a motorbike on its side at speed going through a puddle – everything is tasteful and minimalist in here, from the white dining table and chairs to the pale sofas and rugs.

Rose takes a sip of the crisp, cold wine, her taste buds recognizing that it's more expensive than any she's had before. Moony is such an enigma. She rides a motorbike and smokes like a chimney when she isn't mainlining Haribo sweets. But she also has the tidiest house Rose has ever seen. Even if it does smell so strongly of fags that Rose can feel her resistance to one slipping through her fingers like water. It's been a year since she stopped and the urge still sometimes hits her. But she resists. She doesn't need any more reasons to feel bad about herself.

'So,' Moony says as they settle back into the soft grey sofas, facing each other across the coffee table. 'Gregory Fuller. What do we think?'

Rose doesn't really know what she thinks. Gregory had been adamant that the 'boy in the wall' was behind every odd thing going on at number 42 Wyndham Terrace, from the mysterious banging to the damaged photo and cut flowers, to the even more disturbing 'accidents' that had befallen Anton Fuller over the last few months.

Rose takes a slightly too-big sip of her wine and waits for Adam to reply first. Thankfully, he obliges.

'Well,' he says, 'we either have a very disturbed little boy who needs psychiatric care – and we'll find that out after he's been assessed – or there *is* some kind of presence in that house as he claims there is.'

Moony nods and sparks up another cigarette, her small hands fluttering, inhaling deeply.

'What do you know about poltergeists, Rose?'

Rose puts her glass down on the coffee table. 'Not a lot, to be honest. I mean, I've seen the old film of that name and that's about it.'

Moony looks expectantly at Adam.

'So the most famous case was probably the one that happened in Enfield, in the 1970s,' he says, sitting back. 'I suppose it all happened not that far from where we're based.'

His shirt has come slightly undone and a small triangle of brown skin appears at his waistline. The skin at Rose's throat gets warmer. She takes another sip of the wine, finding with disappointment that she has somehow finished her glass.

Adam goes on to describe the case that became famous around the world, after a single mother called Peggy Hodgson, living in a council house in North London with her two daughters, called the police in 1977 to report that furniture was being moved around and that there was knocking in the walls. The two girls, thirteen-year-old Margaret and eleven-year-old Janet seemed to be the focus of the events, which progressed to supposed attacks on them and episodes of levitation.

'Over that time,' says Adam, 'lots of different people got involved, from a psychic investigator who wrote a book about it, to the *Mirror* newspaper and others. Even the police at the original call-out claimed to have witnessed something if I remember rightly.'

'I remember it,' says Moony, tapping her cigarette into a small, crystal ashtray on the table. 'Was all over the news at the time. The family were quite the stars.'

Her arch tone makes Rose turn to look at her. 'So it was all bullshit?'

Moony makes a face. 'I've read quite a bit about it, for obvious reasons. There was some evidence that the girls had faked some of the events. For example, one of them was caught on camera trying to bend a spoon. So my feeling is that there wasn't necessarily a ghost.' She pauses. 'The girls themselves seem to have got so caught up in the whole thing and it may have been attention-seeking. But there is also an argument that poltergeist activity is somehow caused by the children themselves.' She shrugs. 'I'm not sure I believe that. And it doesn't feel quite like what Gregory is saying anyway.'

All three are silent for a moment.

'Poor kid,' says Rose. 'Whatever's going on in his head, or in that house, that's one unhappy little boy.'

Adam sighs. 'I'm not a psychiatrist but it's possible that the military regime his father makes him live under is giving him murderous impulses that he's trying to name as something else. You know, in order to cope with them.'

'Hmm,' says Rose. 'That might be the case. But maybe we ought to look at the house a bit more closely anyway.' She is quiet for a moment before continuing. 'I don't know which is worse, really,' she says, 'if you're him.'

This disturbing thought seems to subdue them all. The harsh buzz of the doorbell then makes Rose flinch.

Moony gets to her feet.

'The Gods of Deliveroo have smiled on us at last,' she says. 'Come on.'

They eat the Indian takeaway at the dining room table, which Moony has laid out with a tasteful white cloth and heavy cutlery. There are even candles. It all seems a bit much for a Wednesday work meal. Rose is more used to sharing a bag of Chilli Heatwave Doritos with Mack across the desk, but she settles in, grateful for the soft, rosy comfort of the light.

'You still with us?'

'What?' She starts at Adam's voice, realizing she has drifted away from the conversation. The curry sits heavily in her stomach as she blinks her gritty eyes. The cumulative lack of sleep is taking its toll.

'I need to piss,' says Moony with her characteristic bluntness and Rose finds Adam's eyes, a smile on his lips.

'TMI,' he murmurs and takes a sip from the glass of whisky he's moved on to.

Rose smiles and drinks from her glass of water. Needs to slow down on that wine.

In the hall Moony's phone rings. She says, 'Yup?' then lowers her voice to something more intimate.

Adam raises an eyebrow at Rose, who laughs.

'Has she got a man, do we think?' she says.

'No idea,' he says, 'but she's certainly been in a different mood lately. Maybe that's the reason?'

They exchange grins and then Rose gazes down at the table, suddenly lost for anything else to say. The silence seems to expand between them.

'You doing okay?' says Adam. He looks far too attractive in this candlelight and for a moment Rose pictures herself shocking him by leaning over and pressing her lips to his. This forces a weird laugh out of her mouth, which she hadn't intended. Adam looks puzzled.

'Yeah, sorry!' she says, too brightly now. 'I've not been sleeping all that well, you know. Bit tired.'

'I'm not surprised,' says Adam. 'I'm not sure I'd ever sleep again if I'd been through what you did last year.'

Rose looks down again, shocked at the emotion that has come over her, stoppering her throat.

'You know we have to watch out for PTSD, don't you, in this line of work?' he continues. 'Did you end up having the counselling you're entitled to?'

She shifts uncomfortably. Rose moved to a new department not long after it happened and there was clearly an admin error of some kind because she never received the paperwork. The trouble is, the very last thing she wants is to have to sit across from some therapist and lie about the weirdness of her living arrangements. No, she doesn't have PTSD. She just has a complicated life. But she'll cope with it on her own, as she has always done in the past.

Adam places a hand on her arm, only for a moment, but the effect of his warm skin on hers is electric. Her breath hitches in her throat. Their eyes meet and she knows she has betrayed how she feels because an expression of confusion crosses his face. It was simply a friendly pat on her arm, part of his concern for a colleague, nothing more. And now she has made it weird and uncomfortable by wearing her lust like a neon sign on her head. It has been a long time since she has been touched, that's all. The last time someone touched Rose's skin, they wanted to kill her.

This thought, as clear and bold as if someone has whispered it into her ear, is a cold clamp around the heart.

Rose has never felt lonelier in her life than she does in this moment, sitting in uncomfortable silence with her colleague as the candlelight flickers.

Moony comes back into the room now, brandishing a fresh bottle of wine.

'Time for a top-up?' Her eyes are bright and there's something Rose can't read in them. But she doesn't have the energy to think about it. She stands up hurriedly.

'Not for me,' she says. 'I think I'm going to get off.'

'Oh.' Moony looks visibly deflated. 'You're no fun. It's only ten thirty!'

'Sorry.' It feels claustrophobic in here all of a sudden and she wants to be outside.

'Can't I get you an Uber though?' says Moony and there is a note of desperation in her voice that comes as a surprise.

'I feel like a bit of air so I'll walk up to the tube station,' says Rose. 'No problem.'

'Do you want me to come with you?' says Adam, getting to his feet.

'No,' says Rose hurriedly. 'I don't mean to be a downer. I'm knackered, that's all. It's been great!' She knows she sounds shrill and her smile is too wide, lips drawn back in a rictus. But she can't seem to be normal right now. 'I've had a really nice time,' she says. 'I think I'll get off all the same.'

As Rose walks down the elegant black-and-white-tiled path and through Moony's gate, she groans inwardly. How can she be a professional woman of thirty years old – someone who has put actual killers away – and somehow still feel like such a *child*? She may as well have written 'I FANCY YOU, ADAM' in black marker ink across her forehead back there. If she could climb right out of her own skin and walk away from it, she would.

Is she ever going to have that feeling of being with family again with her work colleagues? The way she had at Silverton Street?

Rose contemplates calling Mack for about five seconds until she dismisses the idea. Far too late in the evening for a social call. She could never tell him about why she's cringing so much anyway.

On the High Street, Rose gets out her phone to look for exactly where Woodside Park station is and is distracted by music seeping out of a busy pub a few doors down. It looks like some sort of craft beer pub and it's humming with life.

She needs to get home and into her bed. Maybe a decent night's sleep will help sort out her muddled head a bit. The very last thing she needs is another drink.

But as she looks in the window, she sees a group of people about her own age, quite well dressed but all having a riotous time. There's a woman with similar colouring to Rose and for a minute she imagines she is her. She works for a marketing company, perhaps, and is getting engaged to the guy opposite, who is looking at her with clear adoration. They don't want kids yet but when they do, her lovely mum will help out. She can't wait to be a grandma; everyone says so.

Then Rose pictures herself turning the key in her own front door and coming carefully into the hall to see whether Adele's ghoulish presence is hovering inside the living room. Rose will walk past her and go upstairs to the bedroom, where she will climb into cold sheets, alone, and picture the moment when she woke up to a darkness so thick it had a texture.

James Oakley had disabled the two streetlights outside her bedroom that night and was waiting, like a malignant mass, outside her door. Her body starts to shake, almost involuntarily, and she clenches her fists at the wave of revulsion that threatens to engulf her.

No one has touched you since someone tried to kill you.

The sentence plays through her mind again, cruel and daring at the same time.

Go on, it seems to say, as she pushes open the door of the pub and orders a large glass of Sauvignon Blanc. *Go on,* it seems to say, as she opens the dating app on her phone for only the second time.

Go on, it seems to say, as, five minutes later, with a glass of Dutch courage inside her, she swipes right.

11

Rose Gifford's sexual history has been a lopsided affair.

Her first encounter happened at eighteen, which felt embarrassingly late in comparison to her peers. But when she went to do the A levels required to join the police, it's fair to say she made up for it.

Having to retake all her GCSEs after failing badly the first time around, Rose was a little older than her fellow students and, yet again in her life, an outsider. It was through the job she did several evenings a week in a popular pub in Camden that she discovered, for the first time, that she could have fun.

Rose would be invited to parties all the time there and while she turned down many invitations, she met a number of men that way. The longest relationship was with a plumber and part-time DJ called Josh, whom Rose saw on and off for a year. But she always held back. She could never really talk about her childhood, and she wouldn't take anyone home where Adele Gifford might get her claws into them. Eventually, Josh ended things. He's now happily married with two children, Rose has discovered from some light social media stalking.

There were plenty of one-night stands then too.

One morning, she came into the house in order to shower before college and Adele made a comment about time repeating itself. That this reminded her of Rose's mother, Kelly, at a similar age. Kelly had died of a drug overdose and beyond a fleeting memory of sitting on a woman's knee as she read picture books to her, Rose has no real recollection of her. The barb had reached its target though.

Rose is different to her mother and her grandmother. This is important. No, it is *the most important* thing. So she had reined in the partying and concentrated on her A levels, finally doing well and being propelled into her police apprenticeship.

Apart from a couple of dates here and there, her night with Sam Malik from Silverton Street last year had been the only recent encounter she'd had. But Sam and her clearly weren't meant to be.

Now she extracts her thick hair from the ponytail she wears most days and fluffs it around her face a bit, hoping to look less like a person who has come from a difficult day at the office. She applies eyeliner and lipstick, before undoing two buttons of her patterned shirt.

'Not too bad for a big weirdo,' she murmurs at her own reflection in the pub bathroom mirror.

The guy, who is called Ewan, is a pleasant surprise when he walks into the bar, dark eyes scanning for Rose. Floppy dark hair, beard. Easy smile. He's about six foot two and subtly muscled, his chest and arms showcased by a black T-shirt.

They get talking over drinks. He works for a PR company specializing in the electronics market in Newbury and is here on business. Rose says she works at the head office of Marks and Spencer, simply because it sounds like quite a nice place to work and why not? She imagines all the free knickers she might get in this other, carefree life.

They talk about being native Londoners. They talk about television and they talk about nothing much. They get drunker. Rose notices him catching sight of himself in the mirror behind the bar at one point and fiddling with a bit of dark brown hair that has fallen over his eyes to position it just so. And wait, did he slightly suck in his cheekbones then? Rose is overcome with a desire to giggle.

She leans in close and murmurs, 'You are really, really *ridiculously good-looking*,' then starts to laugh so hard she can't stop. Either Ewan has never seen the male fashion send-up *Zoolander*, or he is choosing to ignore this because he grins and pulls her in for a kiss, warm and soft and lingering.

Half an hour later, they're back in his hotel room. Rose is moving on top of him and thinking he has quite an appealing sex-face, which is a relief. He snaps open his eyes and grins and then skilfully turns her round so she is lying beneath him, and she doesn't think about anything at all apart from bright, focused pleasure for a few moments.

She is almost there, feeling herself begin to ride a wave when a sudden picture comes into her mind of a man in black leaning over her, pressing gloved fingers across her mouth and nose, pressing, pressing, pressing the air from her lungs.

She can't breathe.

Her body stills.

Stop! NOW!

A scream wrenches itself from her throat and she reaches behind and smacks her fist into his thigh.

'Stop!' But he doesn't straight away and so she wriggles hard from underneath him so he almost falls off her, and she semi crawls across the bed and thumps onto the floor, hurting her shoulder.

'I said stop, for fuck's sake!'

He peers down at her, an undignified, terrified naked huddle on the floor, a look of shock and yes, anger on his face.

'I didn't hear you!' he says. 'What the fuck happened then? I thought you were enjoying yourself!'

Rose hurriedly picks up the items of clothing near the bed and begins to stuff her legs into her knickers and her shirt over her head.

'I'm sorry,' she mumbles. 'It's not you. I need to go.'

Ewan swears quietly under his breath and gets up before going into the bathroom and closing the door.

Her heart thuds sickeningly loud in her chest and her ears feel oddly muffled, as though she is under water.

Out on the street, she's trembling and can't seem to get warm.

But most of all, she's angry. She can't have a proper relationship because of the complications of her life, and now, evidently, a bit of quickie sex is out too thanks to what happened last year. It's not fair.

Since she was a little girl, she had been asking the question: 'Why can't I just be normal?'

Nothing changes, it seems.

12

Rose's hangover is a giant, malign hand squeezing her skull in a rhythmic fashion and she's counting the minutes until she can take the next lot of painkillers. She tries to focus on the meeting about Gregory, which takes place the next afternoon.

The bodies concerned are the Child Abuse Investigation Team and a social worker from Camden Council's Family Services and Social Work Division. CAMHS – the Child and Adolescent Mental Health team are not present. No one is available.

'Good job Gregory is a totally balanced kid then,' Adam had muttered, looking angrier than Rose had ever seen him after he had tried to organize their presence. As pressures on the service stand, they were lucky to get someone from CAIT. And that was only because Moony has a contact there who organized this quickly.

Scarlett has made coffees and teas all round and is keeping a discreet distance as the others take their seats in the briefing area.

The woman from CAIT, called Zoe, is around forty, with a careworn face, short, braided hair and what appears to be a heavy cold. She disappears into a tissue to sneeze every few minutes and then apologizes, before dabbing at raw-looking nostrils. The social worker, Angela, is a woman in her fifties, who keeps looking around and blinking hard, then adjusting the floral scarf held together with a brooch at her neck.

Moony isn't present, having been called away to something with only a vague comment about checking in later.

'Thanks for coming,' says Adam, kicking things off. He has a way of speaking with immense warmth in his eyes, even when he isn't actually smiling. It's almost unbearably desirable. Rose forces her mind back to why they are here.

There's a murmured response from the two women, then Zoe sniffles once more into her tissue.

'I'm so sorry,' she says, 'it's hay fever. It happens like this every single year and makes me grim company.'

'Worse for you though,' says Rose and the other woman gives her a small, grateful smile.

'So let's get started,' says Adam. 'We've created a Merlin report about Gregory Fuller, as you know.' Merlin is a database that's used whenever a child becomes involved in any police business and can be accessed by various agencies, police and civilian. 'We have been looking into reports of neighbour harassment at a property in Kentish Town,' he continues, 'and it came to light that the boy, Gregory, believes a "boy in the wall" is out to harm his dad.'

'That's Anton Fuller?' says Angela, checking something on a sheet of paper and writing in the large notebook on her lap. 'And I believe he has been rather accident-prone lately?'

'That's right,' says Rose, and reads out the list of visits Anton Fuller has had to A&E over the last six months.

'Could Gregory be to blame on all these occasions?' says Zoe. 'Because that raises a red flag for me straight away.'

'It's complicated,' says Rose, with a slight grimace. 'We have no evidence that Gregory had any role in the previous accidents and he says he really didn't do anything then. I do believe him on that. This time, though, he admits he was trying to, well, scare his father into being ill.'

'What does that mean though?' says Angela. 'You mentioned it in the report but I didn't understand.'

'No,' says Zoe. 'Me neither.'

Adam explains the basics of the nocebo effect and there is silence for a few moments after.

Zoe rubs at her nose again and sits forward in her seat. 'So,' she says, 'are you saying that Gregory *hoaxed* his dad into feeling poisoned but Anton Fuller actually reacted as though he *had* been poisoned? Surely that's just ridiculous?'

Rose has read quite a lot about the nocebo effect in the last couple of days. It seemed to explain why people who had been 'cursed' by Voodoo exhibited extreme physical effects. On a less sensational but even more tragic level, there was one man who died of liver cancer at the exact time doctors predicted to him, even though a mistake had been made in the diagnosis. The tumour was in fact nowhere near as deadly as they had first believed, but the man was so sure he would die in the timeframe he had been told, he died anyway.

'No,' says Rose, 'it's a genuine physical reaction. I mean, they wouldn't use placebos in medical trials if they were worthless, and this is only the same effect, but the negative side of it. It's a proper thing. Bodies behave as though they're affected by something if the mind is convinced enough of it. In one case, people had more side effects if they were told a drug was stronger than it actually was. It's very weird, but it really happens.'

'And Anton Fuller has a bit of a phobia about accidental poisoning,' adds Adam, 'because of something that happened when he was a child and accidentally ate some berries. For him, this was about the worst thing he could imagine, I expect.'

'It's bizarre,' says Angela, once more glancing around the room as though the next strangest thing will be found there. *Maybe it will,* thinks Rose, and only hopes the ghostly tea lady won't suddenly wander in and silently offer some manner of wartime treat.

Her phone buzzes then and she glances down to see the message from a number she doesn't recognize.

Want 2 know what happened. U made me feel like some sort of rapist. WTF?

Oh God, that Ewan bloke. Rose's cheeks flush and she turns her phone to silent, then places it so she can't see the screen. She's going to have to block him. Adam is speaking but his eyes are on her, a slight frown wrinkling his brow.

'. . . crucially though,' he says, 'Gregory appears to be doing this with good intentions. He said he wanted his father out of the house and this felt like a safe way of doing it without seriously hurting him. I'm not exactly sure whether he intended the effect to be quite so severe.'

'What is he like, this Anton Fuller?' says Zoe, looking down at her notes.

'He's a teacher at a posh school,' says Rose, dragging herself mentally back into the meeting. 'He clearly rules the roost at home. Gregory's mother seems totally under his dubious spell. It's all rules and regulations and no telly. I don't think there are a lot of cuddles in case they interfere with study time. That sort of house.'

Zoe makes a face and writes something down. 'Do you suspect any actual abuse, of Gregory, I mean?' she asks, eyes moving between Rose and Adam, hand poised over her pad.

'I think we'd have to leave that to you to ascertain,' says Adam, 'but apart from being tutored and coached to within an inch of his life, he seems like a reasonably cared-for child. I mean . . .' he pauses '. . . as Rose said about Gwen, I'm not sure Gregory is exactly put first in that house. But I don't think he's in any danger from his parents. I think he really believes someone is haunting him.'

Angela looks from Zoe, to Rose, to Adam.

'Look,' she says, 'can you explain again what your actual remit is here?'

Adam pauses long enough for Rose to realize it's her turn. It's probably about time she forced herself to actually say the words.

'We look into what we call uncharted crimes,' she says. 'So anything that doesn't have an obvious explanation is part of our remit. And there are enough odd details about this case for us to be interested.'

Angela grimaces and pulls her scarf closer around her throat. 'Is that why you're in this spooky old building? I've had a funny feeling about it since the moment I walked in here.'

'It's an unorthodox department,' says Adam, saving her. 'But we're essentially all on the same page here, which is making sure a child isn't in danger.'

'Now, only a psychiatric assessment will help us to determine whether Gregory has an actual psychosis and believes he is seeing ghosts,' says Zoe. 'But as you said, Adam, the fundamental purpose of all this is to work out if he is at risk. If he isn't and is acting out because his dad makes him work too hard, well, I'm afraid there are many, many more deserving cases on which we have to stretch increasingly limited resources.'

Adam and Rose exchange slightly desperate looks. It feels as though this is all slipping away from them by the minute.

Zoe closes her notebook. 'I'm going to be meeting with Gregory this afternoon and I'll get back to you.'

Angela begins to gather her bags. 'I think we're done?' she says. 'I'll also be starting a file on the family, but in all honesty, this isn't going to be getting a lot of attention when there are so many pressures on our resources, as Zoe said.'

Rose accompanies the two women back to the main reception area, down the corridors with their painted brick and signs that are older even than Angela.

When they get to the door, Zoe makes her farewells, and goes, sneezing, to her car.

Angela hesitates and turns to Rose.

'I heard about this department once,' she says. 'But I didn't really believe in it. Sounds a bit too much like . . .'

'. . . *The X Files*, yes I know,' says Rose, managing to hide the weariness. 'But it really isn't like that here. We have to be open to less obvious explanations for crimes, that's all.'

Angela gives her a pinched look. 'I wasn't going to say that,' she says. 'I was going to say, a bit too much like a daft rumour with no basis. Well, I was wrong about that.'

'Seems you were,' says Rose.

'Look,' says Angela, more quietly. 'I am a lot more open-minded than you might think. I grew up in a house where I would sometimes see a young woman holding a baby on the landing. Terrified the life out of me at first; then I found her sort of comforting. I told my parents but no one believed me, of course. I have sympathies for what you're doing here. And I have a lot of sympathy for this boy, Gregory, whether or not he is having a psychotic breakdown, is simply acting out like a kid who doesn't get enough attention, or whether he really does sense something in the house. I'll let you know how it goes as soon as I can, okay?'

'Okay, thank you,' says Rose, surprised and grateful.

She gives one last uncomfortable look behind Rose and hurries out to her car.

Rose sighs then walks back down the echoey corridor, the heels of her boots tapping. Maybe Gregory will need to have some sort of therapy for whatever it is that's driving him. But something isn't right. She feels it. And it isn't only her unwanted awareness of the dead that's driving her on in this case.

It's her instincts as a policewoman.

13

Rose goes to the supermarket on the way home. It's about time she has a proper meal. She is going to make some roast chicken for herself with all the trimmings, even if she has no real idea about how she is going to go about any of it. Still, she has her phone. She'll work it out.

Before she goes inside, she sends Ewan a message saying, *It really wasn't you, but me. I'm sorry. But let's leave it there.*

Dots appear, signifying an incoming reply but Rose swiftly blocks the number before she can see it. No point opening a dialogue. Not with her life the way it is. And certainly not with a man who checks his cheekbones are on point, over her shoulder.

Still, as she picks out the ingredients for her meal, she can't help imagining herself having a different sort of evening. One where she and her imaginary boyfriend eat their dinner at the table and discuss their days with easy familiarity. One where she sleeps in a bed, curled up next to him, rather than huddled on the sofa, flinching awake at every sound.

As she comes through the front door with her bulging carrier bags, the letter on the inner mat catches her eye straight away. It is a formal-looking white envelope but handwritten. After carrying it through to the kitchen, she puts it on the table, while she stows the shopping away, then makes a cup of tea. She'll sit down for a little while and then get cracking on her gastro-nomic adventure.

When she opens the envelope and stares at the letter inside, it takes a few moments for the words to reach her brain. And then she says, 'Oh shit.'

It's from a solicitor's firm called Allen and Isherwood. It says that the man who was her mother's landlord – and then hers – for all these years has died. His son is selling the house. Rose has one month to move out.

Her heart begins to race. She knew this day was going to come at some point but was able to push it to the back of her mind most of the time. It's not that she *likes* living in this dark little semi-detached house in East Barnet. If anything, it's the albatross around her neck and reminds her every single day of her miserable childhood. And that's not to mention the fact that it is haunted by her mother.

But there are several reasons to stay.

For a start, Rose's salary isn't going to go far for a property of her own in London. She could move up to near where UCIT is, but the thought fills her stomach with a cold stone of disap-pointment. It's a bit grim around there. If anything she would like to live more centrally, somewhere with a bit of life. Ironic to say that though when it's death that is also keeping her here.

Her internal logic goes like this: Adele's ghost is tied to the house. If Rose stays here, she can be in control of when she sees it. If she moves away and Adele comes with her, Rose is never going to be able to have a normal life.

She's aware the logic is somewhat shaky. Rose goes to the fridge and pours a large glass of orange juice, still thinking.

The slight disturbance of air in the room is like someone has slammed a door somewhere in the house, even though she hears nothing. It's more like a change in pressure and as she turns her body she lets out a shriek and almost drops the glass.

Adele Gifford is standing right behind her, as substantial as a real woman but Rose knows that an outstretched hand will only meet cool air. Adele is wearing a strapless dress that's far too young for her wrinkled décolletage and has her hair done differently. It's in a twisted sort of bun Rose remembers from when she used to get a hairdresser friend to come round and give her a 'do' as she put it. Her eyes are closed and her mouth works as if she is speaking, her face a picture of distress. Rose notices the sparkly dangly earrings that she used to sometimes try on secretly are somehow reflecting the light, just like real earrings would.

'Get lost,' she says. 'Just leave me alone.' She makes a noise of disgust and backs away from the figure, which reaches out its fingers towards her. The characteristic talons with their shell-pink polish look filthy, and there is thick dirt under the nails. That's new, and horrible. This in itself somehow fills Rose with a terrified sort of rage.

'Get out!' she bellows, with every breath in her body. 'I won't have you here! Get out, get out!' Even though every fibre of her being resists the horror of getting nearer to this thing in front of her, she throws herself forward, hands outstretched as if she could push the spectre out of her kitchen.

Of course, there's nothing there. She falls forward and almost hits the kitchen table.

Adele has gone.

Too upset to cook now, Rose sinks into a chair at the kitchen table. There was a time, not long ago, when she became inured to these visits. She was disturbed by them, of course, but they were so frequent they almost passed for normal after a while. It's somehow much worse having had such a long break. So cruel to make her think that it was over.

But why is she back now?

Rose's eyes skate to the letter on the table. It *has* to be because of that! She experiences a flash of something like hope in her chest. Perhaps Adele really will be gone forever once she moves out? Maybe that's why she's back? It looked as though she were beseeching Rose in some way . . . trying to tell her something.

Maybe Adele knows that whatever is causing this horrendous unwanted reality needs all three sides of the triangle to exist: Rose, Adele and the house itself.

'I'm getting away,' says Rose to the empty kitchen, raising her glass of orange juice to the air. 'Here's to me being shot of you once and for all. You can creep around in here forever for all I care.'

Rose forces herself to cook the meal, which she eats mechanically, barely tasting it. Carrying a mug of tea into the living room, she looks around cautiously, in case the spectre is standing anywhere nearby, but she *feels* alone, in a good way.

Switching on the television, she finds a Netflix comedy that she can numb out to and contemplates her new situation.

The insistent way Adele had behaved was disturbing. She had never reared up behind Rose like that before. That had been horrible and alarming. But maybe it really was due to desperation that her days were numbered?

Rose reaches for her iPad and starts looking at rental properties in her area. She has been paying a peppercorn rent for a long time, she quickly discovers. Suddenly overcome with a vast weariness about the whole business of having to sort out this house and find somewhere else to live, she puts the iPad down again and mindlessly watches the television under her duvet.

The harsh ringtone of her phone sometime later is an aural assault. She hadn't even realized she'd fallen asleep. For a moment she can't find the phone, then feels the vibration against her back and retrieves it from where it slipped behind her body on the sofa.

The caller ID says, *Gwen Fuller.*

Rose heaves a sigh and contemplates not answering. There's nothing she can do about whatever is going on in that house. As Moony said to her when she first started working at UCIT, they're in the business of solving crimes, not carrying out exorcisms. She's not sure what else she can do.

But what if it's Gregory, and he's in some sort of trouble? She's going to have to answer.

'Hello?'

There's such a loud crackle on the other end, it makes her hold the phone away from her ear in shock. It's followed by a *whirr-click, whirr-click*. Like something being turned. A picture comes into her mind of an old-fashioned telephone, where people had to dial the number with a finger. Adele had a broken one that Rose sometimes used to play with as a little girl and she could remember the effort of turning the stiff rotary dial with her small digits.

'Is someone there?' she says again.

Whirr-click, whirr-click.

There's the sound of breathing now, very faintly. Someone's on the other end.

'Gregory?' she says. 'Is that you? Are you all right?'

A manic giggle makes Rose's stomach free fall. It sounds male, but somehow not a child. It's not Gregory, then. But who? She hears the word 'Rose' as if like a sigh and more breathing, which starts to speed up into a shockingly recognizable rhythm.

Uh-uh-uh.

'Oh God!' she says. 'Are you serious? Are you *wanking*, whoever you are?'

The breathing stops and another low giggle fills her ear. It is the single most malevolent sound Rose has ever heard. Every hair on her body seems to stand to attention. She wants to throw the phone down in disgust but makes herself keep hold of it, her palm beginning to sweat.

'Who is this?' she says in a bold, strong voice she really isn't feeling. 'Because it's not very funny.'

There's a silence, then another painfully loud burst of static that almost makes her drop the phone.

The line goes dead.

Her heart seems to be bouncing around inside her ribcage as she hastily dials the number.

It rings a couple of times, then: 'Hello, this is Gwen Fuller speaking?'

'Gwen,' says Rose, conscious that she is heavily breathing herself now with the shock, 'it's DC Rose Gifford here. Has Gregory tried to call me on this phone again?'

'DC Gifford,' says Gwen, 'no, he definitely hasn't. He's in bed. My phone has been with me the whole time. Hang on . . .'

She's quiet for a moment and then comes back on the line.

'The last number dialled from this phone was this morning so I think you must be mistaken.'

'Right,' says Rose, a little numbly. 'Maybe I was. Sorry to bother you.'

'Well if that's all, I'll—'

'Wait!' says Rose. 'Is everything okay there? How is Anton?'

'They have let him come home,' says Gwen tightly. 'Thank God. He's very weak and his tummy is still quite poorly. But there is no long-lasting damage and we're going to try and put everything behind us now and move on.'

'And Gregory?' says Rose. 'How is he doing?'

Gwen sighs before answering. 'Thinking on,' she says, then, formally: 'Thank you for your concern.'

When Rose comes off the phone, she's shivering, and she chafes her arms. First, she has the weirdness with Adele appearing again after such a long absence. Then this vile and creepy phone call.

It definitely wasn't Gregory on the other end. It had sounded like a young male – maybe someone in their teens, judging by the voice, and well, the behaviour. Was it a crossed line? Was that even a thing that could happen anymore? It probably could. But the person, whoever it was, on the other end of the phone, had whispered her name at one point.

Rose turns up the volume on the television with the remote

control, simply to surround herself with something real and normal and pulls the blanket around her once again.

It must have been some sort of technological glitch.

But Rose's skin won't stop crawling.

Because there was something about that voice that wasn't entirely human.

14

By the time Rose climbs into her childhood single bed, she is so tired she can barely see straight.

She hasn't been able to make it back to the double bed yet, the one she was sleeping in on the night of the attack. And even in this lumpy, too-small one, she sometimes wakes up in a panic. But the whole episode with that bloke last night – and she is still shuddering at how it played out – has made her yearn for a bit of normality. She can't face the sofa tonight.

If she had any sleeping pills in the house, she'd take them. But she's resisted, fearing ending up suspended in some horrific paralysis between being awake and asleep, just like Oakley's victims. She has experienced it once, thankfully, but has no desire to be anywhere in between ever again.

Before closing her eyes, she runs through the usual mental checklist. The radio is on in the background. The hall light blazes on. She has her phone plugged in next to her on the bedside table, and a large battery-operated torch just in case. At the side of the bed is her baton, propped up so it's the first thing she touches when she reaches out. A pair of handcuffs are under the pillow, along with a kitchen knife. She's practised what she would do if anyone were in the room many times now in a series of smooth, swift movements. At least, it is when she's fully awake.

It helps. If only she could simply switch herself off for the night, like a household appliance.

As her eyelids finally begin to droop, a memory from last night comes back to her in bright detail, so intense it makes her insides fizz. She was lost in the pleasure of the moment, body moving on top of that bloke. He might be a vain idiot, but he felt very good. Until she made it all weird and showed herself up. Wincing once again, Rose curls herself into a ball and wills sleep to come.

In the wee small hours, the dream comes.

She's walking up the road to her old police station at Silverton Street, feeling light and happy. As she enters, Omar, the giant desk sergeant, is singing something that sounds like opera. He loves musicals but dream Omar is something else again. Rose claps enthusiastically as she passes him and goes through the double doors to the main working area, where she can see all her old colleagues at work. No one looks up when she greets them and they all keep their heads down. That's when she notices the floor is no longer covered in the worn institutional carpet, but in twigs and dirt, like the ground in a forest.

She calls out to her colleagues to 'mind their shoes', which seems eminently sensible but no one pays any attention. Then her own feet are sinking into the ground as though the forest floor is a twiggy quicksand. Rose tries to cry for help but has no voice. She clings to DC Ewa Duggan's desk but her fingers slip and the earth begins to close around her.

Now she is pressed against something cold and flat. She manages to lift her head to see that she's against a wall, the wall in her bedroom, but some force is stopping her from pulling away from it. It's like powerful glue is keeping her suspended there and when she attempts to pull back, the wall bends and warps and comes with her. Then she's free again and the relief is enormous, but now she's scuttling along the wall like a spider, looking down at her own sleeping form in the bed. Rose in the bed is as still as if she were dead. Dream Rose feels the need

to call out to her but can't make her voice work beyond a
hoarse barking sound.

Then she's falling, falling . . . a long way down into a dark
hole. She's surrounded by earth walls that she must scrape at
with her fingernails. Gregory is buried under here and she has
to get him out. The cold, damp soil crumbles and breaks under
her fingers and she can't reach him, can't reach him . . .

Coming awake with a cry, Rose thinks at first she must still be
dreaming. She's in the back garden, fingers buried in the mud
at the far end. Freezing and filthy.

Whimpering, she snatches her hands away from the cold
earth and looks around, dazed. What would be worse? That
she's asleep and unable to wake up? Or finding herself outside
in her bloody pyjamas?

It's only a few seconds before she properly understands that,
yes, she really *is* out here, but it feels longer because it's so hard
to process. *How the hell did she get out here?*

Shaking with horror and the frigid night air, she clambers to
her feet. Hard to tell what time it is. It is as about as dark as
it ever gets in London, which is not very, and there's the omni-
present sound of traffic in the background. But it feels like
morning is still some distance away.

Rose is standing there, unable to move, when a nearby car
alarm shrieks. The blast of shock gets her moving. Shivering
violently and with her teeth chattering, she hurries up the garden
on feet that are almost numb with cold.

The ancient water heater is kind for once. Rose stands under the
steaming jets of the shower for as long as she can, trying to
wash the dirt from her nails and the shocking cold out of her
skin.

Images from the dream tumble through her mind. There was
something about Silverton Street. Then the horrible feeling of
being stuck to the wall and scuttling along it to look down at
herself. The shivering starts up again and Rose starts to cry.

Nightmares are one thing, but if she's going to start sleepwalking out of the house now, she is going to have to get help of some kind.

She pictures herself making an appointment with the GP and attempting to explain any of this. That's not the only thing putting her off; she's almost too ashamed to admit that, even to herself. James Oakley was a family doctor. Ridiculous to think he was in any way representative of his profession! But logic doesn't make her any keener to step foot in a surgery.

No, she thinks miserably, as she dries herself with the towel, the night-time cold already creeping back into her limbs, she's going to have to find a way to live through this and get to the other side on her own. Like she always has.

Her phone rings as she's drinking a second cup of coffee that morning, feeling wretched after her terrible night. The horror of those dreams clings to her and she still can't seem to get warm.

When she sees the caller ID, it's irritation that spikes rather than the queasy blend of fear and disgust she experienced the night before.

'Okay, you ghostly little wanker, what have you got this time?' she murmurs as she answers.

But her sarcasm quickly melts at the terrible sound on the other end of the phone.

'Gwen?' she says. 'What's happened? Is that you?'

More guttural sobbing before Gwen finally speaks.

'It's Gregory,' she manages to force out. 'He's missing!'

15

Rose arranges to meet Adam at Wyndham Terrace. The early morning traffic is already heavy, so she slaps on her siren and tries to blink the tiredness from her stinging eyes.

Gwen hadn't been in a state to communicate anything beyond the fact that her son wasn't in his bed when she went to wake him up. Rose finds herself picturing all the things that can happen to a child, with all the grim knowledge a police officer has.

But maybe he has only wandered off somewhere under his own steam? *Please have wandered off, Gregory,* she thinks, putting her foot down on a stretch of the North Circular that's opened up at her presence.

The temperature has plummeted overnight and according to Capital radio in the car, there's been heavy snow in the north-east. She shivers again at the memory of being in her garden in thin, cotton pyjamas. The wind is a knife in a vengeful hand this morning. It's no weather to be outside if you can help it. And why would Gregory take himself off for a walk without saying anything?

When Rose arrives, she texts Adam to say she's there. A few moments later she sees him jogging around the corner, clearly having parked quite far away. He looks more flustered than she has seen him before, tucking in his shirt as he approaches.

'Late night?' she says, and he appraises her, expression hard to read.

'Something like that,' he says. Rose makes herself brush away the unreasonable feeling of jealousy that he spent the night with someone having hot sex (his ex, perhaps?) while she was being hounded by her dead mother and a horny ghost.

They ring the doorbell and Anton Fuller appears, his skin sallow and his beard looking more untidy than usual. He's wearing a hoodie and jeans that look entirely wrong on him, as though he has dressed up in a costume belonging to someone else.

'Ah, you're here,' he says, averting his eyes from Rose's gaze. 'Come through.' His manner is someone employing great restraint in not barking irritation at them. He almost seems more annoyed than worried, it strikes Rose.

They can hear Gwen sniffing before they go into a living room they haven't been into before. There are two large sofas and lots of dark wooden cabinets and bookcases that seem to belong to a much older, bigger house. A dresser on the far wall is packed with old-looking crockery and the walls are adorned with pictures of horses and red-jacketed people on a hunt.

Gwen gets to her feet from one of the sofas and grasps hold of Rose's arms.

'He's not in his bed!' she wails. 'Where is he?'

'Look,' says Rose, 'we need to get every detail from you so can I ask you to take a deep breath? Is it possible we could have some tea?'

'Yes,' says Adam. 'Okay if I do that?' He directs this at Anton who looks as though Adam has just asked him to donate a kidney. After a moment, he nods crisply.

'You'll find everything next to the sink, and a tray by the toaster!' says Gwen as she swipes at scarlet nostrils; ever the host. But she also sounds like she might shatter into a thousand pieces at any moment.

'Take your time,' says Rose. Gwen sinks back into an uncomfortable-looking wing-backed chair with tufts of hairy stuff bursting through the leather like a creature inside is trying to emerge. 'When did you last see Gregory?' she continues.

'Well . . .' Gwen looks anxiously at Anton before replying. 'We're not exactly sure, is the thing.'

'You're not sure?' Rose's tone is sharper than intended and Gwen's eyes fill with tears again. Anton, still avoiding Rose's gaze, stands awkwardly across the room, one hand on the dresser.

'I mean,' says Gwen, fiddling with the cross at her throat, 'it was such a busy time, what with Anton coming out of hospital earlier than we expected and everything. Gregory and I had our dinner together at six, while Anton slept, and then Gregory went off to his room for the rest of the evening.'

'He was definitely in his room?' says Rose. 'Did you actually see him there, or speak to him after that?'

Gwen looks desperately at her husband, who is staring at his shoes now.

Adam comes into the room, bearing a tray. He's managed to find the milk jug and sugar bowl, all set out neatly as if it were the 1950s. Rose is pleased, knowing this will calm Gwen much more than three mugs of builder's tea balanced between his two hands would have done.

Gwen takes over pouring the tea, her hands shaking so a thin stream of liquid slops over the side of the cup. It's likely no one wants tea but the action of trying to steady herself to do this is working as Rose hoped. When Gwen speaks again, her voice is pitched lower and quieter than before.

'I usually go and say goodnight,' she says, then, more forcefully, 'but as I say, it was rather an unusual evening. Everything was a bit topsy-turvy. I lost track of things a little bit.'

'Did you hear him in his room? Music playing, anything like that?' says Adam.

'Not that I recall,' Gwen says. 'It wasn't our usual evening so I can't absolutely say for sure.'

'Right,' says Rose, glancing at Adam. 'So your last actual sighting of your son was at 6 p.m. last night?'

The word 'yes' rips with a sob from Gwen, who buries her face in her hands.

Anton stares, ashen-faced, at the floor. Rose has the curious feeling again that more than being concerned for his son, he's ashamed and embarrassed. It might be partly the fact that the boy is missing and it reflects badly on him. Or maybe it is all tied up with what happened yesterday. The fact that he had such a dramatic overreaction to something that was essentially a hoax seems to have diminished him somehow.

'Can we see his room?' says Adam, rising to his feet.

'Yes, yes of course,' says Gwen, getting up hurriedly.

She leads them up two flights of stairs and then up a short but steep set into the attic bedroom.

The walls are covered in an old-fashioned print of planes that could have been there from another era. The only poster on the wall is of two Arsenal players Rose vaguely recognizes bowing and doing some sort of celebratory, jokey handshake.

There's a large dormer window, low enough to see out from and she crosses the room to see the neat rectangles of gardens below. The room is tidy. A single bed with a plain blue duvet has a long, squashy cushion thing shaped like a caterpillar along the pillows that looks well hugged. Along with a desk and chair, there's a wardrobe and chest of drawers, plus a small cupboard painted green, tucked into what would be the roof space. Rose crosses to the desk, which is tidy, with a neat pile of schoolbooks and an Arsenal pencil case.

There's been no attempt to make the bed, or hide the fact that Gregory isn't in it.

Rose would have preferred to see a rolled-up pillow in the bed, or something crudely attempting to replicate a human shape. Judging by the neatness of the rest of the room, Gregory is the kind of boy to make his bed diligently, even if he is running away.

'What about friends?' says Adam. 'Have you spoken to any of them?'

For the first time, Anton Fuller looks upset. His cheeks darken as he and his wife exchange looks.

'He's a self-sufficient boy,' says Gwen. 'And he is very busy with all his studies. He doesn't spend a lot of time hanging out with other children.' Her tone is a little defiant.

'Mobile phone?' says Rose, thinking about poor little Gregory, stuck in this spooky house with these two, no telly, and not even able to go on TikTok or Snapchat like a normal kid.

'Certainly not,' says Anton. He has literally moved closer to Gwen as though their united front is more important than finding their twelve-year-old child. 'We told him he could have a basic mobile in Year Nine but not before.'

Rose pauses, regarding him. Then: 'Can I see your own phones please?' she says.

'Why?' says Anton.

'Yes, why do you want to do that?' echoes Gwen. Rose doesn't respond, so, grumbling, they each harvest phones from pockets. Gwen has an oldish Samsung; Anton, an iPhone 11 by the looks of it.

'Do either of you have a Nokia phone?' says Adam. 'Or any other phone at all in the house?'

'No,' says Anton, clearly finding his usual loud voice again. 'Why are you asking about phones, for goodness' sake?'

'Because,' says Rose, 'we saw Gregory with what looked like a Nokia phone when we came to the house yesterday.'

The Fullers look at each other with shock.

'Must have been the landline?' says Gwen. 'Although I can't imagine who he would be ringing.'

'Show us the landline please?' says Adam and they all troop back downstairs and into the dining room they saw on the first visit. The phone sits on top of a writing bureau opposite the piano where the butchered photograph was.

'That's not the phone Gregory had yesterday,' says Rose. 'It was definitely a mobile. So I take it you weren't aware of the existence of this phone?'

'No,' says Anton through almost bloodless lips, drawn tight. 'Not at all.'

'What does that mean, Anton?' says Gwen, hands fluttering at her cheeks. 'Why would Gregory have a phone we don't even know about? Did some, some *paedophile* give it to him? Is that what they do?' She's in danger of breaking down completely so Rose takes a step closer and places a hand on the other woman's trembling arm, which stills her movement.

'We don't know anything at this stage and jumping to the worst possible conclusion is not going to be helpful at all. Okay?' says Rose.

Gwen nods, chest heaving with the effort of holding herself together.

'Now I need to ask if there are signs of forced entry,' Rose continues. 'Was the front door locked or unlocked when you looked this morning?'

'Definitely unlocked,' says Gwen eagerly. 'And that's a good thing, yes?' she says. 'I'm wondering if he, if he went for a walk or something and maybe had an accident?'

'Don't be silly, Gwen,' Anton booms. 'He wouldn't go *for a walk* without telling us! He's not that kind of child.' He makes the activity sound as likely as Gregory smoking crack.

Gwen opens her mouth to reply but Rose cuts in. 'We'll be checking in to see if there have been any reported accidents immediately. Don't worry,' she says. She can't help thinking Anton is right though. Gregory might pretend to poison his own dad but he's so sheltered, it is very hard to imagine him running away.

Gwen nods her thanks.

'So,' says Adam, 'we'll need to get in contact with absolutely anyone who you think might know where he is. Any family friends or relations he might have gone to without telling you?'

Gwen and Anton exchange unreadable looks.

'We're all self-sufficient,' says Gwen after a beat has passed. 'We don't really need anyone else.' Anton takes her hand and she gives him a watery, grateful smile.

An uncomfortable thought pops into Rose's brain as she regards the couple.

Maybe they don't even need Gregory.

Once the Family Liaison Officer arrives, a young woman called Becky Iordanou, Rose and Adam leave.

A missing child case immediately pulls in all resources available and a bigger team is required than even the combined forces of UCIT and the original Kentish Town officers. A major incident room is quickly set up in the headquarters of Serious Crime Command, based at Cobalt Square.

Once Rose and Adam are inside the vast red-brick building with its Met Police blue window frames forty-five minutes later, the rumble of trains from nearby Vauxhall station is immediately silenced.

The DCI in charge – a grizzled, acne-scarred man in his late forties with a Birmingham accent – is called Brian Mortimer. He greets them at the reception desk and takes them through the double doors into the spacious, modern office beyond.

'Glad to have you,' he says. 'I've been speaking to Sheila Moony and she's released you both for this investigation because you've been involved with the family this last week. There are also two officers from Kentish Town who had initial contact with the family as part of the team. Report to me but keep DS Moony in the loop, okay? You can fill us in at the first briefing about your involvement.'

With that he gives them a brisk nod and then walks off.

'Wonder how much he knows about UCIT?' Rose says out of the corner of her mouth.

'Senior officers have usually heard about us,' says Adam quietly. 'Here's hoping we're welcomed with open arms by the rest of the team, eh?'

The briefing room is large and comfortable, with room for everyone. Rose and Adam sit together near the front.

DCI Mortimer stands by the large interactive whiteboard that is currently blank and looks around the room until a hush begins to fall, slowly at first and then it's quiet.

'Thank you, everyone,' he says. 'So this is the investigation into the disappearance of one Gregory Fuller, a twelve-year-old boy from an address in Kentish Town who hasn't been seen since last night, at around six. The team comprises my officers from Serious Crime Command, Kentish Town officers and those from a division called UCIT, which is also part of this case. We can do all the introductions as we go. First up, Gail, get us started with a photo?'

He looks at a female colleague, middle-aged and with cropped blonde-grey hair.

She fiddles with the laptop and a picture appears on the screen. It's the recent-ish school picture Rose saw in the house. Gregory is unsmiling and rather startled-looking. He has overly smoothed-down hair that doesn't suit him. Rose can picture Gwen fussing over it that morning.

Her phone vibrates in her pocket and she glances at the caller on the screen. Scarlett. She rejects the call but it rings again. Then a text pops up.

Call me. Urgent. Rose hesitates, then decides she'll answer in a moment.

'Right,' says Mortimer. 'Can the Kentish Town team please fill us in on this family and the first contact with them?'

A uniformed officer about Rose's age with a turban and wire-rimmed glasses begins to speak. Next to him is a short, rotund woman with long dark hair and thick, feathery lashes.

'Constable Hardit Choran,' he says. 'Me and my colleague PC Amber Garvey here have been called out to the property on several occasions to deal with a neighbour dispute. The Fullers have had a very bad falling-out with the family next door at number 40, by name of Quinn. The chief complaints were about noise disturbance, with both parties blaming the other.'

'And how bad has it got, Hardit?' says Mortimer. 'Could the family next door have done something to the child, as some sort of revenge?'

Hardit makes a face. 'I don't know,' he says, 'but it did feel like a bit of a pressure cooker. We must have been over there at least four times. We handed it over to colleagues at UCIT recently.' He looks around and sees Rose and Adam.

'DC Adam Lacey,' says Adam, looking around the room. 'We've been called out twice in the last week. Eric Quinn, who seems to be in biggest dispute with Anton Fuller, is an ex-con – burglary, a few years back – with a clean record since then.'

'Okay,' says Mortimer. 'Well, he's an immediate person of interest so let's not muck about and get him in straight away. Tell me about the family,' he continues.

Rose glances at Adam and then takes over. 'DC Rose Gifford,' she says. 'The father, Anton, is a schoolteacher at the Beamish School and a bit of a disciplinarian. Gregory is tutored up to the eyeballs from what we can tell. The mother, Gwen, is very under the thumb. We know that Gregory had a mobile phone the parents were unaware of, because we saw it with our own eyes yesterday. Today, it was very clear that the parents had absolutely no idea about the existence of this phone.'

'Hmm,' says Mortimer. 'That could indicate a plan to run away, or it could have a more sinister implication, of course. Without the number or the phone itself, there's sadly no way of tracing it at all.' He pauses. 'Why were you called out yesterday?'

Rose swallows, conscious of the dryness of her mouth and the many pairs of eyes currently trained on her. 'We discovered that Anton Fuller had been rushed to hospital after a suspected poisoning, which turned out to be a false alarm,' she says. 'Gregory told us he wanted his dad to think he had been poisoned to get him out of the house.'

'God,' says someone to Rose's left.

'Why?' says Mortimer.

'Because—' Rose swallows again '—Gregory is convinced there's some sort of ghost in the wall who is supposedly out to get his dad.'

An uncomfortable ripple passes around the room.

Adam takes over. 'We have all relevant agencies looking into the child's mental health,' says Adam, 'but he hasn't even seen CAMHS yet because it isn't classed as a priority.'

Mortimer makes a face. 'Okay,' he says. 'Well, if the child has delusions he could well have run away. But both parents are obviously suspects here and will need careful questioning. I want the property searched. We have a very large window, unfortunately, for when he could have left the house, of more than twelve hours. We'll need a lot of manpower on checking CCTV in surrounding roads, plus the tube and bus network. It's going to be a bit like finding a needle in a haystack but until we catch sight of the child, we really have nothing else to go on apart from focusing on the parents.'

Rose's phone buzzes with another text. This time it's Moony. *This can't wait.*

'Can you excuse me for a moment?' she says, and creeps out of the room.

She rings Moony just outside the door. The other woman speaks quickly.

A few moments later, Rose comes back into the room. Mortimer catches her eye and her urgent expression makes him hold up a hand for silence.

'I've just learned something that may or may not be relevant,' she says. 'But it certainly needs to be on our radar.'

'Go on, Rose,' says Mortimer.

'Well,' she says, 'it seems there was a multiple murder at that address in 2006.'

16

An urgent murmuring goes around the room. The two officers from Kentish Town exchange worried glances.

When officers are first called out to an address, they'll check the database to see whether there have been any previous call-outs to the property, even historically. Something this serious at the address should at least have been noted, relevant or not.

Mortimer's severe look at Hardit and Amber doesn't go unnoticed.

'Details, please, Rose,' says Mortimer, folding his arms and leaning back against the desk by the whiteboard.

Rose reads the information sent over by Moony to her phone. It was Scarlett who discovered this by simply googling the property, which makes the Kentish Town officers look down at their shoes. Rose can't help feeling wrong-footed too. Maybe *they* should have double-checked?

'So,' she continues, 'the headline is that eighteen-year-old Heather Doyle poured petrol through her own letterbox, then set fire to it. She killed her grandmother, Patricia Doyle, aged seventy-five; her father, Michael Doyle, aged forty-seven; and her half-brother, Samuel Doyle, aged five. I have the notes here and will circulate them by email after the briefing.'

'Can I just say,' says Hardit, palms up, 'I *did* run the usual check. There must have been an error on the system.' It happens. Rose knows all about mistakes, having made some blinders of her own in her time. All it would take would be a clumsy error in the postcode or address for it not to log properly. Anyone looking may miss it, especially in a hurry, especially for a relatively minor issue like a neighbour dispute.

'Don't worry about that now,' says Mortimer turning to him. 'It may have absolutely no bearing on anything, considering how long ago this happened, and with no obvious link apart from an address. What about this Heather Doyle?' he says to Rose. 'Is she in or out now?'

'That's the interesting thing,' says Rose. 'She got released from Edgefield Prison six months ago.'

'. . . which is exactly when the supposed neighbour harassment started,' says Hardit quickly.

The room is buzzing as everyone starts on assigned jobs. Gwen and Anton are going to be questioned separately, as is Eric Quinn and other neighbours. The CCTV job is going to be huge, and many officers have been assigned these duties.

Heather Doyle is first on Rose and Adam's agenda and they are going to get up to speed on the notes on the way.

They are in the car, heading towards Archway.

'It's not very far is it, between Wyndham Terrace and her place?' says Adam.

'No,' says Rose, 'only a short hop on the Northern Line or a bus and you're there. You could walk it quite easily, in fact. But what I'm thinking is, why *would* Doyle have any reason to harass them? And more importantly, what reason could she have for taking Gregory?' She's thoughtful for a moment. 'Hey,' she says, 'do you reckon Anton or Gwen have done something to him? Are they capable?'

Adam is silent for a moment before responding. 'I don't know,' he says. 'It wouldn't be the first time seemingly distraught parents are behind it all along. What do you think?'

Rose sighs. 'God, I don't know,' she says. 'I keep picturing a scenario where Anton Fuller lashes out because he's humiliated and weakened by the whole nocebo thing. I mean, look at the size of him. What if Gregory was accidentally killed and so they panicked and covered it up? I don't think it's the biggest stretch of imagination to have Gwen Fuller as the sort of woman who puts her man before her child. I mean, it's very different, but look at the business at the hospital. I'm not saying she's capable of murder but she does have a weird coldness about her when it comes to Gregory. I'm pretty sure she would back Anton, whatever he'd done.'

'Hmm,' says Adam, his expression grave. 'I think I agree. And what about Quinn next door?'

'Again,' says Rose, 'I'm not sure what the motive would be. I mean, snatch or kill someone's kid because you've had a bit of a spat over the garden fence?'

'It was more than that though,' says Adam. 'You saw how things were between those two men. And Hardit mentioned the pressure cooker feeling about it all. Quinn has previous and looks like a man with a temper. Who knows at this stage, though? Maybe the kid just had enough and ran away.'

'If that's the case, it shouldn't be hard to find him,' says Rose. 'He's about the most un-streetwise kid I've ever met. Even with his mystery phone. Which, I have to admit, is bothering me a lot.'

'Me too,' says Adam. 'And him running away isn't necessarily reassuring because he could end up in all sorts of places. Anyway, let me read up on the woman we're off to see so we know what we're dealing with.'

Reading from the notes on his phone that have now been circulated fully to the team, Adam tells her that Doyle was sentenced to fourteen years for manslaughter and up for release after seven years. 'Then she got into something in prison,' he says, 'slashed the face of another inmate with a broken pen after a fight. She got another six years on top of that.'

He is quiet for a few minutes as he reads on.

Then he lets out a puff of air through his lips.

'There's not much to go on here. She just repeatedly claimed she couldn't remember why she set the fire. When she was assessed by psychiatrists from both defence and prosecution teams, they said she was of sound mind and believed she was lying about the amnesia. Pretty soon after that, she stopped speaking to her legal team and prison staff entirely but pleaded guilty on the day the trial started.'

'Well,' says Rose, slowing and indicating right across a busy junction. 'She's going to need to speak to us. It's just up here.'

They drive along a leafy street past once-grand mansion blocks and a Victorian-era primary school of red brick to Heather Doyle's address: an ugly four-storey block of flats with panels of faded blue paint. As they climb out of the car, a hum of high-pitched chatter and laughter drifts over from the nearby playground.

Rose pictures skinny, round-shouldered Gregory with his owlish glasses and his odd outbursts. She tries to imagine him in the sort of secondary school she went to, where fights were commonplace and a lad called Daniel Barrow once broke a teacher's nose with a chair. That sort of thing probably doesn't happen at the famous Beamishes but where the hell was he?

Be okay. Please be okay.

They climb to the top floor up a stairwell in which the smells of urine and weed are in strong competition. Loud music pumps from several directions. It strikes Rose that the Fullers might want to see what living in bad accommodation is really like. This place certainly isn't worth two million quid.

A few moments later, they're face-to-face with the ordinary-looking woman who killed her entire family.

With skin the pasty grey of the long-term institutionalized, Heather Doyle could pass for closer to forty, rather than her thirty-one years. She's dressed in an oversized sweatshirt and leggings, feet shoved into slippers. Lank brown hair hangs like curtains around a doughy face. Her round green eyes behind cheap plastic glasses would be quite attractive with a bit of make-up, Rose thinks. And without the hostility.

They introduce themselves.

'What do you want?' she says, pulling the door a little closer towards her.

'Just a chat,' says Adam pleasantly. 'Can we come in?'

She hesitates. 'Do I have a choice?'

'Of course,' says Rose. 'We could always do this down at the station if you'd prefer.'

With a heavy sigh Doyle pushes the door open and they follow her into the bedsit.

Inside, the curtains are drawn and the room is lit by a single lightbulb with no shade, giving everything a sickly, depressing air. That's without taking in the décor, which includes a sofa with a large tear in the fake leather cover that grins at them like a yellow-toothed smile.

Rose glances over at the tiny kitchen area. On the surfaces there is only a loaf of the cheapest white bread with slices falling out, some own-brand Nutella and multiple packets of instant hot chocolate.

'Is it okay if we sit down?' says Rose.

'I suppose,' says Heather, gesturing to two hard-backed chairs by a small table. She takes the sofa.

'What's this about then?' she says.

'We understand that you've recently got out on licence from Edgefield?' says Adam.

'Yeah, that's right,' says Heather stiffly. She crosses then uncrosses her legs.

'Can we ask you if you've been anywhere near Wyndham Terrace since you were released from prison?' Adam goes on.

Hearing this address makes her visibly flinch. She starts to pluck at the fabric of her leggings; that is, until she realizes both sets of eyes have been drawn to her busy fingers and stops instantly.

Sitting up a bit straighter, she says, 'Why on earth would I want to go back there?'

Adam smiles, but it doesn't reach his eyes. 'I don't know, Heather,' he says evenly. 'Why don't you tell us?'

'I can't tell you because I don't know,' she says hotly. 'I'm not going to risk breaching the terms of my licence by doing anything like that. I'm not stupid, whatever you think of me. I'm only speaking to you now, rather than telling the pair of you to sling your hooks, because of that licence. But I can tell you right now, I have no desire to ever see that house again. I haven't been further than about one hundred metres from this front door since I got out. I would never go *there*. I wish that house was—' She bites the end of the sentence off, lips clamped shut as if she fears words might slip through.

'Wish it was *what*, Heather?' says Rose.

The fingers begin plucking at her leggings again but she doesn't reply.

'The thing is,' Rose continues, 'the family there have been reporting some . . .' she hesitates '. . . strange harassment that we can't really explain. Do you have any thoughts on that at all?'

Pluck, pluck, pluck.

Rose and Adam exchange looks and wait.

Heather is one clenched muscle, almost vibrating with unspent energy. When she sits forward, the movement is so fast for someone of her size that Rose almost jumps.

'Tell them to burn it down,' she says in a harsh whisper, almost baring her teeth. 'Make a better job of it than me. No one should live there. *No one.*'

'Why?' says Rose, forcing herself to sit forward and match Heather's pose. 'What's the problem with the house? Why did you try to burn it down, Heather?'

Heather's breathing so fast now, she's almost panting. She closes her eyes and presses her hands to the sides of her head.

'I'm not talking about this,' she says, then in a rapid fire: 'It's taken me a long time to get myself together and now I want to be left alone to live my life. That's it. That's all I want.'

'We appreciate that,' says Adam, 'but I'd still like to know what you mean about the house. It could have some bearing on this case.'

Heather stares mutinously at her thumbnail, then gnaws on it. Rose experiences a flash of irritation.

'We need to tell you now that a child has gone missing from that property,' she says. 'This is extremely serious and we need you to cooperate with us, or we're going to have to go down to the station and talk properly.'

Heather stares at her, telegraphing hate from her eyes. 'I don't know anything about a child,' she says in a quiet voice. 'I don't know anything about anything when it comes to the house now. I haven't been anywhere near it since I went inside.'

'We're going to be checking that via your tag,' says Rose. 'But if there's anything you want to tell us, now is a good time.'

Heather opens and then closes her mouth. 'I can't help you with whatever it is you want,' she says, rising to her feet again. 'Now do what you need to do to check this kid isn't stuffed under my bed and then please leave me the fuck alone.'

It's no good. She's not going to talk.

'Okay,' says Adam wearily. 'Do you have a phone?'

'Yes.'

'Can you get it, please?'

Heather crosses the room to a cheap cabinet that houses a small television and Freeview box. She picks up a very old iPhone with a curved back and hands it to Rose.

'Thank you,' says Rose. 'We'll be needing the number of this phone, so can I get you to write it down, please? And is this the only one you own?'

Heather gives her a scornful look. 'I can't really afford that phone, let alone another one,' she says, then finds a scrap of paper and writes down the number. Rose rings hers once to make sure she has it.

'Thanks, Heather,' she says. 'Now if it's okay with you, we'd like to have a look around your flat.'

All three are aware they need a warrant without permission but Doyle shrugs.

'Knock yourselves out,' she says. 'There's no missing kid here.'

17

The mood at Cobalt Square is one of intense focus when Rose and Adam get back.

The very broad window of time in which Gregory could have left the house, combined with the wide number of possible routes away from the property in relation to street CCTV, plus the widespread public transport options mean it's going to take days to check every avenue. And when a child goes missing, every minute counts.

Rose and Adam report to Mortimer on everything that happened with Heather, including their thorough search of the property. There simply wasn't anywhere a child could have been – dead or alive.

'Okay,' says Mortimer, taking a sip from a mug of tea. 'I can't see how she's a suspect but we're keeping her firmly in our sights. Get that phone record looked at and identify everyone she's spoken to. Get on to Probation about her and look at her movements over the last couple of weeks. The GPS tag will give us all that information.'

In turn, he updates them on what has been happening elsewhere.

Gwen has been questioned and now released. Anton is currently here, being questioned by two of Mortimer's officers.

'Anything so far?' says Adam.

Mortimer sighs and rubs a hand over his chin. 'Not really,' he says. 'Insisted on a solicitor the minute we talked about bringing him in for a chat, which might raise a flag. But it's more likely he just watches a lot of telly like everyone else. It doesn't take a genius to understand that the parents are always in the frame in this sort of case. I will say that he's bloody controlled for a man whose child is missing though. And that does worry me a little, even taking into account how it takes different people in different ways. We can't assume anything at this stage.'

Rose and Adam's next job is to find and question the young woman they'd seen leaving the property in tears the first time they visited Wyndham Terrace.

The FLO, Becky Iordanou, extracts the information from Gwen. In a quiet voice on the phone she reports that Gwen was somewhat reluctant to hand over the name and number. 'She claims there's nothing she can tell you of any use but I think I'll let you be the judge of that,' says Becky before signing off.

Agnes Barreau, Gregory's one-time French tutor, lives in a small, terraced street in Chingford, which is lined by trees that have fresh, new leaves beginning to unfurl. Despite the chill, the sun is shining and there is a spring-like feeling in the air.

Agnes wears a long baggy jumper with a big star on the chest over exercise leggings. Her bare feet have neat, red-painted toenails and her fair hair is in two plaited swirls at the side of her head. When they tell the young woman why they are there, her eyes flare with shock and she ushers them quickly inside.

They are led into a small living room where a man in his twenties, with close-cropped hair and a thick beard, is engaged in some sort of war against zombies on a wide screen television, bare feet up on a coffee table.

After a hurried conversation in French, he leaves the room and Agnes gestures for them to sit. She offers coffee, which they accept gratefully.

'Gabriel?' she calls. '*Tu pourrais apporter plus de café?*'

'My boyfriend, Gabriel, he is a chef,' she says, sitting down, then picking up and cradling a small bowl of coffee as though needing to warm her hands. 'He works at night and in the day . . .' She gives a sort of hopeless shrug that seems to speak volumes. 'Anyway, please tell me how I can help?'

Rose explains again about Gregory being missing and Agnes shakes her head in distress, then puts down the coffee, undrunk.

'Ah, this is a terrible thing to hear,' she says.

'So we wondered if there was anything at all you could tell us that might help with our inquiries?' Rose says. 'Any friendships his parents don't know about, for example?'

'He is a very lonely boy,' says Agnes. 'He has no friends that I know of at all. All he does is homework and endless lessons. It's not right.'

'Have you ever seen him with a mobile phone?' says Adam. Agnes gives a small laugh.

'Ah, no, he was desperate for an iPhone,' she says. 'But his parents wouldn't let him have any kind of mobile at all.'

'Ms Barreau,' says Adam, 'we know that you had some sort of dispute with Anton Fuller that led to you no longer tutoring Gregory. Can you explain to us exactly what happened?'

Her expression darkens for a moment. She looks relieved when Gabriel brings in a tray containing a cafetiere and two mugs, a carton of milk and some sugar lumps in a box. Rose and Adam gratefully prepare their drinks.

'He is a horrible man,' says Agnes when Gabriel has left the room again. Her English is perfect but she misses the 'h' off 'horrible' now in her emotion. 'I think he is a big bully. He accused me of cutting his flowers! And then he claimed Gregory wasn't "progressing" as he put it, as much as he should, and that my services were no longer required. As if I would cut his stupid flowers! I mean,' hotly now, 'why would I do such a thing?'

'Who do *you* think was responsible for that?' says Adam. Agnes holds his gaze for a moment and then looks down at her lap, cheeks colouring a little.

'You must tell us anything at all you think is useful, Ms Barreau,' says Rose gently. 'Even if it sounds . . . strange. We hear all sorts of things and nothing you can say will shock us. I promise you that.'

'Okay,' says Agnes, cautiously. 'I know how this will sound but I think there is a . . . bad thing. A ghost. There, I said it.' She raises her chin a little defiantly. 'You may laugh at me now.' Her accent has become noticeably stronger and her face is flushed, eyes bright.

'We're not laughing,' says Adam evenly. Her gaze flicks back and forth between them, as if assessing whether to believe him.

Rose decides to tell her about what happened yesterday. When she gets to the part about the 'boy in the wall', Agnes nods vigorously.

'*Oui, oui!*' she says. 'Gregory was obsessed with this boy. He talked to me all the time about the fact that the house was haunted. He was almost a bit proud of it. He said the ghost didn't like his daddy.' She sniffs. 'Can't say I would blame it for that.'

'When you say Gregory was obsessed . . .?' Rose says.

'Well, he wanted to understand what was happening so he could make it stop. He told me he was making a project out of understanding the house's history.'

'Right,' says Adam carefully. 'This is all very helpful. When you say Anton Fuller is a bully, did you ever see any evidence of physical violence from him?'

The young woman hesitates. 'I suppose I should mention this . . .' she says. 'The thing is, Gregory sometimes had bruises. Small ones, like pinch marks.'

Rose and Adam look at each other, clearly thinking the same thing.

But Agnes Barreau is shaking her head fervently. 'I'm telling you this but I don't think it is him, the father. I really don't.'

'Why not?' says Adam. 'Why are you so certain of that?'

'Because one time I was there when Anton discovered some of these marks on Gregory's arm. They didn't realize I could hear them speaking. He was angry . . . asking the boy what he had been doing to himself.'

'And what did Gregory say to that?' says Rose.

Agnes Barreau bites her lip and looks from one to the other. 'He said the boy did it. And Anton, he was . . . ah, he was very angry. He said Gregory would have his radio taken away that night so he couldn't listen to the cricket. Said he had to stop hurting himself and telling such big lies.'

Adam fills in DCI Mortimer in the car, on the phone.

'Right,' says Adam after Mortimer has spoken for a moment or two. 'We'll do that then. Okay, see you later.'

He hangs up and turns to Rose, twirling a finger in the air. 'Change of route. He says we should call in at Reservoir Road and liaise with Moony. See what she suggests.'

'Okay,' says Rose, glancing at him in surprise. 'Is he taking this supernatural thing seriously then?'

Adam gives a short sharp laugh. 'His exact words were, "The clock is ticking and we don't have a thing so far. So if we need to conjure up a fucking ghost to find this boy we're going to do it."'

'Right,' says Rose. 'Fair enough.'

'That's not all though,' says Adam. 'He's also rightly concerned about those bruises. They're hauling the parents in again.'

Scarlett and Moony are both there when they arrive back at the UCIT offices. They convene in the briefing area.

Scarlett proffers a bag of physalis around, muttering that, 'none of you eat enough fruit'. Rose helps herself, peeling away the papery skin and popping one into her mouth. Her blood sugar is low and she resolves to have a hunt in the fridge for any other treats Scarlett may have brought in. Then they settle in for the meeting.

'First up, top work by you, Scarlett,' Adam begins. 'I have no idea whether this previous crime is going to tie in with what's happening but we have to put everything on the table just now.'

Scarlett beams. She's rocking the Land Girl look today in grey denim dungarees, with a T-shirt underneath and a bright red scarf tied Forties-style around her wavy blonde hair.

Adam continues, telling Moony and Scarlett the details of Gregory's disappearance, including the visits to Heather Doyle and Agnes Barreau.

'The bruises that this Agnes Barreau talked about,' says Moony, 'she said they were like pinch marks. Isn't that what you reported in the house, Rose?'

'Yes,' says Rose. 'I don't want to believe it was the parents who hurt Gregory. But I'm not sure I'm keen on the idea of the poor little sod being hurt by . . .' she shudders '. . . *poltergeists* either and no one believing him.'

'Could he be self-harming though?' says Moony. 'I mean, he may be pinching himself.'

'That's also a possibility,' says Adam.

There's a sombre pause before Scarlett breaks the silence. 'Maybe the poltergeist is the spirit of Heather Doyle's brother,' she says matter-of-factly. 'The little boy killed in the fire?'

'Perhaps,' says Moony. 'It would fit. They are often associated with young people, but that's more about the victims than the source.'

'I think, whatever it is . . .' Rose is immediately flustered but she ploughs on, 'is somehow older than that. If that even makes sense.'

'Go on,' says Moony, frowning.

'Well, that phone call I had and the way it . . . sort of touched me. It didn't seem like a little boy to me. There was something sexual about that.'

They all absorb this uncomfortable fact for a moment. Rose has been thinking about it for quite some time already.

'Okay,' says Moony decisively, 'well Gregory says it's a boy, not a man, and you say it's a bit horny. So I reckon we're dealing with a teenager then. I mean, when it was alive.'

'Could be,' says Rose, wondering when, if ever, she will completely adjust to this sort of conversation. It's becoming more familiar anyway, which is both a good and a bad thing all in one.

'Okay,' Moony continues. 'If the kid was "obsessed" with the house, as this French tutor says, it has to be a line of inquiry worth pursuing properly. He might be out there doing his own research right now. Trying to put a name to this supposed "boy in the wall".'

'I agree,' says Adam, 'I think that's pretty much why we've been sent here.'

'I've already been looking at the title deeds for number 42 Wyndham Terrace,' says Scarlett. 'Come have a look.'

They go to her desk and Scarlett points one shiny purple fingernail at the screen. 'So . . . the Fullers bought the flat in 2015,' she says.

'Wonder how they afforded it?' says Adam thoughtfully. 'I mean, that's a prime bit of real estate in Zone 2 and he's only a schoolteacher. It might be a fancy school, but I doubt he's getting paid that much.'

'I think Gwen Fuller comes from money,' says Rose. 'She sounds very posh – much more so than him – and have you noticed some of the furniture in that house? It looks out of place and context. She might have inherited money along with the *Downton Abbey* furniture.'

'Yeah, good point,' says Adam. 'Anyway, go on, Scarlett.'

'They bought it from a woman called Linda Meredith,' she says, 'who was living there with her husband and a daughter.'

'No boys,' murmurs Rose.

'No boys,' says Scarlett. 'I've cross-checked everything here against the available census information too. Someone called Ian Baxter, some sort of property developer, bought it from the council after the death of Patricia Doyle, who was a council tenant. He then bought up the other part of the house and converted it back to being one property.'

'So it was council-owned for a time before then?' says Adam.

'Looks that way,' says Scarlett, 'which might take a little

longer to research. I've put a call in to Camden Council and am waiting to speak to someone there. But in the meantime, I've looked at the census information for each decade going back to not long after the house was built in 1899, which at least tells us who was there on those specific years. Look,' she says reaching across her desk, 'I've printed it out.'

'Great,' says Rose, taking the thin, plastic document case from Scarlett, which contains two sheets of printed paper. She starts looking through and reads what has been written next to each date, ten years apart.

1901 – Alfred Edwin Bates (28) and Margaret Ada Bates
    (27) Lydia Audrey Bates (10)
1911 – As above
1921 – 1951 Stanley Clifford Floyd (32–62)
1961 – Lillian Maxwell-Carter (46)
1971 – No information
Bought by council in 1981 and thereafter was Patricia
Doyle, then Ian Baxter, the property developer.

'Wonder why 1971 was missing?' says Rose, handing the papers to Adam, who quickly scans them.

'Hard to say,' says Moony, 'but it might be that a large number of people were coming and going from there.'

Rose and Adam both look up at her and she makes a face.

'Doesn't make it easy but my money is on finding this "boy" or whatever the hell he is, is during that period of time.'

'It fits with whatever the hell it was I saw playing out on that wall,' says Rose. 'Flares and flower power whatnot. The big 'tache on that bloke.'

'Don't knock the Seventies,' says Moony a little wistfully. 'I had some of my best times then.'

After a discussion, it's decided that Rose and Moony will have another crack at speaking to the old lady at number 40. Old Mrs Quinn seems to be the only other person who sensed something strange about that property. 'And let's not forget the comment about the *wicked boy*,' says Moony.

She's coming along because she thinks 'adding a bit of maturity to the equation' might make the woman talk.

Rose drives. As her boss shuffles in her seat and roots inside her handbag, which Rose knows would have cost more than any outfit in her own wardrobe, she thinks about the last time she travelled with Moony.

They went to see a revolting man called Kenny Wiggins, who kept snakes and claimed to have been able to 'visit' people around his neighbourhood from his own bed using astral projection. Everything about that day felt like an assault on Rose's senses: from the smell of the dinner bubbling on Wiggins' stove, to the bombardment of information about things she didn't want to believe were real. She had been briefly seconded to UCIT to investigate Hannah Scott's murder and had gone in with such a bad attitude – she can admit that now – that Moony had pretty much told her to bugger off.

Sometimes she still can't believe this department is real and that she is one of its small team.

Her thoughts are interrupted by the realization that Moony has shoved a bag of Haribo at her, so close it's practically under her nose.

'Ooh, go on then,' she says and takes out two, which she stuffs into her mouth.

'Don't want you fainting,' says Moony. Rose gives her a quick side glance and then turns back to face the windscreen. The other woman is chewing away and staring straight ahead. Maybe she looks a little pale, she thinks, but this is the first time Moony has shown what seems like any real kindness towards her. It feels odd. Nice.

'What do you think of Mortimer?' says Moony.

'He seems very good,' says Rose, glancing over at her boss.

'Yeah,' says Moony quietly. 'He really is. He and my husband were practically best friends.'

Moony has gone quite still in the seat next to her. Rose flicks her gaze towards her but it feels like an intrusion. The other woman is staring ahead, her expression filled with pain.

She's aware that Moony was married to a policeman and that he died some years ago, but no one has ever really filled her in on the details. She feels like she should say something now but somehow, the appropriate response is entirely eluding her. Scarlett would know what to say. But Rose? Rose hasn't got a clue. Not for the first time, she wishes she knew how to handle difficult situations that didn't involve an arrest at the end of them.

18

Rose rings the doorbell of number 40 Wyndham Terrace and a skinny fair-haired teenage girl in a school uniform answers the door.

'Hello,' says Moony, 'I'm DS Moony and this is my colleague DC Rose Gifford. Are your mum or dad about?'

'Are you the police?' says the girl in a lispy voice, so it comes out as 'polith'. She licks her lips and a row of dark braces on her teeth are revealed. They are evidently quite new judging by the way she is twitching her lips over her teeth, as though trying to make room for the new presence in her mouth.

'We are,' says Rose with what she hopes is a reassuring smile. 'But there's absolutely nothing to worry about.' Awkward teenage girls slay her. Sometimes she thinks she still *is* one, trapped inside the body of a thirty-year-old police officer.

'Mum?' calls the girl.

They can hear an irritable voice from inside. 'I'm just seeing to Gran. Can't it wait, Georgia?'

'No!' calls Georgia, rolling her eyes at Rose and Moony as if to say, 'look what I have to deal with'. She turns and calls, 'It's the *police*.'

The harassed-looking middle-aged woman they saw before bustles to the door. She's dressed in a stripy T-shirt and track-suit bottoms with fluffy pink slippers, her slightly greasy hair pulled into a claw clip. A plastic, throwaway apron has been tied around her ample middle. She blinks almost identical brown eyes to her daughter's, her face tight and unfriendly.

'Have you found him yet?' she says, without preamble. 'The boy next door?'

'Not yet,' says Rose. 'Am I speaking to Mrs Quinn?'

The woman nods. 'I've already told your lot everything I can,' she says. 'I'm very sorry to hear about it but it's nothing at all to do with my family.'

'Okay,' says Rose. 'But we'd still like another little chat.'

The woman sighs and rubs her hand across her brow. 'Fine,' she says, 'come in then.' They follow her into a hallway painted in fresh light blue paint. 'Georgia!' she calls out. 'Let us have the sitting room! Clear up your things then go and sit with Nanna while I do this.'

Georgia is hastily grabbing a range of nail polish and equipment laid out on a towel, having clearly been about to carry out a home manicure as they walk into a neatly organized living room. There's a large flat-screen television on one wall and pale leather furniture organized around a low glass coffee table. She leaves the room.

'Do you want drinks?' says Mrs Quinn. 'Only I really am in a rush. My mother-in-law lives with us, you see, and she needs a lot of care. I had only just finished giving her a wash.'

'No, we're okay thanks,' says Moony, taking a seat. Rose does the same and the other woman hesitates and then reluctantly sits too. 'It's actually your mother-in-law we were hoping to speak to.'

Mrs Quinn looks from one of them and back to the other again. 'Mary?' she says. 'What on earth for?'

'Can we start with both your full names?' says Rose, dodging the question, pen poised over her pad.

'I'm Emma Quinn and my mother-in-law is Mary Quinn,' she says, then hurriedly adds, 'Look what's this about? How can an old lady possibly have anything to do with that boy running away?'

'Why do you assume he ran away?' says Moony, half a second later. The other woman blinks, her cheeks reddening.

'I don't know,' she says, clearly flustered as she begins to fiddle with her wedding ring. 'He never looks very happy, that's all. But I still don't understand what all this has to do with Mary.'

'Mrs Quinn,' says Rose. 'When we were here recently, we spoke to your husband and your mother-in-law in the street and she made a comment about the house next door. We think it might have some bearing on things if she can remember previous tenants at all. Do you think that's possible? I know sometimes with the elderly, what happened five minutes ago is a problem but get them on events thirty years ago, they're sharp as a pin.'

'Well, I guess she might remember something like that,' says Emma Quinn. 'She lived on this street for a long time before she moved into her bungalow. Now she's back with us.' Her shoulders round a little at this. Exhaustion is written into the lines on her face. 'She does seem to remember the past much better than where she is right now, if you see what I mean.'

'If we could at least have a go, that would be great,' says Moony. Then, to Rose's great surprise, she adds, 'My mother had dementia so I know how very hard this is for loved ones and carers. It's not easy taking care of people 24/7, like this.'

Emma blinks hard and offers a small smile, as though close to tears at this small bit of connection and understanding. Rose wonders how often her husband is home to look after his mother and whether the bulk of the work falls to her and her daughter.

'Well, you can certainly try,' she says. 'I'll go and see if she is up to it. Hang on.' She gets up and leaves the room.

They can hear a radio in the kitchen and the gentle ticking of a clock on the mantelpiece. Someone shouts something angrily in a foreign language from the street outside.

Rose looks over at Moony.

'Sorry about your mum,' she says quietly but Moony gives her a peculiar, raised eyebrow she can't interpret.

There's a shuffling sound then and she turns to see Emma helping the old lady they met before into the room. Her bird-like frame is dressed in soft sweatshirt and baggy bottoms that look as though they belong to someone much bigger.

Emma shoots them an apologetic look and murmurs, 'We had an accident and this was all we had to hand. Mary?' she then says in a loud voice. 'As I said, these two police officers want to ask you something, okay?'

The older woman seems to have declined even since they saw her last and Rose has a sinking feeling that this is a waste of time. Mary sits down heavily in an upright chair and peers around with rheumy eyes of palest green, as though age has washed all the colour away.

'Mrs Quinn?' says Moony. 'I'm Sheila and this is Rose.'

The old woman chomps at her own lips for a minute before replying and Rose realizes why her face seems to have collapsed in on itself. She hasn't got any teeth in her mouth.

'But what do you *want*?' she says, imploringly, as if they have been going round the houses for hours already.

'We'd like to ask you about the property next door.' Moony gestures to the left. 'You said something to my colleague about it being a "bad place" recently. Was there a reason for that?'

Mary Quinn peers at Sheila for a long time, then at Rose. 'Well you're a bloody rotten copper if you don't know about them murders,' she says.

'Mary!' says her daughter-in-law from the door. 'There's no need to be rude!'

'It's okay,' says Moony with a broad grin. 'You have a very good point! We do know about what happened in 2006. Is that what you mean?'

'Of course I mean that,' she says. 'Horrible business. Three of them dead, just like that. It was a nightmare living here when it happened, what with all the newspapers and things. Plus we could have been burned to death in our beds too. There's something wrong with that house. It always was trouble.'

'In what way?' says Rose, leaning forward a little.

'Them hippies living there,' says Mary, a sour expression on her face. 'Dirty hippies all doing it with each other and taking drugs. I didn't want any part of that nonsense.'

'You said hippies?' says Moony. 'Do you happen to remember the year? Was it the Seventies, perhaps?'

But the old woman has fallen into a groove of memory now. She seems unaware of their presence, her milky eyes focused on a different time.

'Stop all your filthy habits, I told them! Chucking things over the fence. Condoms and whatnot. The police didn't do nothing either. Went round there myself, with my little Eric by the hand, and I told them they couldn't go on all hours like they did. It's a *commune*, says the one with the buck teeth. Artist, she calls herself. Artist, my arse.'

'This is so helpful, Mrs Quinn,' says Moony, clearly struggling to suppress an amused smile. 'Do you remember if there was a teenage boy living there at the time?'

Mrs Quinn suddenly looks at Moony and her eyes have a fearful alertness about them. 'Him!' she says. 'I remember him! He was the one who put dog mess through my door, the little shit! Should have done national service! That would have sorted that one out. He had a look about him. Something wrong with that one, I tell you.'

Rose is almost on the edge of her seat now, leaning forwards. 'Can you remember his name, Mrs Quinn?' she says. 'The boy?'

Mrs Quinn seems out of breath suddenly and begins to cough. 'My boy?' she says when she's stopped coughing, her eyes reddened. A look of pride suffuses her face. 'My Eric is going to be home from school soon so I'll need to get on now. He will be wanting his tea.'

Rose and Moony exchange desperate glances.

'You were telling us about the teenage boy?' says Moony. 'And the hippies?'

Mrs Quinn the elder stares at Moony as though she has said something extraordinarily cheeky. 'No hippies allowed in my house!' she says. 'I told you, I need to get my Eric's tea on!

We're good people!' She attempts to get up from her seat and all three of the younger women lurch forward to help but Emma waves them away.

'I think we need to stop there,' she says. 'Come on then, Mary, let's get you a cuppa and then you can start on Eric's tea, okay?' She makes a hopeless gesture at the other two women as she hauls the old lady to her feet. 'That's going to be as good as you'll get, I'm afraid,' she says quietly. 'And I don't think Eric would like you questioning her like this. He's very protective of his mum, you see.'

'That's okay,' says Moony, standing up. Rose follows suit. 'You've been incredibly helpful and so has your mother-in-law. We'll leave you to get on now because it's obvious you're a busy woman. I'm going to leave my card there and if Mary says anything else about the hippies, can you write it down and let us know? Even if you don't think at first that it's any use?'

Emma takes the card a little reluctantly and nods.

Out on the street again, Moony lights a cigarette and takes a deep drag.

'So it was some sort of commune,' she says. 'It might be that there's something online about it. There were a few so-called communes in London during that time, I remember.'

'Okay,' says Rose. 'Shall we see if anyone is in next door? Once you've had your smoke, anyway.'

Moony takes two more puffs and throws the cigarette to the ground, where she puts it out with her foot then carefully picks it up and puts it inside the refuse bin in the front garden.

'By the way,' says Moony, 'my mother is alive and well and living it up in Spain.'

Rose can't suppress the laugh that springs up. 'Okay,' she says. That at least explains the look Moony gave her back there.

'Sometimes you have to tell them what they want to hear,' says Moony with a roguish, throaty laugh. Then: 'Come on, let's get ourselves into the house of horrors here.'

19

Rose raps the heavy door-knocker once and the door is opened a moment later by Becky Iordanou, a slim, friendly woman with dark eyes and black hair in a ponytail.

'Come on in,' she says.

They follow her through to the kitchen. Becky must have been tidying up because the surfaces are all gleaming and the table neat. The three women talk in very low tones, with a constant ear for any movement from upstairs.

Gwen has been questioned at the property and Anton is back down at the station again.

'She became hysterical when we brought up the bruises,' says Becky. 'Said it was unthinkable that we could suggest they'd harm Gregory. She got into such a state she started hyperventilating and took some time to be calmed down. She's had to go and lie down for a bit.'

'What's your own feeling about these two?' says Moony. 'Having spent a bit of time with them now.'

Becky sighs and rubs her head thoughtfully. 'Well,' she says, 'we all know what liars people are when their backs are against the wall. But, I don't think *she* could have hurt the kid, to be honest.'

'Hmm,' murmurs Rose. 'That was my instinct too.'

'And him?' says Moony. 'Anton Fuller?'

Becky grimaces. 'He's not a very likeable man,' she says quietly. 'There's no doubt who rules the roost here. But my gut tells me he hasn't done anything to Gregory. He's upset, but it's almost as if he is quite embarrassed by all this as well.'

'I thought that too,' says Rose with distaste. 'Perfect children don't go missing or have illicit phones.'

There's a squeaking of floorboards from above and a distinctive thump and rattle that suggests a toilet being flushed.

'I'll go see how she's doing,' says Becky. 'And I'll get the kettle on when I get back down. She hasn't eaten at all but seems able to drink tea, which is something I guess.'

Moony lightly taps her fingers on the table. One of her many silver rings gently chimes against the wood. Rose has the feeling again of the odd sense of weight around them. It's not about architecture; not walls and joists and roof tiles and floorboards. It's something heavy and charged about the air here. A sense of something paused, waiting. Watchful, maybe.

A murmur of quiet voices outside and Gwen comes into the room, with Becky behind her. She looks understandably terrible, with red-rimmed eyes and greasy hair limp around her face. She's in one of her shapeless dresses with a long purple cardigan, which she pulls around her large frame as if she is cold, despite the fact that the heating is on quite high in the room.

'Hi, Gwen,' says Rose, getting up. 'This is my senior colleague, DS Sheila Moony.'

Moony gets up. Gwen holds out a limp hand and Moony, to Rose's surprise, grasps it with both of hers.

'I know this is a horrific experience,' she says, firmly holding the other woman's gaze, 'but I want to reassure you we're doing everything we can to return him home safely to you.'

Gwen's eyes fill with tears. Rose has never seen Moony like this and to be frank, hadn't realized she had the capacity to come across as so compassionate. She is a constant source of surprise.

'Now then, Becky will make you a cup of tea,' she says,

gesturing to a chair and taking a seat herself. Gwen meekly sits, then worries at her pink nostrils with a crumpled cloth handkerchief.

'Gwen,' Moony continues, 'I'd like to know what *you* know about the history of this house?'

Gwen gives her a startled look. 'Why are you asking me that?' she says. 'What a funny question.'

'It's simply that we're aware Gregory was very interested in this,' says Moony patiently, 'and we need to ascertain if it has anything to do with his disappearance. I can't stress strongly enough that everything is worth sharing at this point. Anything at *all* that we can use towards getting your son back here. Do you understand? Even if it sounds strange or unusual to voice out loud. I know your husband doesn't like you talking about these things but he isn't here right now. You said something to my colleagues before Gregory disappeared about a poltergeist?'

Gwen nods once, lips pursed tightly in an attempt to stop the tears that are brimming on her lower lids.

Becky places a cup of tea in front of her and makes a cup-to-mouth gesture at Rose and Moony, who both nod their acceptance. Rose finds herself hoping some biscuits will appear.

Gwen sips at the tea, her large hands with their rough, red knuckles grasping the cup like a lifeline, her eyes cloudy and lost in thought. After she has taken another couple of sips, she places the cup on the table and looks up, as if steadied.

'I never wanted to live in a house where such a terrible thing had happened,' she says. 'But Anton insisted it would be good for us. He doesn't really get on with public transport, you see,' she says, a little apologetically now. 'He could cycle to Beamishes from here and the price was a bit lower than other houses in the area, maybe because of what had happened here.'

She takes another sip of tea. Wonderful Becky lays a plate crammed with Rich Tea biscuits on the table. Rose doesn't need to worry about taking one too quickly, because Moony reaches for one first. Even Gwen picks one up but only places it by her cup without a single nibble.

'You were saying?' Rose prompts.

'We could only afford it at all because Mummy died and left us quite a bit of money,' says Gwen. 'Before then we had been living in quite a grotty flat in Wood Green. Mummy owned a bit of a country pile in Suffolk that was my childhood home and it was a total money pit. But after it was sold to developers there was some left over, which I used to buy this. If I'd had my way, we'd be out somewhere nice in the countryside where the air is clean.'

Rose can all too easily imagine the way she was steamrollered by Anton on such a major life decision as where to live.

'So you knew about what happened to the Doyle family,' says Moony. 'Have you ever had any contact with Heather Doyle directly?'

'Certainly not,' says Gwen with a shudder. 'Why would I do that?'

'Okay,' says Moony. 'Do you know anything about the house *before* that period? Say, in the Seventies?'

'Not at all,' says Gwen with a frown. 'Look, are you saying that there is something else bad that happened here?' She pulls her cardigan around herself even more tightly and looks around as though expecting a malevolent force to suddenly appear. 'Is that why things happened to us?'

'We're simply trying to find out more about what Gregory said,' says Rose in an emollient tone. 'He talks about this "boy in the wall" and we wondered whether you have ever experienced anything like that yourself?'

Gwen looks stricken. 'Not me,' she says. 'But Gregory told me once that this . . . boy told him to do things. He couldn't remember whether he had done them or not.'

'Didn't you get a psychiatric assessment at that point?' says Moony. 'Surely that was a cause for concern?'

Gwen flushes and looks hunted. 'Well, Anton . . .' She catches herself. 'We thought it was best not to encourage him about all that. It wouldn't have been good for . . . for him.'

Not good for bloody Anton and bloody Beamishes, thinks

Rose. Poor little kid, dealing with all this on his own. She experiences a sudden, cold pain in her stomach at the thought of him lying in bed, so small and frightened.

'Did he ever say anything about what he thought this boy wanted?' says Moony. 'Or describe him in any way?'

'No,' says Gwen. 'It wasn't like that. We tried not to encourage it, you see. I wish I'd listened more now if you think it has a bearing on everything.' She stops speaking abruptly. 'Does it?' she says. 'Really?'

'We don't know,' says Moony. 'But we have to take absolutely everything into account to help us find him right now.'

They talk a little longer but Gwen's eyelids are beginning to droop and she doesn't seem to have anything of much use to tell them. Moony gets an urgent call and says she'll take it outside.

Rose decides to have one more look around Gregory's bedroom.

She climbs to the top of the house and turns a corner into the room then crosses to the window to look down on the rectangles of gardens below.

The heavy feeling presses in on her again but she forces herself to take slow, deep breaths. She walks over to Gregory's desk in one corner of the room and opens the small cupboard to books and toys, neatly piled and no longer used.

It is as she is standing up again that it happens.

It's like something is lifting her off her feet, which sends her slamming head first into the wall.

20

It was meant to be a new start.

And now look.

Curled on the smelly mattress, the music coming from downstairs is so loud it seems to shake his bones, reverberate around his internal organs. He thinks it might be harming him inside. Christ, he's the teenager. He's meant to be the wild one.

It wasn't meant to be like *this* here.

Vincent closes his eyes, thinking of the day their supposed new life started. Remembering the cautious excitement he'd felt is a pleasurable sort of ache now, like pressing on a fresh bruise.

It all seemed to be lying ahead of them, barrelling towards London in the tin can of a car his mother loved so much.

Should have known better.

It was raining hard that day, the wipers of the 2CV battling to clear the windscreen, but mostly failing. Rowan wasn't the safest driver at the best of times but he hadn't felt nervous about crashing. The atmosphere in the car was too buoyant and happy for anything like that to happen.

She was singing tunelessly to something he couldn't identify. She often sang. He'd turned to look at her and thought for the millionth time, that she was beautiful, far more beautiful than anyone else's mother he knew. Her strawberry blonde hair ('come on, I'm a total ginge really, sweetie,' she would say with a cackle) hung loose around her the shoulders of her long white dress. She glanced at him and with a cheeky look in her eye began to croon the words to 'I Can't Live' by Nilsson, which she had been obsessed by and played constantly in their old house.

He rolled his eyes but liked it really when she was like this. Maybe this would be what they both needed after all, he'd thought. So naively.

The happiest time in Vincent's fifteen years on Earth had been when he, his mother, his grandmother Josephine and his mother's friend Carmel had all lived together in Josephine's house in Totnes. The fact that Carmel and his mother slept in the same bed didn't bother him, even though he tended not to mention it to anyone outside of the home. Carmel was such an improvement on what came before that he didn't care.

Vincent's father Tony worked as a long-distance lorry driver and for as long as Vincent could remember, the man had used his words and his fists to hurt and belittle his mother. He lived in terror of the man's booming Northern Irish voice filling the house and hated himself for not being able to protect her.

Vincent had been counting the days until he was big enough to properly fight back but when that day came, aged thirteen, he'd ended up with a broken cheekbone for his efforts. It was worth the pain though, when his mother packed Tony's things the next morning and changed all the locks. Evidently, laying hands on him – that was the final straw.

'People can hurt me, my darling,' she had said, 'but they're not laying a finger on my little prince.' Calling him that name was one of the things that wound his father up, which made the words all the sweeter.

For three nights Tony screamed and railed outside but Vincent had never seen Rowan so resolute, even when she was shaking with fear as she, Vincent and Gran huddled away from the windows.

When Vincent pictures his father now, he still has to clench his fists to stop his hands from shaking. He would still kill him if he could get away with it. There's a certain type of man, oozing aggression and cockiness that brings it all back.

Tony is now shacked up with a woman in Paignton. When Carmel came along, having met his mother at a pottery class, he'd been a little bit disgusted at first about it all, but things were so much better he couldn't mind for long.

He had the biggest bedroom in the house. Carmel taught him to swim, while his grandmother cooked for everyone. He even joined the local Scout pack because Carmel believed it 'good for boys like Vincent, who need a bit of authority'. That was an annoying thing to say and at first he resisted. But it was true that he thrived there. Even though it was a bit soppy, he liked the praise he got from earning his various badges, which his mother sewed on, usually drawing blood and swearing a bit as she did it.

It was the happiest time he could remember and if Vincent sometimes felt suffocated and had the urge to smash things, he decided that was what everyone felt on occasion. They were always saying he was 'the man of the house', which he liked to hear.

But then Carmel upped and left. He hadn't even known she was unhappy, but she told him she needed a 'change of direction' and was going to move back to her native Manchester to retrain as a teacher. She had promised him she would stay in touch and tried to hug him the day she went, but he pushed her away. When she tried again he had called her a bitch and then she finally left. She was crying, which made him feel a bit better.

Rowan – who had encouraged him to call her that rather than mother or mum since he was around five – had gone into what Gran called a 'terrible decline'. She'd stayed in bed and not washed. Vincent found the smell of her, lying in grey sheets with the windows closed, revolting, but tried to encourage her by taking in soups and cakes made by Gran.

Then Gran had a stroke and died, in a period of twenty-four hours, start to finish. He was sorry she was gone. She was such a good cook. He knew he'd miss her chocolate cake especially. Vincent had been sure his mother would get even worse, but to his pleasant surprise, she rallied quite quickly and immediately started making plans to get away from Totnes. 'We're spreading our wings, darling,' she'd said, 'and no one will stop us.'

And now they were on their way to this collective thing or commune, or whatever it was. She'd danced him round the kitchen when she told him about it.

In truth, he was a little nervous about moving away to London and saying goodbye to everything he'd known all his life. He had a little gang of friends at school and he enjoyed the status. His mother called him 'a natural leader' when she had a phone call about something that happened one day involving a really annoying weakling called Paul Dickson. The school let it go in the end, after his mother refused to take any action against him. So yes, he'd miss his gang of mates.

But he was excited too. He thought about sex a lot and imagined London girls to be all miniskirts and shiny boots and lipstick. He was a bit vague on what he might do with them beyond the vivid pictures he'd curated from a well-thumbed porn mag he'd persuaded a kid to steal from his dad's bedside table. It was something to think about anyway.

So yes, maybe there would be advantages to going to this place.

'Light me a ciggie?' said his mother, breaking his train of thought.

Vincent took a Marlboro from the packet in the glove compartment and flicked the Zippo lighter to light it. He didn't like the taste of smoke, but if he ever complained she'd say, 'It kills germs. And it's my only vice,' which wasn't strictly true.

'Will I like where we're going?' he said, handing the cigarette to his mother.

'I think you'll love it!' she said. 'It's a brand-new start for us. I don't need—' she seemed to fumble for some suitable word '—*her* in my life to be happy.' Rowan now only referred to Carmel as 'her' or sometimes 'The Queen Bitch'.

'And how will we live?' he said. This is a question that often worried him. Carmel had inherited money and largely supported them all over the last few years. His mother said she was an artist and she liked to paint large splodgy flower-like shapes on canvas but Vincent privately thought they were a bit rubbish. No one ever seemed to buy them, which surely meant they were no good? When Carmel left, she had put some money in an envelope and laid it on the table but when she was gone, his mother had set fire to it. Vincent managed to jump in and salvage some of it, but they had been living on tinned beans and rice for a little while now.

'We don't need to worry about that,' she said and he could hear a little irritation in her voice now. She looked over and gently pushed his head, her cigarette perilously close to his eye. 'You're such an old worrywart sometimes!' She laughed. 'Trust me. When we get to the Wyndham Commune, everything is going to be shared equally. We won't have to worry about money again. I'll be able to sell some paintings once I'm out of the parochial mindset of Devon. We'll be at the centre of things! It's exciting!'

Vincent couldn't stop himself from smiling at her infectious enthusiasm. When she was like this he felt as though they could do anything, together.

He settled back in his seat and tried to picture the house. In his mind's eye, London houses looked like the big white mansion in the crescent from *Oliver!* which they had all gone to see at the cinema earlier this year. They had all loved it and he had to quash a memory now of he, Rowan and Carmel holding hands and singing 'Consider Yourself' as they walked back through town towards home. Anyway, he hoped he'd have an attic bedroom, because it would be cool to be able to look outside the window and see all the tiny ant-like people below.

There would probably be some girls there, who would do the cooking and maybe walk around wearing short dresses. Maybe with no knickers. He shifted a little in his seat. One time when his mother had spotted the bulge in his pants, she had made a joke of it and laughed, and he hadn't liked that at all.

But anyway, he'd thought, maybe living in this fancy house might not be too bad after all.

Now, a few months on, he wonders how he could ever have been so stupid. He hates it here. He'd do anything to get away.

21

'You're incredibly lucky that you didn't get a serious concussion,' says the nurse, whose name badge says Emily Cheng. She is middle-aged and kind-eyed, with small, soft hands that have expertly tended to Rose's various throbbing wounds.

Rose wonders how much worse this could have felt, considering it's already like someone has stamped repeatedly on her face with Doc Marten boots.

She hadn't even had time to instinctively raise a hand as she was sent hurtling into that wall, so her face took the brunt, along with ribs caught on the side of Gregory's desk.

The bruising is coming up nicely already around her eyes in shades of red that will be a full rainbow over the coming days. Her nose is swollen at the bridge and tender to touch, but thankfully not broken. It's given her an unpleasant congested feeling as though she has a heavy cold beneath the waves of pain.

When the nurse asked how it happened, Rose had been lost for words at first, then said she had tripped and hit the wall. But that wasn't at all what had happened. She was *flung*. Literally, as if unseen hands of incredible strength had lifted her and chucked her like a rag doll. But she could hardly say that.

As she had staggered to her feet, gasping with the pain and

shock, Rose had looked around wildly for her attacker. Anton maybe? She even thought of Gregory, which made no sense but she couldn't exactly think straight. But there was no one else until the emerging, horrified faces of Becky, Moony and Gwen, who had rushed up the stairs to investigate her scream.

'Oh my God!' Becky had said. 'What on earth happened?'

Rose had looked at Moony and then at Gwen, whose expression could only be described as one of utter terror. Rose had made a split-second decision. It would be of no use to this investigation to have the other woman so frightened she lost control of herself.

'I tripped,' Rose had said, nasally, holding her hand to where coppery blood was pouring into her mouth. 'Always been clumsy.'

'Right,' said Moony. 'We're going straight to A&E to get you checked out.'

Rose protested but Moony's expression told her she was brooking no argument.

Moony took the keys and when they climbed in, she turned to Rose.

'What the *hell* happened in there?' she said, her eyes wide. 'You didn't trip, I know that.'

'No,' said Rose, her voice muffled by the ice pack wrapped in a tea towel that Becky had organized for her. At that moment, Rose hated that ice pack more than anything in the world. It was so cold and hurt her face so very much.

'Someone,' she said, 'or *something*, picked me off my feet and threw me against the wall.'

Moony let out a low whistle. 'Bloody hell,' she said, 'that is one pissed-off poltergeist.' She seemed about to say more but after glancing over at Rose, she merely started the car and began to drive.

Now, Rose is waiting for a prescription of strong painkillers and staring down with distaste at the blood streaking the front of her shirt. It hurts to breathe from her ribs. It's only the fear of stuffing up her nose further that stops her from giving in and sobbing piteously.

'Is it okay to come round?' says a familiar voice.

'Sure.'

Adam peers around the curtain, his brown eyes soft with concern.

The mixed pleasure at seeing his face, combined with horror at her own appearance, is a potent cocktail of emotion in her delicate, battered state.

'What are you doing here?' she says in her new nasal voice.

'Moony rang me,' says Adam. 'She had to go. I'm going to take you home in your car. God, you poor thing!'

Embarrassed under his scrutiny, she can merely grunt.

Adam rummages in his pocket and shakes a small, white bag at her. 'Here's your painkillers,' he says.

Rose downs two in one go with the unpleasantly warm water in the paper cup on the bedside table. 'Thanks,' she says. 'It's really kind of you to come.'

'We wondered if there was anyone you wanted us to call?' says Adam. A queasy jolt of something like shame goes through her. She imagines calling Mack. Asking if she could stay at his. But the fact is she has left it too long and it would be weird.

'No, I'll be fine,' she says, looking away. 'I'm okay, really. Not as bad as I look. Anyway, what's the news on the case?' He gives her a curious look then seems to understand she doesn't want to talk right now about the accident, assault . . . whatever she should even call it. She's still processing it in her mind and keeps getting waves of horror at the memory. He's clearly dying to ask her but it can wait for a moment.

'They still haven't got anything,' he says with a frown. 'No steers from CCTV or from talking to the neighbours. The Fullers are going on air tomorrow to do a press conference and an appeal. But so far, it's not looking all that good. It's almost as though Gregory has completely disappeared.'

Rose thinks about her dream – the small body buried in cold, dank earth – and is almost winded by the horror of it. No. He's alive. He has to be.

Adam insists on taking Rose home in her car. Every movement seems to judder through her. Once, she gasps and sees Adam's horrified expression.

'Pothole,' he says. 'I'm so sorry. I've been trying to drive really carefully but I didn't see that one.'

'It's okay,' Rose says, although the pain feels far from okay. 'Please don't worry.' Her voice comes out little more than a gasp.

He's still looking at her.

'Rose,' he says, 'I'm not leaving you on your own. How do you feel about coming back to mine for the night where I can keep an eye on you?'

Heat creeps up her cheeks and she attempts to argue but it's half-hearted. The thought of being alone in her own house in pain is so terrible, she can feel her eyes filling again with a terrible urge to cry. Plus, she's scared. She doesn't understand what happened in the Wyndham Terrace house or how it could have been possible. But there's no doubting it was an act of violence towards her and the last time that happened feels all too fresh. Her body is a cauldron of adrenaline and cortisol right now, as though emergency lights and sirens are going off all over the surface of her bruised skin and inside her brain.

Adam kindly doesn't insist on a reply.

'That's settled then,' he says. 'You're coming back to mine. I think Moony would have my guts for garters if I didn't do this, to be honest.'

'Thank you,' she manages, keeping her face averted to the window.

A beat passes.

'Are you up to telling me what happened yet?' he says. 'Or do you want to leave that until you've had a bit of a rest?'

'It's okay,' says Rose, wincing as she attempts to get comfortable. She's never been in the passenger seat of her own car before. It's lumpier than she feels it should be, but perhaps that's simply because her entire body hurts.

She gathers herself for a moment before speaking. 'So I was mooching around in Gregory's room,' she says, conscious of the clicky dryness of her own tongue as she speaks. 'I was kind of standing there, looking around and then I felt a tremendous sort of . . .' she searches for the word '. . . force.'

Adam is silent for a moment.

'It's impossible to exactly explain what it felt like,' she says. 'But one minute I was on solid ground and then it was like being thrown by, by, I dunno, a giant hand or something. Something really powerful and violent.' She has begun to shake and she clenches her hands together in her lap. 'Something *angry*.'

'Shit,' says Adam, after a moment. 'No wonder that poor little sod has run off.'

'If that's what happened,' says Rose and the sentence hangs heavily in the air.

Rose insists Adam wait in the car because 'I'll only be two ticks' when they get to her house, but the business of gathering clean clothes, toothbrush and toiletries seems to take forever. The house has a sort of clammy coldness, as if the heating hasn't come on, and much as it feels strange to be going to her colleague's house for the night, she's grateful to pull the front door on her own home and walk, slowly and agedly, to the car where he patiently waits for her, engine off.

It's after ten when Adam pulls up in a narrow, hilly street in Hornsey.

'Sorry,' he says, 'this is probably about as near as we can get to my flat. Parking is terrible on this street.'

'That's okay,' says Rose but as they walk up the hill, it starts to feel like a marathon in her current state. When Adam puts out an elbow and nods for her to take it, she can't resist.

His arm, inside the dark blue woollen coat, feels strong and comforting as she slips her hand through. She can picture herself slipping her hands inside the coat and feeling his warm body underneath and supposes this a good sign. She clearly isn't so knocked about that her body can't still produce this pathetic, misplaced heat.

As they get to the top of the hill Adam stops outside a modern block of flats among the brown and white Edwardian terraced houses and looks up. 'That's a bit strange,' he says.

'What?'

'Must have left a light on. Oh well, come on in and I'll get the kettle on.'

The flat is on the first floor, which feels like the tenth. Rose wants to sleep more than anything and is thinking about when she can have another painkiller as Adam unlocks the front door and they step into a brightly lit hallway.

'Daddeeeee!' a skinny girl of about twelve in a yellow onesie and fluffy slippers comes careening from nowhere and throws herself at Adam, thin brown arms around his waist and a bubble of natural curls smushed into his chest.

'Kea!' he says, shock radiating from his expression. 'What on earth are you doing here, baby? Where's your mum? And your sister?'

The girl is clinging to him too tightly for her words to be heard and he has to gently prise her away. She sees Rose for the first time and her face is suffused with curiosity.

'Who are you?' she says.

'Uh, hi,' says Rose, 'I'm Rose. I work with your dad.'

'What's wrong with your face?'

'Kea!' says Adam.

'It's okay,' says Rose with an attempt at a laugh. 'I know I look awful! I fell and bashed my face today.'

'It looks really sore,' says the girl with a genuine look of sympathy.

'I'm okay,' says Rose. The child's words have unexpectedly touched her in a raw place.

Another girl of a similar age, dressed in lilac pyjamas, her hair in multiple braids in a high ponytail appears at one of the doorways. She is eating a piece of toast, with a look as though she is defying someone to take it off her.

'Tandi?' says Adam. 'Can one of you tell me what's going on here?'

'Mum dropped us off,' says Tandi, narrowing her eyes at Rose as she bites into her toast. 'She said she was calling you.'

'Well, she didn't call me!' says Adam. 'Have you been on your own here all evening? When did you get here?'

It's apparent to Rose by the tremble in his hands as smooths the hair back from his daughter's forehead that Adam is trying to conceal how upset he is.

'About six,' says Kea, glancing down and then shyly looking up at Rose through thick eyelashes. 'Tandi made us eggs.'

Adam looks at Rose, helplessly, then back at his daughters.

'Why did Mum drop you here?' he says.

Tandi shrugs. 'Meeting someone,' she says.

'Hmm,' says Adam, then: 'I bet,' so quietly you almost couldn't catch it.

'Maybe it's best if I go,' says Rose, although the thought of driving home seems like an impossible feat right now.

'No!' says Adam. 'Absolutely not. Kea, Tandi . . . this is my colleague Detective Constable Rose Gifford, who is a very excellent policewoman. She hurt herself at work and needs to stay with us.'

Rose attempts a smile. 'I'm a klutz.'

Tandi remains unimpressed. Rose sees her mouth the word 'klutz' as if it's the stupidest word she has ever been presented with.

'Anyway,' says Adam, 'speaking of sleeping, you'd both better get yourselves into bed double quick because it's school tomorrow.'

'We can't,' says Tandi, quickly. 'We haven't been fed.'

'Oh,' says Adam, feigning surprise. 'That's funny because I heard you made eggs. And I know that you make the best eggs in the family.'

Various emotions play out on the girl's face and she suddenly seems less lippy and more putting-on-a-brave-face after being dumped here by her mother and her father turning up late with a damaged woman. It's impossible not to warm a little bit to her, attitude and all.

'You know it,' she says airily, playing with one of her braids.

Adam grins. 'Come on,' he says. 'You go through and I'll come tuck you in. I'm just going to get Rose settled first. Deal?'

'Deal,' says Kea, turning to go. Tandi doesn't reply but seems to slide backwards around the door and out of sight.

They go into a long living area with a galley kitchen at one end, a dining room table and a seating area. It feels like a flat where a single man lives, from the lack of pictures and cushions, plus size of the telly and PlayStation taking pride of place. But there is various girl detritus too. Adam picks up a pair of pink socks that have been left on the sofa and the coffee table has a flowery hair accessory and a sparkly tub of lip balm.

'I'm sorry about that,' he says quietly. 'I shouldn't be surprised by my ex-wife thinking it's acceptable to leave a pair of twelve-year-olds on their own for hours without even telling me they're coming, yet somehow I still expect better. More fool me.'

Rose doesn't really know what to say so instead she gently lowers herself onto a leather sofa, which doesn't have half as much give in it as she would have liked. She leans her head back for a moment, then realizes it increases the pressure in her nose and sits up again.

'I'll go say goodnight,' he says, 'then get us something to drink. Hang tight.'

It's not as if she has much choice.

After a moment she can hear giggling from the other room. Sounds like Tandi has forgiven her father for bringing a strange woman into the house, even if it is only his colleague.

Getting her phone out of her pocket she starts to look at emails but she can't really concentrate on anything. She keeps thinking about being in the attic room at Wyndham Terrace and that horrible sensation of sudden movement, then the shock and pain of the wall meeting with her face. The very thought of going back there makes her shudder. If she had any choice, she would stay far away from that house and never go back. Like that's an option in the middle of a major case. Then she has a curious thought.

Maybe she is connected to what's happening there on a deeper level, whether she likes it or not. Like the house, or something in the house, is trying to communicate, even though it's through violent means?

But what?

There's movement elsewhere in the flat then and the sound of a door closing.

'Sleeping time now, girls!' says Adam loudly and then appears back in the room. He has changed out of his suit into a duck-egg blue jumper that complements his skin beautifully, and black tracksuit bottoms. Rose has already changed into fresh clothes but she is unaccountably cold and is surprised and grateful when he holds out a grey hoodie in the softest wool towards her.

'Thought you'd be cold,' he says. 'It's the shock, I think. Sometimes takes a little while to come out.'

Rose thanks him and puts on the hoodie, which drowns her in size but feels comforting. It smells of the same pleasant washing powder she recognizes from Adam's clothes.

'Hot drink?' he says. 'I'd offer something stronger after the day you've had but I imagine it's not the best idea to mix it with your painkillers.'

'I think it'll be all right,' says Rose. 'I honestly can't imagine sleeping unless I knock myself out a little bit. I'll just have one, if you are too.'

'Right,' says Adam. 'And you definitely haven't got concussion?'

'Well,' Rose begins awkwardly. 'They said I should just . . . keep an eye out, but they didn't think so.'

'Okay,' says Adam, 'well I'm going to be checking on you every few hours whether you like it or not.'

Rose is about to object.

'Whisky okay for you?' says Adam before she gets the chance.

'Okay, and that's great,' says Rose. It's not her favourite thing to drink, but it's for medicinal purposes anyway.

'I'll make us something to eat too,' he says from the kitchen area, as he takes glasses from a cupboard above the sink.

'Don't go to loads of trouble,' says Rose. 'I feel bad imposing on you like this when you've clearly got lots going on.'

He makes a face. 'There's always something going on when it comes to Suzanne. That's the ex.'

'Sorry to hear it,' says Rose. But he doesn't elaborate.

'How does cheese on toast sound?'

Rose hadn't thought she was hungry but somehow, it's the best cheese on toast she's ever eaten. Warm and salty and with some spicy kick she can't identify. The good food seems to warm her blood and dissipate the last of the shivers.

'That was delicious,' she says, wiping her mouth with a piece of kitchen towel and leaving it on the plate. 'I never knew cheese on toast could taste as good as that.'

Adam grins. 'It might be the shock talking,' he says, 'or it might be my secret ingredient.' He waggles his eyebrows, which makes her laugh, even though it hurts to do so.

'Oh yeah?' says Rose, sitting back gingerly in the chair. 'How secret?'

'Not secret at all, really,' says Adam. 'A splash of hot sauce before you put it under the grill. Makes all the difference.'

Rose takes a sip of the whisky and finds she enjoys the peaty burn as it slips down her throat. She rests her head back against the sofa again, but the spasm of agony this brings from her ribs makes her groan, involuntarily.

'Shit, are you okay?' says Adam, sitting forward slightly in his seat. 'I'm not sure they should have let you out, to be honest.'

Rose manages a weak smile. 'There's nothing much they can do about ribs, they told me that. I have to ride it out. Not broken, which is a blessing. I'll be okay after a good night's sleep.'

They meet eyes. Rose can feel her own beginning to droop. Adam looks tired too.

'Look,' he says, 'it's late and I'm going to make up my bed for you. Think you need to hit the sack.'

'I can't take your bed!' says Rose.

'You don't have any choice about it,' says Adam. 'If you want to know where Tandi gets her stubbornness from, then we could debate it. But I warn you now it will be time-consuming and can only end in failure.'

It's impossible not to return his warm grin.

'I wouldn't dream of arguing,' she says.

'If it's okay though,' he says, 'remember to leave the door open and I'll pop my head round later. Make sure you're breathing. I'm still worried about concussion.'

'I will.' Rose briefly frets about being seen drooling on the pillow or snoring extravagantly from her bunged-up battered nose. But the feeling of being looked after is lovely.

And quite alien. Because who, really, has ever looked after Rose?

22

It takes a long time to get off to sleep in Adam's cramped little bedroom.

Along with the furniture, there's an exercise bike in there with a couple of T-shirts hanging over it and a pile of paperback books in one corner that are clearly waiting for a proper home. She'd idly glanced at the titles as she painstakingly changed into her pyjamas. Lots of popular science books, mainly, including ones by Bill Bryson and Richard Dawkins. A couple seem to be on the supernatural, such as one called *The Psychology of Superstition and Why People Believe Weird Things*. Rose wonders anew how someone like Adam ended up at UCIT.

The intimacy of lying in the space where he sleeps is distracting, to say the least. She runs a hand across the cool sheet and pictures his body warming the space. Pointless, and inappropriate, but at least the fantasy takes her mind off the memory of being thrown against a wall by an angry ghost.

It's around 2 a.m. when she becomes aware of a shape in the room, a dark presence. Her sleepy brain is instantly electrified with panic.

Oakley. He's back.

Fuzzy from the mix of alcohol and pills, it's hard to surface.

As panic mounts, she fights the thick, muffling sensation dragging her down until she is sitting upright, properly awake, heart pounding so hard she can feel it in her throat.

'Rose, Rose, it's okay, it's only me!'

At the door, Adam is dressed in a T-shirt and pyjama bottoms, his face stricken, hands up in supplication.

With a gasp of pain, Rose leans back against the headboard. 'Oh God,' she says, 'I thought, I thought . . .'

It's impossible to resist them and the tears finally fall, hotly, down her cheeks. She buries her head in her hands.

'Oh shit!' says Adam. 'I'm so bloody thoughtless. After what happened before . . . I didn't think. I'm so sorry. But you were moaning in your sleep and I wanted to check you were only dreaming and not in any pain. I never meant to scare you!'

Rose can't stop crying. It's literally impossible right now. The memory of what happened last year is like a massive rucksack filled with stones she carries all the time, every minute of the day and the night too. It has become her version of normal. But right now she's aware of how very heavy it is, lying here in pain and in her lovely colleague's bed.

Adam hovers near the door and then disappears, coming back a moment later with a box of tissues.

'God, I'm so sorry,' says Rose, gathering herself, her voice so thick it's almost unrecognizable. 'I didn't wake your girls, did I?'

'No, it's fine, don't worry about that,' says Adam. 'They're sound asleep. Look, is it okay if I come over there and give you a tissue?'

'Yes, please,' says Rose.

Adam approaches and hands her the tissue box at arm's length. She takes one gratefully.

'You must think I'm such a fruitcake. Please,' she says, then: 'Sit down for a minute. It was so kind of you to check on me.'

Adam sits, but so far away on the bed, he practically has one buttock and leg hanging off it.

The room is quite well lit, thanks to a streetlight outside.

Rose doesn't really know where to put her eyes but she doesn't want him to go either.

'Look,' he says after a moment. 'It's not my business but can I tell you something?'

'Of course.' She dabs gently at her sore nose.

'When I worked in Vice,' he says, 'back at the start of my career, I was stabbed by a man who was running a brothel of trafficked Eastern European women. A right piece of work he was. It wasn't that serious, only in my bicep, and we disarmed him pretty quickly. It could have been so much worse. I've got a nice little scar to show for it now. But I tell you, for months after, I kept reliving when that knife came at me. I would replay the moment over and over again. For all that he was a nasty little man, it came as a shock. This fat little bloke of fifty-odd in his cheap suit, suddenly whipping out a bloody great hunting knife.'

Rose doesn't say anything.

'What I'm trying to say is, I can't even imagine what it would be like to be assaulted in your own bed like you were,' he goes on. 'I felt a bit embarrassed at the time that I couldn't stop thinking about what happened to me. I mean, it's not like that sort of thing doesn't happen all the time in our job.' His voice is quiet and low. 'A big bloke of six foot two, a copper? I mean, I should be able to shrug that stuff off, shouldn't I? But I couldn't.' He pauses. 'And that's the thing, Rose,' he says. 'Just because we *are* coppers, it doesn't mean we're any more able to cope with threats on our life than the next person. They're still bloody scary when they happen. And what happened to you with Oakley was so goddamned creepy and unusual, well . . .' He trails off.

There is a long silence where their eyes are locked together, the distance between them very close yet somehow very far too.

'Thank you,' says Rose softly, after a moment.

'Ask for proper help if you need it, is what I'm saying,' he says and his voice is so gentle, Rose can barely hear the words.

Adam lifts a hand, then hesitates and puts it back down.

Rose thinks he was going to pat her reassuringly on her leg, but felt it wouldn't be appropriate, even in these circumstances. She wishes he would touch her. What she really wishes is that he would wrap her up in his arms and hold her until she sleeps. Nothing else, just that.

In the morning, her face looks awful with a new darker purpling around her eye, and her bruised ribs seem to stab her with every breath.

It's awkward, seeing the two bright, curious faces of the girls eating breakfast in their school uniforms as she finally enters the kitchen. Thankfully, Adam hurries them out of the door not long after.

Forty-five minutes later, Rose has gingerly driven herself to Cobalt Square, Adam following behind, when her phone rings. She answers via Bluetooth.

It is Gwen Fuller, crying hysterically and saying something about letters.

She is almost incoherent and after a moment, Anton takes over. He too sounds shaken for once.

'Your lot have found a bunch of letters,' he says. 'They've taken them away. I want to know what's happening. Whether that woman has my son.'

'Mr Fuller,' says Rose, pulling into the car park. 'Please speak slowly and tell me what you mean. What letters?'

'The ones that Heather Doyle woman, that multiple *murderer,* has been writing to my son.'

They go in Adam's car, lights and siren on, to Heather's flat in Archway. Officers from Kentish Town station are already on their way there.

She and Adam meet a young PC called Nasreen and a slightly older man called Rob, who was responsible for breaking down the door.

'This room is a potential crime scene,' she says to the two

uniformed officers, 'so can you please not touch anything and secure the scene accordingly.'

Rose dons a pair of gloves before stepping properly into the room, which is much tidier than when she was last here. Checking a cheap chest of drawers by the bed, it's clear the clothes have been cleared out.

'She's gone, hasn't she?' says Adam grimly.

'Adam,' says Rose and the alarm in her voice makes him look up sharply.

'Look at this . . .' She's staring down at the side of one of the cracked kitchen cabinets, which is spotted with what looks like hardened grease. But that isn't the only stain.

There's a small dark patch of something.

Something that looks very much like blood.

23

Rose and Adam almost run into the building at Cobalt Square. DCI Mortimer is heading towards them, his face grave. He winces when he looks at Rose.

'Christ, you look terrible, Rose. Should you be here? I heard you fell?'

'I'm all right,' says Rose. 'Really. I'm okay.'

'If you're sure,' he says. 'Anyway, I'm holding a briefing right now so you're just in time.'

'Okay, everyone,' says Mortimer and a hush falls over the room.

'So,' he says, 'during a search of the Fuller property this morning, an envelope and some letters were found partially burned in a barbecue in the garden.' An image appears on the whiteboard, blown up, showing the inside of a barbecue, with the charred remains of some paper. The image changes to the remains of an envelope. The words HMP Edgefield are at the top.

'Several other letters have been burned beyond any hope of reading them,' Mortimer continues, 'but we have two we can still read. It looks as though someone – maybe Gregory himself – panicked and put the lid down, starving the fire of oxygen before it had done its work.'

The image changes to a picture of one of the letters, which is written in blocky, childish handwriting.

'This is the first one, dated six months ago,' says Mortimer, zooming in so everyone can read it.

Dear Gregory,

I am happy to help with your school project.

To answer your questions, yes it is very boring in here. They make us stay in our cells for hours and hours and there is nothing to do but watch telly or read. Do you like reading? Please tell me what your favourite books are and I will tell you mine next time.

The food is horrible probably but I don't really mind it anymore because I have been here so long. You asked what my favourite food is and the answer is chips but especially ones from McDonald's. Do you like those? Not that I get to eat them!

Your other question is a bit harder to answer. I know I did something bad but it's very hard to explain why.

I'm also sorry your mum and dad don't believe you about your worries but you can tell me about them and I will always listen.

Best wishes,

Heather Doyle

'Here's the other letter,' says Mortimer, swiping the white screen to change the picture.

Dear Gregory,

Yay! It's not very long now and I can't wait to meet you properly.

It might not be very easy to do that though so we will have to be clever, okay? I know you are a clever boy or you wouldn't go to that posh school! I am going to get you a special phone that will be only for calls to me. It will come in the post so you need to keep a close eye out for it in the way you normally do. I know you know what I mean!

Then we can speak privately without anyone knowing.

Best wishes,

Heather Doyle

'Christ,' says someone.

Mortimer's eyes are hooded with stress and exhaustion as he turns back to the room.

'Heather Doyle is not at her property and it looks very much like she's done a runner,' he says. 'Now, it goes without saying that she's now a major suspect in the disappearance of Gregory Fuller. Any possible motive is unclear as yet, but while female paedophiles are rare, they are not unknown.'

A few people, including Rose, grimace at these words.

'There's something else too,' says Mortimer, posting the image on the board initially snapped by Rose's phone. 'This looks like a bloodstain on the side of the kitchen cabinet. We're fast-tracking a test on that to see if it's Doyle's or, more worryingly, Gregory's.' He pauses for a moment before continuing. 'So I want every possible detail on this woman. Most recent movements, habits, financials, phone use – we're already looking into that and there's nothing, so I think she would have another burner. Anything we can get. She hasn't had a tag for a few weeks now but I wanted a renewed focus on all her movements. We're going to have to rely on the usual methods. Where Gregory was between the day he disappeared and the last time Heather was spotted is one big question, so I want a renewed search of anywhere he might have been hiding or kept out of sight in the area around her house. I want a full intelligence package on Doyle. I want to know every single person who ever visited her in prison, every possible location she might have, any remaining family, every bit of correspondence that came in and out over the years she was there. I'm getting an immediate recall to prison authorized, which means when we get her, she'll be off the streets straight away and we won't have any issues with custody time limit.'

He starts giving out jobs.

Rose and Adam are tasked first with finding out how Doyle got the letters to Gregory without the distinctive envelopes being recognized by his parents.

Rose starts with Gwen, who is hopeless, and she is almost on the verge of giving up when Anton, in the background, remembers the partwork magazine on space that Gregory has been collecting for ages. It comes in a cellophane wrapper and would be easy for someone to slip something inside and reseal, before posting on again to the Wyndham Terrace address.

Heather's Probation Officer is a man called Frank Stenson, who, he tells them as he clears space to sit in his small, cramped office in Camden, has been in the job for thirty years and is counting down the days until retirement.

'It was never an easy job at the best of times,' he says, absently scratching his grey-flecked beard, 'but with all the cuts and the creeping privatization of the last few years, it's been a bloody nightmare.' He pauses. 'It's terrible to think a lack of contact with this Heather Doyle may have played a part in what's happened.'

He points to a photograph of a caravan stuck to his computer. 'That's what I'll be doing in six months' time,' he says. 'I'm going to attach the van to the back of the car, and me and my wife are going to spend the whole winter in Cornwall, working out where we're going to buy.'

Rose and Adam make polite noises and he scans each of their faces.

'I'm waffling on,' he says. 'Sorry, but the point is that under the old system I'd have seen Heather Doyle every week since she was released, but the fact is I've probably spoken to her about twice since she got out. I wish I'd had time to build a bit of a relationship with her. But if you've met her a couple of times you know her about as well as I do.'

'What sort of prisoner was she,' says Adam, 'according to your notes, I mean?'

Frank pushes his glasses up his nose and turns to his computer screen, where he taps with two fingers for a few moments in a way that reminds Rose sweetly of Mack.

'Just refreshing my memory,' he says, 'but it seems she was a model inmate until the violent incident in prison. The woman concerned had, let's say, a certain reputation and there was undoubtedly a self-defence element to this but she still slashed open a person's face and we only had her word for what happened. After that, she reverted back to being a very quiet presence. Became a library orderly after two more years and worked very closely with the librarian there.'

'Can you get the librarian's name and number?' says Rose, leaning forwards in her seat. 'And see if you can find out about any visitors she had?'

They ring the librarian, who is called Sanjita Warren, from the car.

She speaks quite fondly of Heather but says she was always very quiet and she never really got to know her in the way she does the other library orderlies.

'She liked books about the supernatural,' says Sanjita, 'now I think about it. Anything remotely factual – using the term loosely there – was her preference, although I remember she read *The Amityville Horror* novel – which has been in the library for about thirty years – and then borrowed it again and again.'

'Sanjita,' says Rose, 'I have to ask you something, I'm afraid. Did you ever post letters for Heather to anyone outside of the prison?'

Sanjita's shocked sucking in of breath transmits loud and clear down the line.

'Oh my God, no!' she says. 'Is that what someone was doing?'

'I'm afraid so,' says Rose. Sanjita could be lying but it is Rose's very strong instinct that she isn't.

'I had to ask, I'm afraid,' she says. 'Also, do you know if she had many visitors?'

'Now that I might be able to help with,' says Sanjita. 'There was only one in all that time, which I always found awfully sad, but I guess when you kill your whole family you aren't going to be getting a lot of love.'

'But she did have one?' Rose prompts.

'Yes,' says Sanjita, 'she would mention this one lady who apparently had known her a long time. I think her name was . . .' she pauses for a moment '. . . something like Jane? Janet? Oh, no, I've got it. It was Jeanette! No idea of her surname, but I'm sure we could get the details to you.'

Rose feels a stir of excitement that takes her mind off her aches and pains for a moment at least.

Fifteen minutes later they have a number and address for a Jeanette Peters, the only visitor Heather had in her thirteen years in prison.

24

The sun is out by the time they drive through the market town of St Albans. Rose has never been here before and she marvels, as she always does, at the amount of space people have when you get beyond the M25. The High Street is busy with shoppers and the sunshine falls pleasantly on the restaurants and upmarket shops in a jumble of architectural styles.

Jeanette Peters' address turns out to be on a wide, tree-lined street of large, mostly detached houses. They park on the road and look up at the house.

'Nice,' says Adam and Rose murmurs agreement. The front garden is a blaze of tulips, which immediately make Rose think of the butchered daffodils at Wyndham Terrace. Even to Rose's non-gardening eye she can see that this one has been lovingly tended. Two neat bay trees bookend the front door and as she walks up the path she catches the sweet scent of some sort of plant delicately threaded along a trellis on the garden wall.

There's a large black Range Rover parked on the driveway. Rose is wondering how this Jeanette woman knows Heather. Maybe she is some sort of prison volunteer.

As she raises her hand to press the doorbell, which is one of those digital Ring ones, the door opens and Rose finds herself looking down at a small girl of about five clad in an oversized Manchester United football shirt, half tucked into a bright pink tutu. She has golden hair that is pulled back into a curly pony-tail and some sort of glitter on her cheeks.

The little girl stares silently at Rose and Adam, while holding onto the wall next to her with an outstretched arm and rocking in and out a bit.

'Did you know my nanna was dead?' she says in an accent that to Rose's ears could be Lancashire or Manchester. 'Are you here to see her? Because you can't.'

'Billie, I've told you before about opening the door like that. Who is it?' says a voice from behind her.

'It's a quite pretty lady and a black man,' says the little girl and then, losing interest, dances off, leaving the door open.

A woman in her late thirties appears, eyes swooping upwards before she speaks. 'Sorry about my daughter,' she says. 'She just says whatever comes into her mind.'

Rose smiles. 'Well, it's the best compliment I've had in a while,' she says. 'I'm DC Rose Gifford from the Met Police and this is my colleague DC Adam Lacey. It's nothing to worry about but am I speaking to Jeanette Peters?'

The other woman's expression instantly tightens. 'No,' she says, 'I'm her daughter Freya. Freya Bond. I'm afraid my mother died two months ago. We're down from Sale to sort out the house.'

'Oh, I am so sorry to hear that,' says Rose, weariness settling over her. Is this going to be a waste of time? Tiredness pricks her eyes.

'But what was it about?' says Freya, lifting her own fine, blonde hair and twisting it into a ponytail with a thin band that was round her wrist. Her gaze flicks between them, curi-ously and with a little wariness. She is slim and freckled, dressed in a pair of jeans and a fitting striped jumper, a pair of red plimsolls on her feet.

The little girl pushes her way past to stand next to her mother. She's eating a red lolly now and her little tongue is the same colour as it flicks in and out of her mouth.

'Where did you get that?' says Freya with exasperation. 'I told you not to have anything until tea!'

'Nanna left it for me in our secret place,' says the child matter-of-factly. 'I found it.'

Freya's eyes cloud with tears, quite suddenly. 'She probably did too; she was that soft with you,' she says and places her hand gently on the little girl's head. Then to Rose and Adam: 'Sorry, sorry,' she says. 'Tell me why you're here?'

Rose glances meaningfully at the little girl.

'Go and see what else Nanna left for you,' says Freya, looking down at her daughter's upturned face, 'and we can talk about it after your tea, okay?'

The little girl looks quite delighted by this and runs off quickly, seemingly before her mother changes her mind.

'Thanks,' says Rose. 'It's nothing to worry about and I really am sorry to disturb you at this sad time, but your mum was a regular visitor to Edgefield Women's Prison over a period of thirteen years to see a woman called Heather Doyle.'

Freya's eyes narrow and her pale cheeks flood with angry colour. 'Ugh, that woman,' she says. 'I could never understand it! I tell you if she hadn't passed away that Heather would probably have moved in here!'

'They were close then?' says Rose, then, hurriedly: 'Look, I know it's not the best time, but can we come in?'

Freya hesitates for only a moment. 'Sure,' she says, 'of course.'

They step inside. There's a herby, meaty smell of cooking that makes Rose's mouth flood with saliva. She hasn't had that sort of hearty meal in ages.

Inside the house Freya directs her into a large living room, with an elegant fireplace and various bookshelves that are in the process of being emptied into packing crates.

Rose wonders whether the little girl is going to come down again but then hears her singing, lustily and off key to herself upstairs.

Freya gestures for Rose and Adam to sit on a comfortable red sofa. On the table next to where they sit is a large pile of magazines called *Tribune*.

Most of the pictures have been taken down, leaving pale

rectangles on the walls. They are neatly stacked by the television, awaiting packing.

One or two pictures are still up. One is a framed poster from the Smithsonian National Museum of the American Indian and the other is a poster saying, *Ban the Bomb, Aldermaston, 1960,* with a large black sign Rose recognizes as the CND symbol.

On the mantelpiece there's one picture: a framed photo of a group of scruffily dressed but smiling women holding a banner that reads, *NO NUKES!* in roughly painted letters.

Freya sees Rose looking and hands her the picture.

'That was my mum all over,' she says with a little pride in her voice. 'It's her protesting at Greenham Common in 1982. She got double pneumonia from doing that. Got arrested three times in her life, God love her. She'd get in her camper van and go wherever she was most likely to get into trouble, or "help", as she called it.'

'She sounds like an interesting woman,' says Rose, handing the photo back. 'How did she know Heather Doyle?'

Freya grimaces. 'We lived in Tufnell Park growing up and I went to school with her,' she says. 'She always was a bit of a weirdo. Always watching people and looking a bit sly. I had a birthday party when I was twelve at the house and my mum insisted I invite all the girls in the class. I kicked up hell about it, but I had to do it.'

Rose swallows the feeling of discomfort in her throat. She would have been the unwanted kid at the party too. Not that she ever got invited, not once everyone found out she lived in a house where people paid money to speak to ghosts. Rose's childhood was one that wasn't neglectful in comparison to the horrors she has witnessed as a police officer – after all, she had food and warmth – even if she largely fed herself from the age of eight. But there was no real love or security, which contrived to make her one of the quiet, odd kids who never had nice things. The sort others knew, with the unfailing social-preservation radar of children, to avoid. For a moment she feels a flicker of sympathy for Heather Doyle, despite herself and despite what the woman has done. What she may be doing right now.

'Anyway,' says Freya, with a weary sigh, pushing her fringe back from her face. 'My mum found her skulking in the kitchen and felt sorry for her. She ended up baking biscuits with her!' Freya gives a snort and Rose feels a wash of something close to dislike. She pictures awkward, dumpy Heather in the kitchen while the girls in the other room whispered hot spite about what a freak she was. It's all a little too close to home.

'Okay,' says Rose, 'so what happened after that? Surely she didn't visit her in prison because she had been in your house that one time?'

Freya looks down at her feet, a frown between her eyebrows. 'She tried to get me to invite her over again after that because she felt sorry for her. But I wouldn't do it.' She looks up, eyes bright. 'And I was right not to encourage her, wasn't I? After what she turned out to be and everything. I mean, who knows what she could have done to us!'

Rose makes a noncommittal noise before continuing. 'So how did your mum end up visiting her in prison then? I still don't understand.'

Freya sighs and fidgets with a fingernail. 'Mum took it badly when she heard what had happened in that house. She kept saying that Heather was a very unhappy girl and she should have done more to help her. I tried to talk her out of it so much and to be honest, it was only recently I discovered it was something she had continued to do for years. She was just one of those people, Mum. She wanted to help everyone and she took all the world's ills on her own shoulders.' Freya's voice thickens and she pulls a tissue from the pocket of her jeans. 'Sorry,' she says, dabbing her nose. 'I still can't really believe she's gone, to be honest.'

'We're sorry,' says Adam. 'We don't want to make you think about any unhappy memories. But if you don't mind bearing with us a little bit longer. Did your mum ever find out why Heather did it? The fire, I mean?'

Freya blows her nose and then pockets the tissue again. She draws her legs up on the chair and tucks them neatly beside her, one hand on her slim ankle.

'Not really,' she says. 'I remember that Heather's mum died when she was very small. Her dad married again and the woman ran off with someone and left them all, including the little half-brother . . . well,' she says, 'you'll know he was one of the victims of the fire, the poor little soul. That's what I can't forgive. That she killed a child.'

She gives them both a curious look now.

'I'm sorry,' she says, 'but can you tell me why you're asking about this?'

'We're interested in her in relation to another inquiry we're pursuing. That's all we can really say right now,' says Adam.

Freya's expression darkens.

'God, I bet she's done something else awful. There's something seriously wrong with that woman. Can you believe my mother left her money in her will?'

'Oh yes?' says Rose, sitting forwards a little. 'How much?'

'Five hundred pounds!' says Freya with wide, outraged eyes. 'We had a proper row about it when Mum was talking about making the will.'

'You mentioned a camper van,' says Adam. 'Where might that be now?'

Freya laughs a little bitterly. 'We finally persuaded Mum to get rid of that, thank goodness, after she almost crashed it in Somerset,' she says. 'Sold it off to someone in Scotland a year ago.'

Rose can feel disappointment settle inside at this news.

Freya gives a visible shiver. 'Makes my flesh crawl to think she was sitting across from my mother all those years,' she says.

'Did your mum ever get any indication from her about *why* she committed the crime?' says Adam again. 'The motive?'

Freya laughs, a little bitterly. 'She once tried to tell Mum that a ghost made her do it! That's how desperate she was to dodge any responsibility for her actions.'

Rose feels her heartbeat quicken and clears her throat before continuing.

'What did she say exactly? About the supposed ghost?' she says.

'Just that,' says Freya, 'that she was "made to do it" by a ghost. I don't really know any other details. My mother found this desperately sad and believed Heather wasn't able to consciously face what she'd done, so created this fiction to make it all the more bearable.' Freya sniffs. 'If you ask me,' she says, 'that was just taking the piss.'

25

Back at the incident room, there have been a couple of developments.

'Firstly,' Mortimer tells the packed room, 'there are a series of lockups a street away from Doyle's address under a railway arch. One of them has clearly been broken into and someone has been spending time in there, judging by some food detritus – a number of drinks cans, a banana skin, and a packet of Pringles. We're treating this as a possible location where Gregory was kept before Heather's flight. There's an unidentified stain on the Pringles wrapper, which we're fast-tracking. Which leads me to the other development.' He looks around at everyone, his expression grave.

'We've identified the bloodstain in Doyle's property as belonging to Gregory Fuller. Now we want to know if it's his blood in that lockup too, but we're fairly sure we know who's behind this now.'

'Shit,' says Adam quietly, to Rose's left.

'Okay,' Mortimer continues, 'there's a vulnerable child out there, possibly injured, in the hands of a manipulative, multiple murderer. I shouldn't need to remind anyone in this room of the high priority of this case. We'll be working night and day until we can find that boy, return him safely to his parents, and put Heather Doyle behind bars again. We've had a helicopter out all afternoon. But our last confirmed sighting of Doyle is at 3 p.m. on the 10th, when she withdrew £400 from a Halifax cashpoint on Camden High Street, which appears to be the nearest branch to where she lives. We then tracked her on buses all the way back to the corner of Archway Road and Pauntley Road, which is the last CCTV sighting.'

'Where did she get that money in her account?' says Gail. 'She's not working, is she?'

Rose lifts a hand to speak. 'Guv, we've just got back from meeting the daughter of the one visitor Heather Doyle had in the entirety of her time in prison,' she says. 'The visitor was a recently deceased woman called Jeanette Peters, who seems to have been a bit of do-gooder. She knew Heather from way back because her daughter, Freya Bond, went to school with her. Bond wasn't friends with Doyle though and she was actually very unhappy about her mum visiting her over the years. Even more so about the fact that she left Doyle £500 in her will.'

There's a murmuring in the room.

'Okay,' says Mortimer. 'Look closely at this woman Peters. What property did she own? Is there anywhere that Doyle could be headed that's connected to her at all?'

'She had a camper van,' says Adam, 'but the daughter says that was sold over a year ago. I'm planning to look into it.'

'Good,' says Mortimer, 'please do that.'

He pauses and takes a sip from his water before continuing. 'Surveillance team, let me know if you need any extra resources on this because it's an *absolute priority* that we track the movements of the child and Doyle during the window of time after last sightings. Any information we can get about intelligence leads of family or friends too, with cell-site overlay. I want live feed surveillance on her address and am getting that authorized by my superintendent as soon as I finish here. Look closely at her bank account. I want to know everything about any possible phone use too.' He pauses for breath. 'Okay, people,' he says, 'we have plenty to do here. Rose and Adam, can I get you to speak to Gail and Jamie about the contact you've had with the prison so far? If I need you as back-up on that, I'll let you know. Other than that, let's get started. We have a lot to do and I don't need to stress again what is at stake here. Thank you.'

Conversations bloom and there is mass movement as the meeting room empties. Gail is regarding Rose and Adam warily. She says something quietly to her fellow officer – Jamie, who's about Rose's age. He's tall and slimly built with a reddish beard and bright blue eyes.

'So you got the impression the daughter disapproved of the friendship between her mother and Doyle?' says Gail, in a soft Northern Irish accent.

'Definitely,' says Rose, 'she practically shuddered at the mention of her name.'

'Hmm.' Jamie and Gail exchange glances. 'We'd better tell surveillance to watch her anyway and do a check on her just in case.'

There's a pause during which Gail regards Adam and then Rose a little suspiciously. 'I don't quite understand how you fit in,' she blurts. 'Sorry.'

Here we go, thinks Rose, but Adam rescues her before she has time to open her mouth.

'We're a specialist division that investigates the kind of thing the Fullers had reported,' he says, meeting Gail's eyes coolly. Rose feels a prickle of admiration at the way Adam lays it out without fanfare or apology. This, she thinks, is what she needs to learn to do.

'Do you mean neighbour interference or all the mad stuff about ghostly presences?' says Jamie. He looks like he is trying to keep his face straight.

'Both,' says Rose crisply, willing herself not to give in to her thumping heart and blushing cheeks right now. About time she got used to this. She could swear there's a slight snigger from Gail, but it's quickly covered up when Mortimer approaches the desk.

'Rose, Adam, a word?' he says.

They follow him into his office. He lets out a sigh and takes a swig from the can of Red Bull on his desk.

'Tell me more about the house and the obsession with this so-called ghost,' he says, 'and please, take a seat.'

'Heather Doyle told Jeanette Peters that a "ghost" made her carry out those killings,' says Adam once they're sitting. Mortimer's bushy eyebrows rise over his pouchy eyes.

'Well, I've never heard that one before,' says Mortimer. 'Did she have a psych assessment when she was originally arrested for the triple murder?'

'Not as far as we know,' says Adam. 'She said surprisingly little at the time. Claimed she couldn't remember anything.'

'Maybe she thought prison was better than living in the house,' Rose says suddenly and she feels as surprised as her two colleagues evidently do. 'I mean,' she adds hurriedly, 'it could be that she knew she had no real defence but what if she *was* trying to burn it down in order to, I don't know—' she searches for the right term '—exorcise a ghost or something.'

Mortimer regards her silently for a moment. 'If Doyle thinks she's somehow saving this boy, that would be one of the better outcomes I can picture right now,' he says wearily. 'But I want you to ramp up efforts to find out whether previous occupants of the house have been contacted by either Heather Doyle or Gregory. We need to know where they are or where they're headed. Anything else at all on that front might help.'

'Right,' says Adam.

'And, Rose?' says Mortimer. 'What happened with this?' he does a circular motion around his face.

Rose feels her stomach swoop. It's one thing telling her UCIT team members but quite another saying it out loud to the SIO of this case.

'I wish I knew what happened,' she says. 'I was in Gregory's room, standing still, and the next thing I knew, I was thrown face first into the wall.'

Mortimer makes an appalled face. 'You mean like in a, a . . . *supernatural* way?'

Rose takes a large gulp of breath, then registers the pain in her ribs. These injuries are very real, however weirdly she got them.

'There was no one in the room,' she says in a quiet voice. 'That's all I can tell you for sure.'

'Christ.' Mortimer rubs a hand across his mouth. 'This case gets stranger by the minute.' He seems to give himself a shake. 'Anyway, get yourselves back to your division and see what you can find on this house. I don't know how it ties in but my instinct is that it does. Somehow. And look after yourselves. Both of you.'

'Thanks, guv,' says Rose. 'We will.'

Scarlett's eyes fill with genuine, fat tears when she sees Rose walking into the office.

'Oh, love,' she says and comes in for a hug, which she does gingerly. 'Your poor sore face. Can't you go home?'

'I will, soon,' says Rose. 'But we have nothing at all really on where Gregory is right now.' She tells her about the blood-stain and Scarlett lifts a hand to her lips in horror.

'Oh God,' she says, 'I can't bear to think that funny little guy might be hurt, or frightened. He seems even younger than twelve in some ways.'

'I know,' says Rose, 'it's appalling.'

Adam arrives shortly after, looking more stressed than when she left him. Scarlett goes off to make coffee and Rose sits with him in the briefing area on opposite sofas. He taps frantically at his phone screen then puts it into his pocket with a grim expression.

'Okay?' she says.

He closes his eyes and leans his head back for a moment before replying.

'I won't bore you with it,' he says. 'Christ knows I'm bored with it myself.'

'Your ex?' says Rose gently and he nods.

'It's her mission in life to cause me as much aggro and worry as she can, let's say.'

'Are the girls with you again tonight?'

'Yep,' he says, 'and I wish they were with me full-time. But she won't allow that and prefers to play games instead that are no good for me and certainly no good for them. She calls the shots all the time and I don't know quite how she gets away with it, to be honest.'

'I'm sorry, Adam,' says Rose. 'That sounds like a nightmare.'

He shoots her a tired, grateful grin. Scarlett brings over a tray laden with coffee cups and a Tupperware container.

'The wife's been baking again and she's going to kill us both with it,' she says, ripping off the lid and offering the container to Rose. Inside are four golden muffins, crusted with nuts and banana chips.

Adam and Rose both fall on the muffins gratefully.

'Where's the boss?' says Adam through a mouthful of crumbs.

'I don't really know,' says Scarlett. 'She went off in a tearing hurry earlier and didn't say.'

'You were here all on your own?' says Rose.

Scarlett laughs. 'I don't mind,' she says with a grin. 'I never feel lonely here for some reason.'

Rose isn't in a rush for Scarlett, who shares Rose's unusual abilities, to tell her about any more ghoulish occupants of this creepy old building. 'Anyway,' she says hurriedly, 'tell us what you've got on Wyndham Terrace.'

Scarlett has already tracked down the living occupants of the house in the Eighties and Nineties. No one had anything unusual to report and hadn't been contacted by Gregory. She was also able to find information about the commune in the late Sixties and early Seventies online. The artist the old lady mentioned could have been one of a number, but a painter and sculptor called Celeste Allingham came up a few times.

'She runs an artist's retreat in Winchester now,' says Scarlett. 'I got her on the phone and she wasn't much use, but she was a bit of a hoot, actually, once she got going.'

'In what way?' says Adam, taking a sip of his coffee.

'Well,' says Scarlett, 'once I got her back on that period, she was full of it. I think they had pretty wild times at that place. She said young people never understand they weren't the ones to invent raves! She was very frank about it all. Said something about "losing count of the gorgeous young men I shagged, darling" and that most of them were off their faces half the time.'

'Was there anything actually useful, though?' says Rose, feeling a bit dispirited.

'I asked her about teenage boys, or any young men and she said something about how it depended on "what my definition of young" was because, quote: "We were all young then, you see." People came and went all the time, but never families as such. It was always just single people having a good time. She couldn't recall anyone who wasn't at least a young adult there anyway.'

'Did you ask her if she ever witnessed anything out of the ordinary?' says Adam.

'I did.' Scarlett shrugs helplessly. 'Her precise words were: "It was the swinging Sixties and Seventies, darling. The whole world was out of the ordinary then."'

Rose directs Scarlett to keep digging to see if she can find reference to anyone else living there at the time.

'I think you should go home and get some rest,' says Adam, as he regards Rose. 'You got quite a bash from whatever it was. And not much sleep at mine.' He pauses, then looks away quickly.

Rose registers Scarlett's blonde head shooting up, and forces herself not to acknowledge it.

Rose visits the ladies' before she leaves.

The huge room has barely changed in decades and still has rusty vending machines on the wall. She goes to the toilet and then takes two more of the Co-codamol, even though she isn't due for more until another hour and a half has passed. Because they make her constipated, her stomach feels bloated and uncomfortable, but the let-up from the pain is such a welcome relief she can't worry about that right now. Has to keep going.

As she leaves the bathroom and walks down the long corridor to the main entrance, she hears a squeaking sound and her heart begins to beat a little harder. Not really wanting to look, she forces herself to stop and glance down the short corridor that branches off this one to unused offices. The figure of the tea lady is there again, the one only Scarlett and her can see. Scarlett affectionately calls her Hilda. The trolley holds a metal urn that looks so real Rose can see the shine on it. Hilda appears to be fiddling with cups, her scarved head bent. Slow and steady, in eternal service to no one.

Why has she appeared now?

It feels, to Rose, like the dead are ganging up on her.

26

It's been four months now and nothing about living in this hellhole has improved.

When they arrived that night, tired and sore after the journey in the shit-box car, Vincent was craving a proper meal and then curling up in his own room to sleep for at least ten hours.

But when they pulled up in front of the house, it was clear some sort of party was going on. The front door was wide open and music was pumping out into the night air. A man and a woman with matching brackets of hair down the sides of their faces were passing a bottle of wine between themselves and snogging between sips.

Rowan and he looked at each other. His mother grinned, instantly energized despite the long drive.

'Maybe this is our welcoming party,' she said. 'Come on, let's go introduce ourselves.'

Inside, a sweet, smoky smell was so strong, Vincent immediately started coughing. In the hallway a skinny girl with buck teeth and glasses giggled as though this was funny.

'Haven't you ever smelled pot before?' she'd said, holding out what looked like a cigarette in his direction. Ignoring it, he'd clenched his fists and tried to swallow back the humiliation that burned in his throat. She didn't even look that much older than him. He'd sincerely hoped she was simply a party guest, but as he later discovered Fern, as she was called, was one of the ever-changing inhabitants of the house.

When his mother had located the person who'd invited them to the commune, a drippy woman of forty something who looked absolutely out of her skull, it transpired there had been a 'silly mix-up'. Those were Rowan's words, avoiding his eye in that nervous way she had when she'd made a spectacular error of some sort. Turned out they hadn't been expected at all and the room they were supposed to have had been given to someone else. But 'there was plenty of space and we all muck in here' the woman had cheerfully announced before getting distracted and floating away on a cloud of patchouli oil and pot smoke.

The house was absolutely packed with people and they'd had to push their way through the baying, yelling bodies to find a kitchen. Some sort of gungy lentil thing with an odd smell was congealing in a large pan on the stove, but it was better than nothing. Vincent found a heel of slightly stale bread on the dirty, cluttered tabletop and ate it with that, darting furious looks at the bodies pressed around him. Rowan had evidently made friends with everyone within about five seconds of being there.

He'd finally slept – or attempted to – at 6 a.m., surrounded by snoring bodies and huddled under his coat in a corner of the big sitting room. Vincent had insisted on lying on top of the bag that contained all the money they had, even though Rowan insisted it 'wasn't that kind of place'. But she hadn't looked especially convinced. And this was a good thing. There was no way they would stay here. Even she could see that.

Well, more fool him, because here they still are.

Once the party was over, it was clear that there were many more people living here than rooms. Vincent had found himself wandering up to the attic in the first few days. A couple called Beth and Frank were living in there with their spectacularly ugly baby. Frank called himself a 'performance artist' whatever that meant, and she seemed to spend most the time with a tit stuffed into the baby's mouth, greasy hair framing her wan face. Vincent decided the room was the best one in the house because it had a modicum of separation from the rest.

He'd always fancied an attic room and anyway, it gave him a project.

The first unfortunate thing that happened was the baby crawled down the stairs and onto the landing, where anything might have happened. Imagine if it had crawled right out the door and got in front of a car? Almost too terrible to think of. Beth had been sleeping and not paying attention; that was the problem so really, it was her fault. Then the whole family got sick from something they ate and even the baby got a bit of it in the milk so it had to go to hospital. When they announced, Beth shaking and pale, that they were going back to her mum's in Swindon and leaving the commune, Vincent pointed out to Celeste, the self-appointed 'leader' of the commune, that he and his mother had been next in line for a room.

Beth had given him an odd fearful look as she'd left, which he had returned with a broad smile.

And it got a little better after that. Or at least, he'd got used to it. He didn't go to school anymore, instead choosing the maximum number of books he could take from Kentish Town library at the weekend and spending his time reading. His mother was painting again and somehow, even though no one here seemed to have a job, the food and booze kept coming in.

He didn't like the pot, even though his mother had become quite the fan. But he was becoming very fond of the lax approach to alcohol here. He could take a bottle of whatever was going from the heaving table in the big living room and sit in the corner, watching what was going on or reading his book.

Vincent was good at blending into the background. There was a lot of near-shagging in plain view (and perhaps, sometimes, actual shagging) that he was particularly interested in, providing him with a rich bank of material for when he was on his own. He'd even had an encounter himself, with a stoned girl who called herself Harmony.

She was about twenty and had seen him watching her one evening, then, to his amazement, she led him by the hand to dance with her. Rowan wasn't around and so he'd swallowed back his embarrassment at not being able to dance by holding her tightly by the hips and grinding himself into her.

She'd only laughed and then moved his hands, putting them more gently on the silky skin at the tops of her legs before coming in and kissing him. He'd never felt anything so smooth as those thighs. That and the shock of her tongue probing his mouth had almost finished him off there and then. But then she had taken his hand and moved it up under her skirt, up and up. She kept going and then, instead of material, as he was expecting, there was hot wetness and the shock of hair against his fingers. It was too much. He'd let out a groan and then felt the shameful dampness in his underpants. She'd whispered in his ear that it was a compliment and told him to get himself sorted.

Vincent hoped she would come back but he never saw her again.

Anyway, it wasn't perfect but he'd had to admit it was better than going to school. The neighbours weren't happy with any of it and the woman on the right was always calling the police on them, but nothing much happened. Vincent chucked dog shit through her door one night, because she annoyed him by the way she looked at him on the street.

Things had been bearable, anyway.

Then *he* had arrived.

Hugo, or Huge Ego, as Vincent privately thinks of him.

Hugo has been living in San Francisco, which he likes to bore on about ('. . . the quality of the light, man, you should see it' and other utter crap).

He's well over six feet tall, with wavy hair and a moustache Vincent can only dream of ever achieving. He plays the guitar and sings, which makes all the women in the house, and some of the men, wet their knickers. Vincent has tried to tell his mother what a big fake he is. He told her about seeing Hugo with Mattie, one of the long-standing residents (and the prettiest, if you ask Vincent). They'd been at it, in one of the rooms with the door open and Vincent had been passing. He hadn't been able to stop himself from looking in. Hugo was naked from the waist down so Vincent could see his tanned, hairy arse pounding between Mattie's thin legs, her dirty soles in the air and her hands holding the headboard behind. She was making little squeaking noises like a mouse. He'd wanted to walk away but it was impossible and then Hugo must have heard something because he turned his head and saw him watching. All he'd done was give Vincent a large, white-toothed grin and Vincent scurried away.

He told his mother, who had looked a bit upset and said he shouldn't be spying on people. Then later, he'd seen her with Hugo, Hugo whispering something and playing with a lock of her hair.

Now Hugo makes jokes all the time at his expense. He says things like, 'Okay, Tiger? How many hearts have you broken today?' and stupid shit like that. Rowan is completely under his spell and tells him to 'live and let live' and that he is really 'spiritual and cool when you get to know him'.

When they pass each other in the hallway, Hugo pretends to punch Vincent in the stomach. Much as Vincent would like to smash the stupid git's face against a wall until it turns to raw meat, he can't help flinching every time, which makes Hugo laugh more.

Vincent has been trying to do push-ups to bulk up his puny arms and concave chest but there's never any privacy here and he has no money for some of the stuff advertised in the local paper to get muscles. If only he was bigger and stronger, he'd show Hugo exactly what he thinks about all the stupid 'jokes'.

Not that there's anything funny about them. There's a gleam of something malicious in Hugo's eyes, like he wants to humiliate Vincent and reduce him right down to nothing. Vincent knows it's all wound up in Rowan and becoming her number one. He would have thought this could *never* happen at one point in his life, but now he's not so sure. He sees the way his mother looks at Hugo, like her nerve endings are all on the surface of her skin.

Vincent thought he hated Tony when that loser was on the scene, but his feelings towards Hugo are something else again.

The feeling burns so brightly, it's all that warms him in that damp little bedroom.

27

By the time Rose is reluctantly leaving the office, Adam has discovered that the 'camper van' mentioned is a 1999 Peugeot Boxer Way Finder motorhome, still registered in the name of Jeanette Peters.

'So she lied to her daughter about selling it then,' says Rose. 'I wonder who she might possibly have gifted it to?'

'Yep,' says Adam, already lifting the phone to tell the Cobalt Square team. This van is now a priority for ANPR.

Rose gives in to the exhaustion at 11 p.m. and drives home on autopilot.

She thumbs a food delivery app as she comes in the door, knowing she needs a decent hot meal but too tired to cook anything for herself.

The house is freezing and she swears under her breath before going to the ancient boiler and seeing the pilot light is out again. With everything going on, she hasn't had a moment to think about the eviction notice that's still lying on the kitchen table.

But maybe it's a *good* thing, she reminds herself. Being forced to move on from a house of so many unhappy memories, not least being attacked in her bed by a serial killer. Surely that's a positive move?

She has run out of wine, which is disappointing, so she makes a cup of tea and then, while waiting for her chicken bhuna and naan bread to arrive, walks around the house to do a cautious check for whether Adele is lurking about anywhere.

But it's all clear.

Not that this means anything, because the old witch might appear at any moment. Rose goes back to the kitchen and sits at the table, sipping her tea and tentatively touching her swollen cheek. She takes two of the strong painkillers prescribed by the hospital and waits for the pleasant blurring sensation to take effect.

Something occurs to her then and she hesitates, before picking up her phone to send a text.

The reply comes quickly. 'Yes. Ring me.'

'Rose?' says Scarlett when she calls. 'What's wrong? Are you all right?'

'Yes!' says Rose with a laugh. 'I'm sorry, I didn't mean to give you a shock then. Sorry to bother you so late.'

'You're not bothering me at all. I'm just watching some incredibly depressing Scandi drama the wife has roped me into.' There's a sound of another voice, gently scolding, and then Scarlett gives a peal of laughter. 'She hates it when I call her that but I can't seem to stop doing it.'

Rose pictures the two women enjoying a comfortable evening together and a wave of tender longing washes over her. But it reminds her why she called.

'Yeah, look, it's nothing urgent but I have a question,' she says. 'I feel like you understand these things a bit better than me. But what would you say was the main reason for, well, hauntings of any kind? I'm not sure I've ever asked you that.'

Scarlett is silent for a moment. 'Are you talking about Wyndham Terrace?' she says gently.

Rose swallows, then gives a bright laugh. 'Yeah, of course. Hard to think about anything else.'

'Right,' says Scarlett. 'I can't possibly "know" the answer to this, not least because there are probably myriad reasons that relate to that person's period alive. But . . .' she pauses '. . . I can't help feeling that some sort of unfinished business has to be one of the biggies, don't you? That something has to be understood by those of us still here, you know?'

'What kind of thing though?' Rose hadn't meant her tone to be so pressing and Scarlett's pause seems loaded.

'Well,' says Scarlett, more carefully now, 'something about that person's death perhaps. Or maybe something they regret and need to make right. Something important the living person has to understand.'

The doorbell signals that Rose's food delivery has arrived so she hurriedly thanks Scarlett and hangs up.

But Scarlett's words stay in her mind as she eats her curry, slowly. She hasn't thought through the fact that chicken and naan bread require quite a lot of chewing, which tests her sore face. She only manages to eat half before putting it optimistically into the fridge for another time.

With a sigh, she looks around the bleak little kitchen, wondering what manner of unfinished business her mother is trying to convey. Something about the house itself? Something Rose must know before she moves out? Because why else did Adele appear just as that letter arrived? She can't know for certain that Adele was money-laundering here. But she strongly suspects so. Maybe there's a big bag of dirty money sitting at the back of the attic. The thought makes Rose laugh; it would be exactly the kind of compromising thing she can imagine happening to her when all she has done is try to be straight up. But then a serious thought douses this moment of humour. If Adele was breaking the law like that, might she have been breaking it in other, more sinister ways? Could she have killed someone?

The trouble is, whichever way she looks at it, Rose can't imagine she's going to like the answers to any of these questions.

Shivering a little with tiredness and the sluggish efforts of the boiler, she decides she's had enough of today.

As she brushes her teeth, she regards her appearance in the mirror. The swelling across her nose is going down a little, but her black eye is shaping up nicely. And the effects of the pain-killers are already wearing off so her ribs have begun to complain if she takes anything other than a shallow sip of breath.

It's all a bit much.

Rose begins to cry then, tears dripping piteously down her bruised cheeks and mixing with the froth from her toothpaste.

But if she is hoping to get a break from her own mind that night, she's disabused of this by a series of nightmares, starting with Gregory being buried in a shallow grave in the back garden of her own house by a grim-faced Anton Fuller, and ending with her drowning in quicksand as she tries to reach him, her mouth filling with suffocating grit that feels so real, she would swear it has a taste when she comes to, with a gasp of shock.

She gets up early and is at Cobalt Square by 8 a.m., where she finds DCI Mortimer and a few of the CCTV team, looking as though they have been there all night, which they probably have. Rose takes over on CCTV from a grateful middle-aged officer called Neil, who is going for a sleep. It's a job that's mind-numbing but requires constant vigilance and she forces herself to focus.

Unfortunately, the mobile home hasn't pinged on any ANPR at all in recent times, which suggests Doyle has moved it some-where in advance.

Back to square one.

At three in the afternoon there's a development. A seventy-eight-year-old woman called Dorothy Blake rings in to report a stolen car. Her Volvo station wagon, which she last saw parked on a nearby road a week ago, has gone. That road happens to be the next one along from Heather's address. Mrs Blake told officers that she only uses it once a week to turn the engine over and visit the supermarket. Heather Doyle could easily have watched her and worked this out, before breaking into the car.

Heather Doyle could have driven this car to wherever that mobile home has been parked.

It doesn't take long to find the car and they are back in the briefing room within the hour.

'Right,' says Mortimer. 'What have we got?'

Jamie speaks. 'We were able to track the car travelling north from Tottenham Hale on the evening Gregory disappeared, around midnight,' he says. 'Cross-checking with CCTV shows what seems to be a lone driver – an elderly woman – but that would be easy enough to do with a wig. The kid could be lying down in the back seat.'

There's a brief moment when Rose imagines everyone's thinking the same thing. Hopefully, he is lying down because he has been told to and not because he is incapacitated.

'We were able to follow its progress all the way to the A1 and then the M1,' Neil continues. 'It looks as though they travelled all night in that direction. They got petrol, using cash, at a service station near Birmingham but she manages to hide her face from all cameras. We lost them for a bit north of Leeds and she was obviously driving carefully enough that she wasn't caught on any speed cameras along the way. The current situation is that we're following the trail from Durham but need as many bodies on this as we can get.'

'Okay,' says Mortimer. 'We need to find that car. They seem to be travelling further away from the highest density areas and that's going to make ANPR really difficult. They could end up anywhere. I think it's time for a public appeal and for the parents to do a press conference. The rest of you, I want you to question everyone again about any possible connections for Heather Doyle in the North of England or Scotland. Speak to the dead friend's daughter again. Speak to the Fullers to find out whether the location has any relevance to them, however tangential it may seem at first. This isn't good enough, people. We have to find out where they're going and we have to do it as soon as possible. As far as we know, that kid is injured. Let's make sure it doesn't become anything worse.'

28

It's early evening and Rose is drinking full-sugar Coke and taking another two of the painkillers, fretting about how quickly they are going down. She needs to keep going – that's all – until they can find Gregory and get him safely home again.

The atmosphere has been frenetic all afternoon, since the car that Heather Doyle was driving, which almost certainly contained Gregory, went off radar briefly after Perth.

A different approach was needed. Speed cameras also clock number plates but the information gets overwritten quickly and getting hold of the information from local police involves GDPR permission and authority at superintendent level. This was secured fairly quickly because of the seriousness of the crime, but still added on a little time.

Now all available eyes are on where the car went between Perth and Inverness. They're closing in, but the north of Scotland is a big place with plenty of blind spots in terms of cameras.

Rose has been on the phone all day, talking to everyone connected with the case and trying to find out whether there's any connection at all with that part of the country where Heather seems to be headed. Freya can't help at all, saying her mother 'went to all four corners of the country in that thing until her eyesight got bad'. But she couldn't specifically recall a Scottish trip.

Rose becomes aware of a change in the air and looks up from the desk that's her temporary home to see Anton and Gwen Fuller arriving in the office. There's a woman with them. She's in her forties, with such a thick thatch of long ash-blonde hair that it can only be extensions, lots of make-up and long silver earrings. Her expression is a strange sort of benign but superior one.

Rose rises and goes over.

DCI Mortimer comes to greet them and Rose introduces the people she knows, looking expectantly at the mystery woman. Gwen is looking even thinner and more exhausted than when Rose saw her last. Anton has an imperious expression on his drawn face, lips pursed tightly. He gives Rose a nod.

'Thanks for coming in,' says Mortimer. 'We're going to try and make this as quick and painless as we possibly can.' He pauses. 'Sorry,' he says, 'and you are?' to the woman.

She holds out a plump, freckled hand and smiles, revealing small, even teeth.

'Felicity Gordon,' she says, 'intuitive healer.'

There's a moment of perplexed silence, broken by Gwen. 'She's helping us to find out what happened in the house,' she says, eyes flicking to her husband and then away again. He looks straight ahead, jaw set.

'Like a researcher?' says Mortimer.

'Like a medium,' says Rose and the woman's eyes meet hers. 'Am I right?'

'Yes, some people call me that,' says Gordon and there's an edge of steel to her voice now. 'But I work across the board on promoting wellness and harmony in all dimensions.'

'Jesus Christ,' says Anton quietly but loud enough that everyone hears it.

Felicity's smile remains fixed.

'Anton,' says Gwen in a tone Rose has never heard her use with her husband before. 'Can you just do this *one thing*, this *one time*, without making one of your bloody big fusses about it? Please?'

Anton Fuller's cheeks colour but he raises both hands as though warding off an attack.

'Whatever you say, dear.' Sarcasm drips from his voice but Gwen doesn't seem to hear.

'Felicity has the answer for what has been going on in the house,' she says, addressing Rose now. 'I thought we could tell Gregory in the press conference and then maybe it would, I don't know, help.'

Rose and Mortimer exchange glances.

'And what do you think has been going on?' Mortimer asks, expression neutral.

'I think there is a very unhappy soul in the house,' says Felicity with a great deal of self-importance. 'I communicated with it and it is the spirit of a girl who died of TB there when the house was first built.'

'A girl?' says Adam, who has crept up and joined the conversation, clearly catching up with what has been going on. 'Because Gregory seems to think whatever it is, is male.'

Felicity's eyes flick around the room and she licks her lips.

'I think in the other realm, gender has no real meaning,' she says.

'Right,' says Mortimer after a moment. 'Well . . .' he seems uncharacteristically lost for words before recovering himself. 'I think we need to get this press conference started. But please don't confuse things by bringing your, um, research into this. Keep it simple, okay? Like we discussed on the phone?'

'But I hadn't spoken to Felicity then,' says Gwen. 'I simply want to get my son home.'

'We all do, Mrs Fuller,' says Mortimer. 'But if you start talking about the ghosts of Victorian kids, the press is going to have a field day with this. Do you really want that? It's crucial that you get the public on board with this appeal, do you understand?'

'Listen to the man,' says Anton drily. 'If we don't handle it the right way, my dear, the public will turn against us like a pack of wolves. It's happened before.'

'Okay,' says Rose hurriedly as the little remaining colour in Gwen's face blanches away. 'Look, you don't need to think about any of that, just concentrate on speaking from the heart. And stick to specifics for now.'

'It's okay,' says Gwen surprisingly firmly. 'I know what I have to do.'

The room chosen for the press conference is heaving with reporters, both seated and standing. Gwen and Anton file in after Mortimer and take their places at the tables. Behind them on a movable board are blown-up images of both Gregory and Heather Doyle, who looks about as sinister as she possibly could: greasy hair, squinty dead eyes. The picture was clearly taken in prison.

Mortimer introduces himself as the SIO on the case as Adam leans in to Rose and whispers in her ear.

'Do you believe what that woman said?' he says. 'About the girl? I mean, the Victorian waif thing is a bit of a cliché, isn't it?'

Rose shakes her head. 'Exactly,' she whispers. 'Trust me when I say I've met her type before.'

They tune back in to the statement Mortimer is now reading out.

'We believe that twelve-year-old Gregory Fuller has been persuaded by a woman called Heather Doyle to run away. At this stage we don't understand why but believe Gregory has become fascinated by the details of a crime committed by Doyle at that property in 2006, when a fire caused a multiple murder. We are appealing to anyone who may have seen them, driving a red Volvo station wagon V70 and heading towards Scotland. I will now hand you over to Gregory's mother, Gwen Fuller. After this there will be questions, which I would ask you to direct only at me. Thank you.'

Gwen clears her throat and begins to speak in a voice that is faltering to start with but gains strength as she goes on.

'We have now been without our boy for forty-eight hours,' she says, 'and every moment has been agony. I want to make a direct appeal to you, Heather.' Gwen's eyes are fixed firmly on the camera in front of her, hands twiddling a tissue that she hasn't used yet. Rose can't help being a little impressed at how strong she's being in this intimidating setting. So far anyway.

'You can tell my son,' she continues, 'my beloved, darling boy – that he doesn't need to worry about getting into trouble when he gets back. We just want to give him a hug and tell him . . . tell him how much we love him.' Her voice wavers here but she clears her throat and when she continues her words come out in a fast stream, as though she'd been waiting for this moment above all else. 'And, Gregory?' she says. 'If you're watching? We'll move away when you get back. We won't stay in that horrid, haunted house a moment longer.'

Anton's look of surprise is almost comical. Clearly, moving house wasn't discussed until now. But Mortimer appears even more dismayed, raising a hand as questions from the press all start jabbing at the Fullers at once.

'All questions to be directed to me, please,' he says and the noise abates a little.

A reporter from the BBC goes first, asking if it is their belief that Gregory had gone away with a convicted murderer by choice.

'We don't have information confirming one way or the other and because of that we have to work on the assumption that he needs to be found and brought home as soon as possible,' says Mortimer. 'Next question.'

'Surya Kahn, Sky News,' says another reporter. 'What did Mrs Fuller mean when she referred to the house as being "horrid" and "haunted"?'

'We don't have that information at this time,' says Mortimer, 'but we are aware Gregory perhaps felt disturbed by events that had taken place there in the past.'

'Why would he go with the person who committed those

terrible acts though?' another reporter calls out. But Mortimer has had enough.

'That will be all for now. Thank you for your time,' he says, getting to his feet and hurriedly guiding the Fullers out of the room, which echoes with the buzz of excited conversation.

Rose and Adam walk to the top of the room and follow them out.

Felicity Gordon is waiting outside the door and she embraces Gwen, who collapses, weeping into her arms.

'That wasn't very helpful, Gwen,' says Anton, expression thunderous. 'What was all that nonsense about moving? And why did you mention the supposedly *haunted* house at all? The gutter press will be all over this.'

'I'm sorry but the bad energy needs to be addressed!' says Gordon, clearly loving every moment of this. She meets Rose's eyes and Rose looks away.

A few moments later, the Fullers are in conversation with Mortimer. Gordon hangs back then comes over to where Rose is standing, leaning in to speak in a conspiratorial voice.

'You think I'm a phoney, don't you?' she says, a small smile playing around her lips.

Rose coolly meets her eye. 'I couldn't possibly comment,' she says. 'I'm just concerned that Mrs and Mrs Fuller aren't exploited, that's all.'

The smile drops off the other woman's face. 'I have nothing but good intentions for that family and that missing child,' she says. 'I hope you can look beyond all your prejudices about the kind of work I do and see that I am genuinely trying to help.'

'*Work.*' Rose can't help the scornful way this slips out. Gordon takes a step forward, looking hurt. 'Why are you so closed-minded? Why can't you be at least open to the possibility that I am helping the Fullers. Don't we all want the same thing? Gregory home safe and sound?'

'Maybe,' says Rose. She realizes her hands are shaking and her cheeks are flooded with colour. Something about this woman, standing there with her intuitive-this and her other-realm-that is pressing all of Rose's buttons. Wasn't this exactly what Adele did? Feed off other people's pain for her own gain?

She knows she needs to keep her mouth closed now because she is seriously close to calling the other woman a vampire but then she notices that Gordon has gone deathly pale and staggers a little, so she has to place a hand on the top of a chair.

'Are you okay?' says Rose, looking around for help, but Gwen and Anton remain in deep conversation with Mortimer. Everyone else is too busy to be paying any attention to the micro drama unfolding right here.

Gordon sways and makes a moaning sound.

'Ms Gordon,' says Rose, 'Felicity . . . what is it? Are you sick?'

Gordon does a sort of heaving motion then shudders dramatically. Fearing for her shoes a little, Rose wants to step back but forces herself to reach out and touch the other woman's arm.

Felicity Gordon flinches as though she's been burned, then opens her eyes. Her eyeballs have rolled back into the sockets, showing only the whites, grotesquely. She starts to speak then, in a quiet, low hiss, all the words almost running into each other. Her accent is somehow rougher than the well-spoken voice she had before this bizarre episode.

'You never listen; you never look,' she hisses, 'always busy-busy-busy, always turning away from it, always running. Too scared to know the truth. Never get your hands dirty, do you? Not really dirty, down in the muck with the worms and the dead things. Block it all out, ignore it ignore it ignore it. Pretend and pretend and pretend but you can't get away. Have to stay have to stay have to . . .'

As abruptly as she started, Gordon stops speaking and her eyes snap open. She's trembling all over, her skin ashen.

'What happened?' she says, her hand flying to her mouth. 'What just happened?'

Rose tries to slow her galloping heartbeat. Her insides have turned to icy sludge.

'I don't know,' she says. 'You had a sort of fit and were talking . . . nonsense.'

'What did I say?' says Gordon, looking terrified now. 'That's never happened to me before. I couldn't control that. It was, it was . . . Oh God—' she presses a hand to her chest '—really intense.' Rose can see that her shock has turned into something else. She's thrilled. 'Someone in the other realm really wanted to communicate,' continues Gordon, 'and they used me as a conduit even though I hadn't invited them in.' She pauses and her focus on Rose intensifies. 'Who was it?' she says. 'Who wants to speak to you, DC Gifford?'

Rose regards her icily.

'I think it's time for you to go,' she says, turning away.

Hurrying down the corridor, Rose battles to get her breathing under control. Nausea roils in her stomach as she goes over what just happened.

It was as though Gordon was inhabited by someone else entirely back there; turned into a grotesque costume made of skin and bone and clothing, rather than a living breathing woman.

No prizes for guessing who that someone was.

Have to stay have to stay have to stay . . .

A deep shudder travels up Rose's back, so intense it prompts a jab of pain from her ribs. Why is her mother so desperate for her not to leave that house? She doesn't have time to dwell on any of this now. A bracing wave of anger replaces the cold horror.

There's a missing boy who needs to be found. Rose needs to be on her best game. She walks into the briefing room and takes small, slow sips of breath as everyone else piles in.

Shut the fuck up, Adele, she thinks. *Just leave me alone.*

Needless to say, Mortimer isn't happy about the way the press conference went.

'For God's sake,' he says, 'someone give me some good news.'

'I wish we could,' says Jamie. 'We have a last sighting of the car from the camera at Kessock Bridge, Inverness,' he says. 'Obviously, the possibilities of where they can have gone after that are very wide. They have the whole of the Highlands. She hasn't used the phone registered to her since the day before she left London, so we can't track mobile phone use. She's using cash rather than cards.'

'What about getting petrol?' says Adam. 'It's a long way to the north of Scotland so is it worth checking garages for someone who paid for a tank of petrol in cash? I mean, that's probably unusual these days?'

'Yes,' says Rose, turning to him, heart quickening. 'If you know the make of the car, maybe it's possible to work out exactly where on the road they might need to fill up?'

'Good idea,' says Mortimer and gestures to a man sitting nearby. 'Steve, can you work on that? We last have her on camera getting petrol near Birmingham, and yes, using cash.'

'Small garages in the country might be more likely to remember though,' says the officer called Steve, who is about Rose's age, with a shiny bald head and neat beard. 'We can call all the garages within a certain radius and see if anyone remembers.'

'Good!' says Mortimer. 'And have we had any responses from the press conference? Gail?'

Gail grimaces. 'Absolutely nothing useful so far,' she says, looking down at her pad. 'But I've had a persistent reporter from the *Standard* asking about what Gwen meant about the house. I've tried to put her off but now there are a few papers who are ringing about that.'

Mortimer grimaces. 'Well, it's unfortunate. But if there's any chance at all of Heather Doyle seeing the press conference, it might nudge something in her and make her rethink whatever the hell it is she thinks she's doing. Okay, people, let's get back to it. I want every single garage in the Highlands contacted. It's time to hammer those phones.'

29

It isn't perfect but it will have to do.

Vincent puts down the container of Vim, from which he's managed to eke out a thin crust of powder. It's taken off the worst of the brown stains from the bathtub when combined with the Brillo pad he'd found in the kitchen. The enamel is scratched with grey lines now and his hands are sore and flecked with dirt and pink, grimy foam, but at least it's clean. He can't do anything about the black mould on the ceiling and he's not going near the disgusting sink and toilet but he can have a bloody bath at last.

He turns the key in the lock and gives it a jiggle. It never feels very secure and he longs for a bolt he could slide across. If he had a radio he'd put it on to alert people the bathroom was occupied but that wouldn't necessarily make any difference. No one seems to care about privacy here, apart from him.

The thin stream of water is nowhere near as hot as he would like but there's an old box of Radox on the side and he throws in a lavender-scented handful of grit along with a squirt of shampoo for bubbles.

When the bath is ready, Vincent removes his clothes, catching sight in the flecked mirror above the sink of his pale scrawny chest and the fresh crop of spots scattered across his cheeks. Grimacing and turning away, he climbs into the tub and lowers his substandard, disappointing body into the water.

He wants to lie there and not think of anything but what happened last night keeps playing out in his mind. He and his mother haven't spoken a word to each other since then.

It all started when Hugo had teased him about how slowly he was eating his vegetable moussaka. They never got to eat meat anymore, even though his mother had once been as keen on a bacon sandwich as anyone. Now she says she doesn't eat 'anything with a soul', which is such bullshit. The constant beans and pulses make Vincent fart and give him pains in his stomach. He looks paler than usual these days but his mother doesn't even seem to care that he is a growing boy who needs fuel.

She's changed so much since they've been here. When he thinks about them being in Devon and her once working at the solicitor's office, wearing smart skirts and heels, she seems like a completely different woman. These days she has a permanently glazed look in her eyes from all the pot, which she smokes or cooks into disgusting cookies that Vincent tried and was so sick he is never going near that stuff again. She never wears a bra anymore and it makes him uncomfortable to see her pointy tits moving about under her T-shirts. They're all like that here, and while it was thrilling at first to see so many breasts, now it has turned him off a little. There is one woman, called Catherine, whose tits hang down practically to her waist and are always popping out the side of her dungarees.

And they all do it for Hugo.

His hatred for the man is starting to feel like something tangible he could touch and shape with his hands. It sticks in his throat and makes his belly hurt and sometimes he pictures it like a big lumpy tumour growing inside him. He's starting to feel that he hates *all* men or at least the swaggering confident ones, who look down on him and get women to behave like pathetic slaves.

So he'd been making a face as he looked down at the meal Hugo had made. Hugo said, 'What's up, Vincent – too good for this?' and Vincent had dropped his spoon into the bowl so a little tomato sauce splashed onto the table.

'Yeah,' he said, meeting Hugo's amused gaze with a hostile one of his own. 'It tastes like shit.'

Hugo's eyes flared for a moment. He'd got under his skin. Good.

'Vincent!' His mother finally seemed awake after monotonously spooning food into her mouth. 'Don't be so nasty. You shouldn't speak to Hugo like that when he's been good enough to cook for us all!'

'But it does taste like shit,' said Vincent evenly.

Hugo surprised him by starting to laugh. Then he did a slow hand clap. 'No, Rowan,' he said, 'it's all cool. Vincent is at an age when he wants to assert his male presence. It's like stags, rutting in the wild.' As he said the word 'rutting' he ran a lazy finger along Rowan's bare arm. Vincent wanted to stab him with a fork, right there and then.

'I understand,' said Hugo with fake sincerity. 'I was once just like you, frustrated and desperate for my real life to begin. It's normal for you to feel threatened by the older, more dominant presence.'

'I don't feel threatened by you,' said Vincent through clenched teeth. 'I simply think you're a total wanker.'

'Vincent!' said Rowan, apparently appalled. 'I'm so sorry, Hugo!'

Hugo was still smiling as he hitched up the sleeve of his long blue poplin shirt and placed his elbow on the table, hand raised.

'It's okay,' he said. 'Why don't we have a little man-to-man tussle and see where we go? It's good for a boy to let off some steam.' He waved his tanned hand in the air and grinned. 'What do you think, Champ? Want to take me on?'

Vincent's heart was beating so fast he could feel it throb in his ears. There was no way he could beat Hugo at arm wrestling. But he wasn't going to refuse either. He glanced at his mother, who was chewing her lips as if she wanted to eat herself up from the inside.

'Yeah,' he said, flexing his own arm and placing his bent

elbow on the table. 'I'm not scared of you, even though you *are* twenty years older than me and much stronger.'

Hugo's eyes flashed then. He was too stupid to understand sarcasm but he knew he was being got at.

'I don't think this is a good idea,' said Rowan. 'Can't we stop this silly game now?'

'It's all right, sweetie,' said Hugo with an easy smile. 'I'm not going to hurt him. I'll go . . .'

He didn't reach the end of the sentence because Vincent had already begun, taking him by surprise. Even though he was thin, he had been doing press-ups in the attic through sheer boredom and his wiry arms were getting a little bit stronger.

As Hugo's face reddened and his fist gradually got closer to the scuffed, Formica table, Vincent felt a beautiful power rush through him. He wished it was Hugo's stupid, smug, handsome face he was going to grind into the hard table instead. Even though Hugo doesn't hit his mother (as far as he knows) something about him brings the memories of his father flooding back. That swagger. That sneery air of 'you can't hurt me, you little insect' that makes him feel so small.

Then Hugo simply smiled and before he could even take a breath, Vincent's arm blazed with pain as it was smashed back onto the table the other way. He'd simply been toying with him; letting him think he was winning.

'Not bad, Champ,' said Hugo. That he was a little out of breath wasn't particularly gratifying.

'Darling,' said Celeste in a drawl from the other side of the room, where she was sketching with her legs crossed on a beanbag. 'Don't be a prick. He's just a kid.'

Hugo's sister Celeste is almost as bad as him. She's constantly coming up to Rowan and touching her hair or lifting her chin with a finger and saying she wants to paint her. She hasn't yet, mainly focusing on crap paintings of huge triangles that all look the same to Vincent.

Being called a kid by that ugly whale was the final straw and he'd neatly tipped over the bowl of slop with a finger. Sauce spread like blood across the wooden surface of the table.

'Oops,' he said, with a little smile and then walked out of the room.

Rowan had come upstairs to find him straight away and began shouting at him that he wasn't giving living here a chance.

Vincent told her she had no self-respect. Also, that she was a whore. She slapped him and began to sob. It was a good job she had collapsed into tears because Vincent had come very, very close to hitting her back.

This uncomfortable thought makes him slosh down abruptly so his head is under the water. *Think about something else. Harmony. Think about her instead. Think about that silken skin and the short dress.* The shock of that moment when she'd put his hand between her legs . . .

His eyes are squeezed shut and he is very, very close to getting there a couple of minutes later, which is why he doesn't notice the bathroom door opening.

'Didn't your mother warn you you'd go blind?' The voice is such a shock that Vincent cries out and flails, cracking his elbow painfully on the side of the bath. Water sloshes over the side.

Hugo, in the doorway, is grinning at him. 'Don't worry,' he says with a conspiratorial wink. 'It's bullshit about going blind. Celebrating our own bodies is nothing to be ashamed of.'

'Get out!' The yell comes out high-pitched and girly, such is his distress, but that's the least of his worries. 'Get out, get out, get out! You fucking bastard!'

Hugo puts up both palms and adopts a wounded expression. 'Hey, easy, tiger! I didn't mean to walk in but the door wasn't locked. You should be more careful.'

As Hugo closes the door and walks away, he's chuckling to himself.

Bastard.

Vincent bows his head and can't help the hot tears of humiliation and rage that splash into the now tepid bathwater.

30

Gregory

Gregory's hand really, really hurts. It looks all puffy and red around the cut. Washing it hasn't helped at all and infections can be really serious. Is he going to die from a stupid *cut*?

Heather keeps sleeping. She's like some sort of hibernating creature. Gregory looks over at the hump of her back turned away on the narrow, greasy sofa that barely holds her. She told him she hadn't slept properly since she went to prison. That can't possibly be the truth, but she does sleep a lot. And she constantly sips from a bottle of gin or vodka; he hasn't seen the label so can't be sure. Daddy says women drinking anything other than a white wine spritzer, like Mummy, is 'chavvy'. He gazes over at her. It's so cold, she's wearing all her clothes at once – so is he – and she looks enormous.

It's partly that everything is smaller in the 'van' as she calls it. It's cold and damp and everything has a sort of fishy smell. He keeps thinking about the beach that's nearby but he's not allowed to go outside to see it.

*

She'd made it sound like an adventure, hiding out here.

He hadn't even really believed her at first, when she said they could run away together. It seemed like a joke. But then the stuff happening got worse and worse and he started to want to leave the house more than anything. The pinching was the new thing. The final straw.

He kept thinking about Heather killing those people – her own family – after the boy in the wall told her to. It all started just the same way as it had for him. Her dad, who she says she fought with constantly even though she knows from prison he could have been so much worse, started having accidents around the house. Just like his daddy.

Then the voice started whispering to her and telling her she should do bad things. Finally, it told her that the only way to get rid of the evil was to burn the house down and that everyone in it needed to be 'purged' of it. She gets all upset and says she 'just wanted it to stop'.

She couldn't tell anyone about that after because they would think she was mad and put her in a mental hospital, which terrified her. There'd been some film she saw as a child that was set in one; something about a cuckoo nest? He's confused about that bit of her story. Anyway, it all frightened her so much she couldn't say anything about hearing voices, even when the psychiatrist tried to get her to say why she'd done it.

Gregory heard those whispers too. The boy had started saying that Daddy was a really bad man and that Gregory and Mummy wouldn't be safe with him. But he didn't want to hurt him, even if he was a bit too strict about things like television and having a phone.

So he'd tried the nocebo thing but it hadn't worked at all. Daddy wasn't even kept in overnight once they realized he wasn't actually poisoned and it was all in his head.

Daddy hadn't been very happy about what Gregory had done. He didn't shout, which was much, much worse than the Arctic disapproval that chilled him to the bone.

So maybe it's better to be here, even though he doesn't like the thought of his parents being worried. He wanted to leave a note but Heather talked him out of that.

Still, he wishes he could speak to Mummy just for a little while.

Instead, he makes himself think through some of the worst of the things that have happened. Reassuring himself that he hasn't done a terrible thing in running away.

There was the time when the rug was all rolled up at the top of the stairs and Daddy fell all the way down. And the time when the water coming out of the tap was suddenly as hot as kettle water. The plumber hadn't been able to find any reason for it, which made Daddy shout at the plumber and then at Mummy.

But the thing with the razor blades was the worst.

They'd had their dinner of steamed fish, potatoes, and broccoli. Gregory hates that meal, but he knows it's 'brain food' so he forced himself to eat almost all of it, only leaving a horrible broccoli stalk on his plate.

He was in his room doing some test papers after dinner, one earbud secretly in his ear as he listened to the cricket match on the radio. It was a very exciting match in Antigua. England had enforced the follow-on and the West Indies were about to bat again. If Daddy knew he wasn't concentrating properly he would be annoyed. Daddy doesn't like cricket and says rugby is the only decent sport, but Gregory likes cricket and football more than anything. Rugby is stupid and violent, while football is full of grace and beauty. Gregory misses the poster that he bought with his birthday money, of Aubameyang and Lacazette doing their funny celebration handshake after one of them scores a goal. He's planning to buy an Arsenal scarf that he can hang across the big mirror in his room when he has birthday money.

Drifting into a pleasant football-related daydream for a moment, he's disturbed by a shiver of cold running through him as he remembers what he was thinking about before.

Needing a wee that evening, he'd gone down the hallway to

the bathroom and heard Mummy on the phone to someone. Pine bubble bath smells tickled his nose. Daddy liked to spend ages in there when he'd finished all his work for the evening.

Gregory walked into the bathroom and did a long wee, quickly, before anyone came in. He hadn't really been paying attention when he came into the room but as he turned to the sink to wash his hands, his blood seemed to turn to electricity in his body; shock zapping cold all the way through him.

Razor blades – the type Daddy buys off Amazon and uses to trim his beard – had been taken out of their packets and laid all around the edge of the bathtub. He stepped a little closer, his heart throbbing in his chest with dread.

They looked so neat; like someone had taken a ruler and placed them so they were an exact distance apart all the way round the bath. It felt like a machine or a robot had done it, it was so precise.

Gregory's fingers had migrated to his mouth, a bad habit he was trying to give up, so he took them out before grabbing a big wodge of toilet roll. Then he carefully picked up the razor blades and laid them gently inside the paper. Even though he was being really careful, he cut his hand and a single drop of blood fell into the bathwater and spread in tiny swirly circles. It was sort of fascinating and for a minute he'd stood and watched as the blood dissipated, which meant he didn't hear the sound of anyone coming into the bathroom until it was too late.

'What the hell is going on in here?' Daddy's voice had been so loud, Gregory had almost jumped out of his skin. 'Are those my razor blades? What are you thinking, Gregory? You could seriously injure yourself!'

His father began to pick up the blades very carefully between his big fingers and somehow, they had all been collected and put away before Mummy came into the bathroom, looking confused by the scene. Daddy told her Gregory had cut his finger in his bedroom and left Mummy to clean it and put on a plaster. Neither of them told her what had happened. Daddy had given him The Look; the one that meant he should keep quiet and not make things worse. He wanted to tell Daddy that it wasn't him who had put out those razors on the bathtub. But Daddy never believed him. He probably thought Gregory cut all the flowers too. The trouble was, Gregory couldn't say for a hundred per cent certain that he hadn't done it. When the strange things happened in the house, he sometimes wondered whether he had done them without even knowing it.

When he told Heather that, she'd said that was 'how it started' and how he would end up doing something really terrible if he didn't get away.

And at first, it really *had* been exciting. He hadn't liked being in the garage thing that much though, hunkered down in a sleeping bag, even though he had a book to read that he had brought with him. But Heather said she would be one of the very first people they would interview, and she was right. She didn't go to a good school like Beamishes but she's still really smart about a lot of stuff. He hadn't wanted to tell her he'd been fiddling with the lid of the can of Coke and opened up the cut on his hand until after they were on the road and then she told him he should wrap it in the kitchen roll in the car. It bled so much it stuck to the paper but it finally stopped.

Heather isn't that great at looking after him. When he complained about the clothes she had brought for him – a horrible red hoodie that was like a girl's, jeans that were a bit small and a couple of T-shirts, along with pants and socks – she snapped at him really nastily. For a moment he remembered that, actually, she may be his friend but she'd still killed three people. This is a thought that has to be kept right at the back of his mind because it's too scary to face directly.

His hand really, really hurts.

He looked all through the van for antiseptic but there's nothing like that. At home they have a first aid box that is stuffed with all sorts of plasters and medications. How can you clean a wound properly without antiseptic?

Then Gregory remembers something and sits up a little

203

straighter. He was only little and they were on holiday in France. He remembers he wasn't allowed an ice cream because Daddy said he had been too whingey on the way to the beach, so he'd stomped off down to the water, where he'd trodden on a sharp shell, cutting his toe. When he ran back to Mummy, trying not to cry, she said that the salt in the sea was the very best thing for it and made him come with her to walk in the freezing-cold water. He remembers the sharp bite of it and Mummy saying it would be okay in a soothing voice, holding his other hand tightly.

Maybe if he would get some sea water on his hand now, it would be better than nothing? He looks over at Heather, who is absolutely silent and still, like she's dead. He wonders what will happen if she did die because he would be here all alone then. A tiny secret thought worms its way up that instantly makes him feel ashamed.

If she was dead, I could go home.

Heather murmurs in her sleep. If he's going to do something, anything, he has a tiny amount of time left in which to do it.

He eyes the window. It's not raining for a change and the sky is a watery blue.

Gregory bites the nails on his good hand, thinking hard.

He'll run down to the water and dip his hand in, then come straight back. No one will see him. He won't speak to anyone. What harm can it do? And it might stop his hand from hurting for a little while at least.

31

Rose has drunk so much coffee that she's simultaneously jumpy and exhausted but she's contemplating another all the same when there is a shout from across the room.

Jamie gets to his feet as everyone looks over at him.

'I've just spoken to a tiny garage on the A9 at a place called Tore,' he says. 'It's a bit north of Inverness. The guy there remembers a woman matching Heather's description coming in to buy petrol in the early hours of that morning. Cash sale.'

'Brilliant.' Mortimer crosses the room and leans against a desk, arms folded. He's vigorously chewing gum, stubbled jaw working hard.

'Where does that road lead?' he says and Jamie turns back to the screen. 'There are a few places you could go from there, but according to the guy at the garage, it's on the road to a little seaside town called Dornoch. There's a big caravan and camping park there.'

Mortimer taps a pen against his bottom lip, thinking hard.

'The mobile home could have been taken there ages ago,' says Rose, 'and it would be a good place to hide.'

'Yes,' says Jamie, nodding, 'I've rung the office number but at the moment there's only an answering machine message about calling back when the season begins in May.'

'What's beyond Dornoch?' says Mortimer.

'Mainly mountains, going by this map,' says Jamie, pointing at the screen. 'I mean, there are lots of small towns, and they may follow the coast road all the way to John o'Groats, but I can't see why they would. They'd literally run out of country before too long.'

Mortimer jumps to his feet. 'Right!' he says. 'We're going up there. Tonight.' He looks over at Rose and Adam. 'I'd like you two to be part of this, because you've had interaction with Gregory. Okay, everyone. Do whatever you need to do. We're leaving as soon as possible.'

Adam rushes off to make hurried childcare arrangements and Rose goes home for a flying visit to pick up some things.

There are no more flights to Inverness at this late hour, so the plan is that they'll drive up in two cars. Rose and Adam in one and Mortimer, Gail and Jamie in the other.

Rose insists on doing the first shift because she knows she has a limited shelf life after her lack of sleep.

'Music?' says Adam as they get onto the M1.

'Yeah,' says Rose, 'depending on what it is. I need it to be lively enough to keep me awake but not annoying.'

'Hmm.' Adam focuses on his phone for a few minutes. 'I've got some death metal that will certainly stop you nodding off but am guessing it might come under the annoying banner?'

'Just a bit,' says Rose, smiling. Then, glancing quickly at him: 'I wouldn't have put you down as the death metal sort. Your hair isn't long enough for a start.'

Adam yawns expansively. 'I like loads of different kinds of music actually,' he says after a moment. 'I'm looking forward to sharing my extensive collection for the entirety of this journey.'

'Oh I can't wait,' says Rose drily.

'There may even be a quiz afterwards,' says Adam.

Rose lets out a laugh. She can feel him grinning next to her. It's going to be a long night but there are far worse people she could be sharing this journey with.

And it is all taking her mind off what happened today with Felicity Gordon. For a moment, Rose contemplates telling Adam. All of it. But just as quickly the urge burns out. *No. Keep it to yourself, Rose.*

Adam puts on some low-key music with a haunting female voice Rose doesn't recognize and she settles in for the long drive.

'Okay if I grab some kip now?' he says, reaching into his bag for a sweatshirt to put under his head. 'I'll take over when-ever you want.'

'Go for it.'

It is impressive how quickly he falls asleep, even in this uncomfortable position. When he gives a gentle snore, it makes Rose smile. He even snores quite nicely.

But as the black motorway unfurls beneath the wheels, it's impossible not to let Gordon's words, when she'd channelled Adele, play out again in her mind.

Could it be that there is money hidden somewhere in the house? Or, *oh God*, a body?

Rose thinks about the night some sort of disturbance happened. Mr Big was round and Rose had been banished to her room as usual. But she'd heard someone else come in at some point and there was shouting, including another female voice she didn't recognize.

Then everything had gone strangely quiet. Rose had crept out of bed and peered through the rails on the stairs into the hallway. Adele was there, her face streaked with make-up like she'd been crying. She'd been aghast at the sight of Rose and screamed at her to get back to bed. It had always stuck out in Rose's mind; seeing Adele in such a state because the other woman seemed to pride herself on being tough. Adele had drunk more after that episode.

Dismissing any wild and morbid thoughts about murder or

hidden money, Rose concludes she will probably never know what happened.

One thing is for sure anyway: she has to get out of that house soon whether Adele likes it or not.

32

Gregory is breathless and his head feels all fuzzy. He tries not to think about dying, or his mum, or any of the things that make him feel worse, but it's really hard.

He should have run off to get help at the beach yesterday. He thinks it was yesterday anyway.

It was so nice with the sun out. No one was there, apart from a lone dog walker absolutely miles away. He'd washed his hand in the sea and it hurt so much. That was probably a good thing, though, like TCP, which stings like crazy and stinks the place out.

After cleaning his hand, he thought he'd have a little walk, only to stretch his legs. He wasn't going to wander off anywhere. But walking on sand was so tiring, he'd decided to go up the dunes to where there might be a road. There was a car park there and a bench.

And that was where he'd seen his own face looking back at him.

It was the *Sun* newspaper with a headline that read:

WE'LL ESCAPE HAUNTED HOUSE OF HORRORS

Tragic mum makes promise to missing lad.

His heart had almost stopped beating. It was such a stupid picture of him, taken last year when he still looked like a child, but he couldn't focus on that for long. He'd snatched it up and begin to read.

The mother of missing twelve-year-old Gregory Fuller made a tearful plea for the return of her son yesterday, promising they would move from the 'horrid HAUNTED' house in which Gregory's abductor Heather Doyle, (36) slaughtered her own family. Just eighteen at the time, Doyle deliberately started a fire that swept through the Kentish Town flat, killing her father, Michael Doyle, 47; grandmother Patricia Doyle, and brother, Samuel Doyle, just five.

It's unclear why a sinister friendship developed between Doyle and Gregory, but a source says the boy has been experiencing ghostly presences, perhaps the spirits of Doyle's family. It's thought she may have been manipulating him into what one psychologist called a 'Stockholm syndrome' relationship (see 'What is Stockholm syndrome? on p5).

It is believed that the two are in the north of Scotland, possibly staying on or near a campsite in a light green Way Finder mobile home. The public have been asked to look out for any unusual use of buildings, or any mother and son duos who may have moved into the neighbourhood in a secretive way. It is asked that the public do not approach Doyle directly but to report any sightings to this special helpline: 0333 566 723.

Gregory barrelled through the door into the caravan.

'Heather!' he cried.

She was up, looking as if she had been crying and when she saw him she began to shout in a way that made him shrink back towards the door again.

'Where did you go?' she yelled. 'Did you speak to anyone? Fucking hell, Gregory! Do you realize what you did?'

She got up and grabbed him by the shoulders, and he let out a sound that was really pathetic and girly but he couldn't help it.

Maybe this shocked her, because she released him and stood back, her expression aghast. He could smell her sour breath and her eyes were piggy and red.

'I'm sorry! All right!' she cried and made a sort of frustrated growl in her throat. 'I just, God, I wondered where you were and thought some SWAT team was going to come through the fucking ceiling and get me!' She gave a high-pitched laugh, which sounded out of place and wrong. 'Who did you talk to? Tell me!'

'I didn't talk to anyone, I promise!' said Gregory, then, gaining more courage, 'I only went to wash my hand in the sea then, look! I found this!'

He'd been holding the paper behind his back, fearful she would take it but now she looked curious as he held it out for her to read.

'Shit,' she said, reading hurriedly. She was silent for a few moments and then: 'I'm not thirty-six for a start,' throwing the paper across the room.

Gregory went to retrieve it. 'No, but look at the headline!' he said, excitement bubbling up inside him. 'Mummy said we could move! Isn't that the best news ever!'

Heather turned to look at him, scowling. 'You don't believe them, do you?'

'What? Why wouldn't I?' He hated that his voice had gone so small.

'Because they're *LY-ING!*' she said, snatching the newspaper and waving it as she said the word in a nasty, sing-song voice. 'Can't you see that? They're not going to move! Who would buy the house now it's been called the House of Horrors in the fucking national press, for the second time! They couldn't even if they wanted to!'

Gregory's legs began to shake. 'Mummy wouldn't lie,' he said quietly.

'God, I wish you'd stop calling her Mummy! You sound like you go to Eton or something! You're about to be a teenager! No wonder the other kids are mean to you!'

Gregory's eyes filled with tears. He should never have told her about school.

'. . . And yes, yes she would lie,' she yelled. 'People always lie when it comes to that house. They need to make it stop. Even if they did manage to sell it, the very next people in would go through what we went through! Don't you understand that?'

The tears were coming now and he couldn't stop them.

'But I don't care about other people who move in!' he shouted. 'I want to go home! I don't want to be here anymore with you! My hand really, really hurts and it's cold and I'm sick of eating . . . eating shitting crisps!' He was too upset to be shocked at his own audacity. Heather stared at him, goggle-eyed and he tried to make himself smaller.

'You're so ungrateful!' she screamed. 'I am trying to help you, you daft little sod! Don't you understand that? I'm trying to save you from that, that *thing* in the house! I'm not the monster here!' She sank onto the sofa. 'Shit,' she said, rubbing her face. 'This is such a mess. How many people did you see? Tell me.'

Gregory hesitated. There was a car in the car park, with someone inside but he didn't think they were looking at him.

'None,' he said. 'Not a single soul. I promise.' His breath was coming out really fast now. 'It's so quiet round here, there was really no one.'

Heather's expression softened 'Let me have a look at your hand,' she said. 'Come on.'

He held out his palm towards her and she took his hand in hers, which felt clammy and cold. He tried not to shrink back because he didn't want to hurt her feelings.

'Hmm,' she said, looking worried. 'It might be infected. You might need antibiotics. Shit, let me think.' She began to pace, pulling at her hair. Then she rushed to her handbag and reached inside and pulled out her phone.

'What are you going to do?' he said, hope and fear all mixed together fluttering in his chest.

'I'm going to put it on just for a second,' she said, 'to look up hospitals.'

'You're going to take me to hospital?' He didn't mean to almost shout and she winced at the sudden pitch of his voice. 'Sorry,' he said. 'But are we turning ourselves in?'

She looked at him, her expression blank now.

'I'm not turning myself in,' she said. 'But I'm not having you getting gangrene or something on my conscience. The whole point of me doing this was to protect you, not bloody hurt you. Not that they'll see it like that. I'll drop you outside and then I'll come back here, or, I don't know, go on somewhere else. I'll work it out.'

Gregory pictured a clean, white hospital with drugs to make him feel better and Mummy coming rushing in to hug him. And Daddy too. He was surprised how much he wanted to hear that booming voice taking control of things and being in charge. They'd sort everything out.

But now it's the morning again and they haven't been to hospital. He's shivering so hard he feels like his teeth are going to shatter. At one point in the night he dreamed that actually happened and he came to with a cry, coughing and spluttering in panic. But there was nothing in his mouth at all, apart from lots of spit.

His hand feels monstrously big, a vast throbbing landscape of pain that's all he can think about. Gregory imagines it as a purple colour inside him, filling him up and obliterating everything else.

He'd thought they would go to the hospital straight away, but Heather had been insistent that they could wait until the morning when she was what she called 'fresher'. He knew she was scared of driving on the roads around here by the grim way she'd clutched the wheel on the way here. And she'd been drinking and wasn't in the right state to drive. She spent ages washing his hand under the cold tap with shower gel. He hadn't even bothered to hide the tears, it hurt so much.

They ate what she called 'their last supper' of rolls and Nutella but he hadn't had any appetite. She told him one more night wouldn't make a difference, and that they would go first thing in the morning, she promised.

But Gregory knows she finished off the bottle of gin because when he stumbled to the toilet to pee as the first light came, he saw the empty bottle. She wasn't waking up when he jiggled her shoulder and she sort of groaned and went back to sleep. It's like she is the child, he the sensible one, but he hasn't got the energy to argue.

Instead, he curls up in the corner of the room, cradling his monster-sized hand, which now has funny red lines coming up his arm, and he waits. He doesn't feel well enough to go anywhere now anyway. He's hunkering down into himself, living every single second of the shivering and the horrible doom feeling. Maybe he really is going to die. This probably is what it feels like. It must be because he has never felt so ill, not in his whole life. This is what the boy in the wall experienced, he thinks, at least, the dying part. No wonder he's so angry if he feels trapped in it. If you die you should be allowed to rest.

When he becomes aware of Heather's shouting sometime after, it sounds like it is coming from far away. He doesn't care anymore. He's too cold and shivery and ill even to think about going home now.

The pain has a rhythm, *DOOF-DOOF-DOOF*, like when a car has the music up too loud inside and all you can hear is that.

His heart beats in time to it and he lets himself get washed away on a wave of sound and bright, shivery pain.

DOOF-DOOF-DOOF.

33

Rose, Adam and Mortimer are in the car with an Inspector Lennox from Inverness CID – a man near retirement age with seen-it-all eyes and a soft Highlands accent – heading through the green countryside to Dornoch. Another car holds the rest, including two officers from Lennox's team.

Rose had one cup of weak coffee when they arrived at the station and were greeted by the officers coordinating the search locally. The little bit of sleep she managed to get in the car is enough, combined with the adrenalin, to get her through if she ignores the sharp pain in her ribs and the dull throb from her bruised face. It keeps her awake, anyway.

A cell tower registered Heather Doyle's phone for only a few minutes last night. No call was made but data was used.

They're about five miles from Dornoch. Staring out of the window, Rose is soothed by the incredible variations of undulating green she can see. Every now and then a little light peeks out from the heavy clouds and shadows dance playfully over the landscape, washing it in a new palette all over again.

The radio comes to life. Lennox has a conversation, which he then relays to the back of the car.

'Seems local officers have got a sighting of the Volvo and it's on the B9168, Poles Road, out of Dornoch. That means she's heading towards the A9 and that means . . .' He tails off.

'. . . she's heading our way?' says Adam, leaning forward in his seat, eyes lighting up with new focus.

'She is, right enough,' says Lennox. 'We'll have to wait and see whether she goes left back to Inverness or turns right to who knows where. Thurso maybe.' He has another brief conversation via the radio.

He turns back to them again. 'There's a house right near that junction. We can pull in there and then follow her as soon as she shows herself.'

'Are we going to apprehend her here?' says Rose, picturing a tactical pursuit and containment move. That would be very frightening for Gregory. Mortimer's face is scrunched in thought and he doesn't reply for a moment or two.

'No,' he says then. 'We're going to keep a low profile and follow her until we're in a situation where she stops. Gregory's safety remains our top priority here.'

They drive in silence for a couple more minutes amid the light flow of early morning traffic on the A9. It's one of the major roads in the Highlands, and according to the little bit of trivia from Lennox as they left Inverness, the longest road in Scotland.

'Here,' says Lennox and the car abruptly slows and turns left up a short driveway to what might be a farmhouse, or a home with a couple of outbuildings. They are a little across from the junction, which is the main road down to Dornoch.

They wait. No one speaks.

Then the radio crackles and a voice says, 'Suspect almost at the junction. Get ready.'

There's a sudden flow of two or three cars that everyone is silently cursing as they see the red Volvo appear at the junction and turn right.

'Here we go,' says Mortimer as they pull out onto the main road. Officers from Golspie station a little further along are going to join them and make a formation around the car at a distance, but for now, it is only them and the officer who came from Dornoch who are in pursuit of the car, which is being driven at a careful speed, well within the limit.

They are two cars behind now. Rose cranes her neck to see if she can see Gregory. Lennox produces some binoculars and looks from the front seat.

'I cannae see the kid,' he says. 'But he might be lying down on the back seat. Officers on the ground are still going door to door in Dornoch but we have to assume the boy is in that vehicle.'

'Agreed,' says Mortimer, drumming his fingers against his knee, seemingly unaware of the nervous gesture.

A light rain begins to fall and the windscreen wipers' *thwick-thwick* sound would be almost hypnotic, were it not for the crackling tension in the car. They pass fields dotted with splashes of bright purple heather and some kind of yellow plant, stark against the green. Here and there, cows stand sentry, heads down as if in formation. A field filled with piles of bales tightly wrapped in black plastic whips past, then a long white building that looks like a bed and breakfast.

Mountains rear up in the near distance and then there is a silver expanse of sea to the left, another band of rain hanging low in the sky like a swathe of grey cloth.

'We're nearly at Golspie,' says Lennox.

'What's at Golspie?' says Mortimer.

Lennox rubs his face. 'It's just a pretty wee seaside town,' he says. 'Lovely castle. Lots of golf.' He pauses. 'A hospital.'

At this he turns and makes a see-saw motion with his head. 'But maybe she's going to pass straight through and keep going. There's pretty much only mountains to the left and straight ahead you'll go through a number of small places and maybe end up in Thurso. We'll have to follow her and see what she does.'

A tractor pulls out ahead, with a blasé regard for the speed of passing traffic, causing a groan from everyone in the car.

'Bugger,' says Mortimer. Heather's car is now three ahead of them. The other police car is behind. There have been no stretches of dual carriageway so far; the road entirely two lanes all the way.

Majestic pines surround the car on both sides of the road now and in the thrumming rain, it's like being in a tunnel – almost claustrophobically so – until the road opens up a little again.

When they finally get to a big junction, the tractor chugs off to the left and there's an almost simultaneous letting out of breath in the car. They're now only two behind Heather. Rose can make out the back of her head and her round shoulders.

So close . . .

As they get to the outskirts of the town, they begin to see a smattering of houses with their distinctive drystone walls, and pass a sign for the council offices. A band of glinting sea appears again on the right as they enter the town. And then they see Heather's indicator blink on and off.

'She's heading to Lawson Memorial Hospital right enough,' says Lennox as they approach the entrance. Wrought-iron fences top a low wall with ornate pillars.

Lennox is on the radio now, calling for the back-up vehicles.

Please let Gregory be all right, Rose thinks, her palms sweating as they pull up a short distance from where the Volvo backs clumsily into a parking space, so it's facing the larger of the three buildings of the hospital. There's one new building and two much older ones, but it's clearly a small hospital befitting small health crises.

Is that what *this* is? Or something more serious?

Heather gets out of the car, painstakingly slowly, like a woman much older.

'Everyone wait,' says Mortimer, hand raised. 'Let's see where the boy is before we act.'

Heather goes to the back of the car and opens the door. She leans in and then, with a frustrated look around, reaches inside.

Then the small, crumpled form of the boy gets out of the car, inch by inch. He seems barely able to stand. He has a coat around his shoulders that's far too big and looks about himself for a moment, bewildered, before Heather ushers him through the doors of the nearest building. She's evidently going to leave him there because here she is now, alone, hurrying back towards her car.

'*Now!*' barks Mortimer and they jump out of the vehicle at once.

'Heather Doyle, stop!' he shouts. Sirens fill the air and two more police cars career at speed up the hospital driveway, headlights swirling in the soft, grey light as they park near the buildings, blocking the way forward.

Heather's face is a picture of shock as they all surge towards her.

'Get back!' she yells and draws something out of her pocket. A kitchen knife. She waves it around.

'Heather!' calls Rose, pushing ahead, despite the jolting pain that travels up her feet and encases her sides. 'We can help you. Put the knife down and we can talk.'

'What's wrong with Gregory?' says Mortimer. 'Why is he needing hospital? Is he hurt?'

'Like you care!' shouts Heather. 'You didn't give a shit about him before!'

Rose holds up her hands and steps forward, a little closer. 'Heather, please listen,' she calls as the woman takes a step back, knife held up. 'We do care. We want to find out what happened in that house. We're close to getting to the bottom of it. Will you help us?'

There's a moment when Heather seems to hesitate and then her expression shifts again. 'None of you lot will ever understand.' She wrenches open the car door and gets inside with surprising speed. Rose shouts her name and runs closer. The car engine roars into life and it surges forwards, towards the road that runs around the back of the hospital.

But she must see that now one of the police cars has skidded around the other way, blocking her route.

There's a painful sound of gears crunching in the elderly car, the engine screaming in protest.

Heather reverses and comes back the other way. Two uniformed officers have laid a 'stinger' – a jagged line of metal designed to rip car tyres and immobilize vehicles – and there's another police car now at the end of the driveway.

No way out.

She's trapped.

Heather's face scrunches into tearful fury through the windscreen and Rose thinks, *This is it, nowhere to go now.*

But the engine bursts into life like a growling beast. Heather drives straight across the tidy lawn, bumping and scraping on the small hills of it, right towards the fence that separates the hospital from the busy A9.

The car smashes straight through it and onto the road.

The blaring of horns is brief but the sickening sound of metal crunching into metal seems to go on and on.

34

Rose climbs gingerly into bed in the cosy little hotel that overlooks the River Ness and pulls the thick, soft duvet up around her chin. Sleep feels a long way away, despite the lack of it the night before and the long and traumatic day.

She closes her eyes but the very moment her mind is given a blank screen, it helpfully replays the whole scene outside the hospital in high-definition detail.

It had been a terrible moment. Running across the damp grass, gasping breaths, skidding as she went, to where the car had smashed through the fence.

Heather Doyle's car went right into the path of a van that was delivering seafood from the fishing port of Scrabster to restaurants in Inverness.

There had been a moment when she wanted to cover her face like a child and block out the sights and sounds of it all. The Volvo, upside down on the other side of the road. The van with 'The Seafood Company' in jaunty blue on the side, its driver hidden from sight. Then she remembered she was a police officer. It wasn't an option to turn away. Running straight towards the terrible things was the very nature of the job.

So she'd forced herself down there, into what was quickly a hive of activity.

It was surprisingly quick getting the road blocked off and preventing further accidents because there were so many police officers already in situ.

Lawson Memorial is only a cottage hospital and has no resources for dealing with a major emergency of this nature, although medical staff on site rushed to do what they could before more help arrived. The nearest big hospital, the Raigmore, is in Inverness, and a helicopter and ambulance came directly from there. The fire brigade also came from Inverness.

It could have been so much worse. The driver of the van, a Polish father of three called Pawel Wójcik, sustained relatively minor injuries, including a broken nose from the air bag and two broken ribs as he swerved to try to avoid the red Volvo that came from nowhere.

There'd been a moment's lucky lull in the traffic that meant no other vehicles were involved. It could have been a massive pile-up.

But Heather had to be cut out of the car and sustained multiple serious injuries. She is now in the Raigmore in an induced coma to prevent further swelling on her brain.

She hadn't been wearing a seatbelt. Rose keeps wondering whether she panicked and acted as she did, or whether it was a deliberate act whose consequences she was fully aware of and actively seeking.

Gregory has sepsis. It's a potentially catastrophic infection, which has festered in a cut on his hand, the cause of which is unknown. Every time Rose thinks about this, about the fact that Heather was so remiss in caring for the boy, she feels a surge of rage and the tiny bit of sympathy she has at the other woman's smashed-up body and hopeless future dim a little more.

Gregory was also airlifted to the Raigmore, while Pawel had gone in the ambulance.

*

Once Rose and her colleagues had got to the Raigmore, a young and very perky female doctor with hair shaved on one side, had assured them that children can bounce back from sepsis quickly once the intravenous antibiotics get to work.

Rose feels something twist inside as she replays looking in at Gregory lying in the hospital bed. He'd looked very small indeed, lying there fast asleep, the drugs saving his life snaking into his skinny arm from the drip next to the bed.

'Honestly,' said the doctor, whose name Rose never caught, 'you'll be amazed when you see him tomorrow, I'll bet. But we really were just in time.'

Anton and Gwen are coming on the first flight to Inverness the following morning.

Rose attempts to turn over but her ribs still hurt so damned much. Then she thinks about poor Pawel Wójcik, who must be in much worse discomfort.

She wishes she felt a bit more satisfaction about where they had got to.

Getting Gregory back home was the absolute priority. But she's also keenly aware that nothing has changed in that house – not really.

If anything, his parents may well take an even more over-protective role now, controlling every aspect of the poor kid's life. And what of the haunting? What of the presence in that building that supposedly drove a woman to murder her family and to snatch a child from his home? When is that story going to end?

In the end, sleep comes, blissfully heavy and dreamless.

In the morning she wakes early and stands under the shower for as long as she can bear it, the heat offering some respite from the discomfort.

She has forgotten to bring make-up and when she contemplates her bruised, tired face in the mirror over the sink in the bathroom – with its pale blue and white nautical theme – she grimaces a little. She attempts to finger-comb her thick chestnut hair and then reties it into a ponytail, noting how much it needs a wash. Still, it will have to do.

When they all arrive at the hospital a little later, there's no change in Heather, they're told, and no possibility that she can be moved in an unconscious state. The decision is made that they will return to London without her and organize for her to be flown down once she's well enough to travel, should that time come.

It strikes Rose that she may be coming home in a body bag.

All the same, there's a police guard outside her door, who won't be going anywhere for the foreseeable future.

They make their way to the Highland Children's Unit, where they saw Gregory the night before. It's painted in a cheerful bright blue and turquoise with murals on some of the walls. They pass one painted like a forest and meet a doctor coming out of Gregory's room. He's in his thirties and has curly blonde hair and very pale skin, his eyebrows almost invisible. Introducing himself as Dr Mike Bloomfield, he updates them on Gregory's condition.

'The wee lad is doing extremely well,' he says. 'He's going to need to be on antibiotics for a while but we can take the IV out later today and it might be that he could even travel home by this evening.'

'Oh, that's so good to hear,' says Rose. She looks at Mortimer whose face splits into a wide grin she hasn't seen before.

'That is very good news indeed,' he says. 'Are his parents here yet, by any chance?'

It's almost as though by saying this, he conjures them into being.

Rose becomes aware of movement behind her and then a booming, familiar voice says, 'I'm here to see my son – Gregory Fuller.'

She turns to see Anton at the nurses' desk, Gwen hurrying behind him.

Anton's face is drawn and flushed but he's dressed in a smart charcoal coat with a checked scarf neatly folded under his chin. Gwen wears a voluminous mackintosh that looks as though it may belong to Anton and boots that are a short hop from wellies. Her hair and eyes are wild.

'Where is he?' she calls, almost pushing past the small knot of people to get through. 'Where's my son?'

Dr Bloomfield looks momentarily alarmed at the number of visitors for this one small patient before he holds out his hand and introduces himself. To Gwen first, which immediately makes him rise in Rose's estimation, then Anton, who barely acknowledges the extended hand and merely gives a distracted nod.

'Now, I can let Mum and Dad in,' says Bloomfield, looking around the group, 'but the rest of you can wait. I can't have that many people around one bed on the ward.'

'Thank you, Doctor,' croaks Gwen, grabbing hold of his hand.

In the meantime, Rose and the remains of the team head to the café, each involved in different tasks. Rose is struggling to hide how terrible she feels. Her ribs hurt with every intake of breath now the adrenalin from yesterday has burned away, and her face throbs.

She's run out of the strong painkillers and feels like a walking bruise. When she touches her cheek and winces, she catches Adam looking at her intently from where he's buying a coffee and a pastry. A few moments later he has a quiet conversation with Mortimer, who looks over at her and nods in a decisive way.

'What was all that about?' says Rose as Adam comes over.

'Mortimer is flying back this afternoon and you're going with him.'

'Wait, what?' says Rose. 'I can't do that!'

'Why not?' says Adam, looking her directly in the eyes. 'You've clearly been injured in the line of duty and are in pain. I'm going to drive back with Gail and Jamie is going to do it alone but stop off and see a friend in Dumfries to break the journey.'

His eyes soften. 'We've got Gregory home,' he says. 'The job is over.'

Rose opens her mouth to protest again because it still seems unfair but she sees that Anton is now at the entrance to the café, looking around with an irritated expression.

He marches over and she arranges her face into one of polite helpfulness. There's something about this man that gets her hackles up the moment he comes into her airspace.

'Everything okay, Anton?' says Adam, although his face seems to telegraph that no, everything most definitely isn't okay.

'It's Gregory,' he says curtly to Rose alone, 'for some reason he wants to see you.'

'Me?' says Rose. 'Me specifically, or my SIO, who's been in charge of the case?'

'You,' says Anton, mouth turned down sourly. 'I told him no but Gwen . . .' He bites off the end of the sentence. 'Well, let's say that she's feeling rather indulgent because of everything that's happened.'

'Right,' says Rose, 'I'll come right now, in that case.'

But Anton doesn't move. 'If you ask me,' he says, 'I don't think any of you were any bloody use.'

'Right,' says Rose again. Tiredness and pain are leaching what little tolerance she has for him. 'Well, we did find him, to be fair.'

He practically snarls. 'Well, you found him after he was made very sick by that . . .' he pauses '. . . that woman.'

'Yes,' says Rose, 'I do understand how upsetting it must be to have learned he was in hospital. But thankfully it looks as though he'll make a full recovery and you'll have him home in no time.' The words feel robotic as they leave her mouth.

'And what about *her*?' says Anton. 'Doyle? I hope they'll throw away the bloody key this time.'

'Well,' says Rose, 'she'll certainly serve more time for this. But at the moment it's not clear whether or not she'll survive the accident.' She gestures past him. 'Want to lead the way?'

The curtains are drawn around Gregory's bed when Rose and Anton approach. Anton says, 'Knock knock,' in a loud voice. A man with a Sikh turban who is sitting by the bed of a small, bald-headed girl across the way looks up sharply.

Anton pulls back the curtain to reveal Gwen sitting close to the bed and showing Gregory something on her phone that's making him laugh. They seem to spring apart almost guiltily at the sight of Anton and Rose.

'Here she is,' says Gwen in a too-bright tone.

It's cramped with the curtain closed but Rose smiles broadly at Gregory, who looks very pale in the bed, his dark hair sticking up all over his head. One of his arms is hidden inside a clean white bandage, small fingers curled over at the end.

'All right, Gregory,' she says. 'You've had quite the time of it, haven't you?'

'Is Heather going to die?' he says without further preamble. 'Mummy won't tell me and I want to know.'

Rose hesitates before replying, conscious of the eyes of his parents on her. 'I can't answer that, Gregory,' she says. 'I'm not going to pretend she's okay because she had a very serious accident. I think you're a really smart boy and you know when people are bullsh— when people are trying to pull the wool over your eyes. She's very gravely injured, but the doctors are doing everything they can for her.'

'Why do you *care* what happens to that woman?'

'Oh shush, Anton,' says Gwen. 'It's not the time.'

Anton's eyes widen. Rose feels much the same surprise.

Go, Gwen.

Gregory sniffs loudly until his mother hands him a tissue from the box next to the bed.

'It'll be my fault if she dies,' he says in a tiny voice. 'If I hadn't been clumsy like Daddy always says I am, then I wouldn't have cut my hand and got sepsis.'

Rose casts a quick glance at Anton, who seems uncharacteristically lost for words.

'Now,' says Rose, moving a little closer to the bed. 'I need you to listen to me very carefully as a police officer, okay?'

Gregory nods miserably, top lip puckering with the effort of not crying.

'None of this is your fault,' she says. 'Heather is a grown woman and you are a child and it was very wrong for her to take you from your home like she did.'

'I chose to go though,' says Gregory, pitch whiny. 'Because she was the only person who understood.'

'*I* understand,' says Rose and Gregory searches her eyes with his own, desperate to believe her. 'I mean it.'

Gregory swipes his nose with the tissue.

Rose continues, 'And aside from doing a bad thing by taking you away, she drove her car deliberately onto a busy road. She could have killed people.'

'*More* people,' mutters Anton. Everyone ignores him.

'I just wish we could find out what he wants, the boy in the wall,' says Gregory. 'That was all I was doing. It was why I wrote to her. I thought she might know. But she didn't. She said it wouldn't ever stop and I had to get away. I just want to *know*.'

Gwen looks shiftily at Rose and then back at her son.

'I told you, darling,' says Gwen, revealing her horsey teeth. 'I have a clever lady who's helping with all that.'

Gregory looks at her, guardedly. 'Yes you said. But when *exactly* are we moving house, Mummy?' he says. 'Will I have to go back at all or will we stay somewhere else while we look?'

Gwen looks properly at her husband for the first time, stricken.

Anton clears his throat. 'We have plenty of time to talk about all that,' he says, the fake jocularity in his tone as unnatural as if he had suddenly donned a comedy moustache and clown trousers. 'We need to get you fighting fit again first, little man.'

'We *are* moving though?' says Gregory, looking only at his mother. 'I mean—' his words are coming out faster as he speaks, almost skidding into each other '—I wish we could help the next people who live there but at least it won't be our problem anymore, will it?'

'Darling,' says Gwen, reaching for her son and realizing he has no hand available, so her own hand lands in an awkward pat on his leg. 'Let's not worry about it today.'

'No!' Gregory shouts. 'I want to talk about it today! I don't want to go back there and you can't make me!'

Rose is thinking she may need to leave this family drama to play out on its own, a sad, sick feeling curdling in her stomach, and then she sees that Gregory is glaring right at her.

'You said you understood,' he says, starting to cry. He turns his head away from all the adult faces staring down at him and sobs.

35

They fly in the afternoon. As the plane takes off from Inverness, bright sunshine momentarily floods one side of the aircraft. Rose settles into her seat, thinking guiltily about that long drive back the others are making. But really, she's mostly relieved. So very kind of Adam to ask on her behalf.

She's distracted from this pleasant thought by an image of Gregory's little unhappy face in that hospital bed, turned away, with tears flooding his cheeks.

He'd looked at her as though she'd betrayed him. That was no doubt how he felt.

Rose has a very strong feeling that the Fullers are not planning to move away from Wyndham Terrace at all, despite what Gwen had blurted out during the press conference. She wonders if Gregory has been told yet about the supposed Victorian girl, or whatever the hell she was meant to be. He was going to see through that about as swiftly as Rose had.

The worst part is that Rose knows how it feels, to be a kid with no power, trapped in a household that makes you miserable.

Trapped with ghosts.

Much as she wants to go home and properly change her clothes, she decides she'll speak with the team first. There has to be *something* further they can do with this case.

At least the Fullers haven't ended up being on this flight. Gregory had got so upset the nurse had seen a small spike in his temperature, which meant he wouldn't be released until probably the following day.

Rose is sitting next to Brian Mortimer on the plane and worries she will be required to make small talk for the duration of the flight.

The seatbelt light pings off and flight attendants appear with a trolley at the front of the plane. A few minutes later she's contemplating whether to find her earbuds and try to nap when Mortimer puts down his iPad and turns to her, expectantly.

'So,' he says quietly, 'now I've got you on your own and the case is over, I was meaning to ask something. Is it true what I heard about UCIT?'

'I don't know,' she says, with a slightly nervous smile. 'It depends on what you heard.'

They're interrupted by the flight attendant offering drinks. Mortimer surprises Rose by asking for a gin and tonic. She looks at him.

'Figure we've earned it after the seventy-two hours we've had, don't you?' he says. Rose smiles and orders the same.

She waits until the drinks are poured and the flight attendant has moved to the next row before speaking again.

'So what've you heard then?' she says. 'Although if it's freaky or disturbing there's a good chance it's going to turn out to be true.'

Mortimer laughs. He seems quite different now that Gregory has been found and she can imagine he might be fun when not embroiled in a high-stakes case like this one.

'I know all about what you do over there,' he says. 'I used to be good friends with Sheila Moony's ex and we stayed in touch for a while after he died.'

'Oh?' says Rose, thinking of that photo in Moony's house. 'I don't really know anything about the circumstances around that. Do you mind if I ask you what happened to him?'

His brows knot and he takes a sip of his drink. 'It was a

really bad business,' he says. 'They were such a happy pair. It was him who introduced her to the motorbikes and they used to go off all over the place on those things.' He sighs. 'Yeah, a really bad business all round.'

He seems to have become momentarily lost in his thoughts but Rose quashes the feeling of impatience inside and waits. Mortimer takes another sip of his drink and then turns to look at her.

'Have you heard of a man called Michael Cassavetes?'

'Don't think so,' says Rose.

'Bit before your time. What are you, twenty-five?'

'Thirty actually.' One day, she is forever being told, this will be a compliment.

'Ah,' says Mortimer. 'Well, in the Nineties there was a massive criminal network operating that was carrying out one of the biggest money-laundering enterprises the city – well, the country – had ever seen. A crook called Michael Cassavetes was the kingpin of the whole thing, a Greek national who came over here in his twenties. He started small and then gradually built this network of businesses to funnel funds from prostitution and drug money.'

'Go on,' says Rose, enjoying the drink slipping down her throat, even though it is lukewarm.

'So, he had a number of lieutenants,' says Mortimer, 'including a man called Bigham. God, *Terrence John Bigham*.' He lets out a grim laugh. 'He was a proper charmer, him. He tended to do the dirty work, dealing with the businesses directly.'

Bigham. Money laundering.

Something seems to twang inside her brain like a note played off key.

'What kind of businesses?' says Rose. She takes a big sip of her drink. Her heartbeat bumps up.

'All sorts,' says Mortimer, 'everything from massage parlours to scrapyards, to things people were running from their own front rooms. Having multiple very small businesses worked well for him. There was all sorts. There was even talk about one of them being some sort of crystal-ball gazer or something in that vein.' He laughs. 'Anything where it might be easy to pay cash and stay under the radar.'

Rose is silent; temporarily robbed of speech. Luckily, Mortimer is lost in his story and hasn't noticed.

'Anyway,' he says, 'the big part of the Cassavetes story is that he ended up turning evidence and becoming the biggest super-grass the Met has ever known. He turned thirty-four people in, including, get this, his own wife and his brother-in-law.'

'Wow,' Rose manages.

'He claimed that there was someone really high up in the Met who was in on it all but they were never identified. He blamed a bunch of coppers actually, including Charlie Moony, who'd been working undercover to try and get Bigham for some time. Nothing was ever found to back this up and no one who knew Moony would ever have believed it. But Charlie took it very badly. Went into a depression and started drinking . . . then . . .' he pauses '. . . came off his bike one night in Kent and hit a tree. Killed instantly.'

'God,' says Rose, 'that's awful.' But her tired mind is racing so much she can't think how else to respond to this. Terrence Bigham? Could it be the 'Mr Big' who Adele used to see all the time? And could the 'crystal-ball gazer' have been *Adele*? Her hands are sweating and she feels a sudden wave of nausea as her past rushes at her like a speeding truck.

Moony had already told her that she was the policewoman Rose remembers seeing as a child one night after some sort of altercation at home. The policewoman, in fact, who Rose had kept in her mind all those years as the symbol of a potential new life. But how much does Moony know about Rose's upbringing? And how much did it impact having taken her on?

It's all too confusing and she rubs her tired eyes, wanting very much to stop having to make conversation now. But there's something she still hasn't heard.

'Hey,' she says. 'You still haven't told me what you meant before? About rumours?'

Mortimer looks awkward now and his eyes skitter away from her gaze.

'Ah it's probably not my place,' he says. 'But I'd presume in such a small team that you'd already know.'

'Know what?'

'About them pulling the plug. Closing down UCIT.'

36

Coming into the house where she has lived her whole life that evening, Rose stands in the hallway and feels memories sweeping over her in a wave. All those so-called clients, trooping through and going into the incense-stinking living room, with its curtains drawn and its atmosphere of confession and connection.

It was all fake.

All of them cogs in a great big machine that involved huge amounts of money being 'cleaned' to line greedy, violent people's pockets.

Rose remembers one of those 'cogs' now: an elderly woman, white head bent and eyes downcast, who wanted to connect with her dead husband. Adele told her he was lonely 'on the other side' but wanted her to keep talking to him. She must have come for close to two years, blissfully unaware that not only was she being systematically lied to, but that she was a player in a crime network that involved hundreds of people.

At least hundreds, anyway, according to the intensive googling Rose did for the entire rest of her journey back after her conversation with Mortimer.

She thinks of Bigham and the nights he used to visit. That one night – not when Moony came as a young officer – but the other one that has been in the back of her mind all these years. Shouting and banging. Then the terrible hush.

As for the other thing Mortimer said – about UCIT closing – Rose's feelings around this are taking some unpicking. She would have been grateful for this a couple of weeks ago, perhaps. But now . . . she feels part of something. Is it about to end almost as soon as it began?

By the time morning comes, after a restless night filled with snatches of dreams, she is feeling one main emotion: anger. How dare Moony entice Rose away from a job where she was relatively happy to a department that was in such an uncertain position? Especially as it sounds like she had some complex reasons for taking her on. Reasons that had nothing to do with catching a serial killer. Does she still hope to find something out about the man who played a part in her husband's death? From Rose, who was only a little girl at the time?

Rose doesn't know if she could even go back to Silverton Street. Would her old boss, DCI Rowland, welcome her back when she never liked her? Rose resolves to call Mack as soon as possible and be honest with him.

Also on her mind is that little boy in a hospital bed.

A kid who was so frightened of his own home that he was prepared to run away in the company of a convicted killer.

She goes in late to the office. Adam is absent, apparently dealing with something at home. This is good news because Rose wants to speak privately to Moony. But Scarlett is there too and she greets her warmly, going in to give her a hug before stopping herself when she sees Rose flinch.

'Oops, sorry,' she says. 'Are you still feeling a bit sore?'

'Just a bit,' Rose says, 'but I'll be okay.'

The three of them sit down in the briefing area with cups of good coffee and Rose tells them everything that happened after she arrived in Inverness.

'God,' says Scarlett once she's told the whole story from beginning to end, 'do you think Doyle is going to survive?'

'No idea,' says Rose. 'I haven't had any further news this morning.' She takes a welcome sip of coffee. 'Did you manage to find out anything further about the previous occupants?'

'Not a thing,' says Scarlett. 'I'm really sorry. No teenage boys anywhere that I can find.'

'I'm going to speak to that artist myself, I think,' says Rose, frowning. 'Just in case there's anything at all rattling around in there that she didn't think was important.'

'Wait,' says Moony, 'there's no need to do that. We're done with this case.'

'What?' says Rose incredulously. 'But what about Gregory?'

'What about him?' says Moony.

'What about him?! What do you mean, "what about him"? The poor kid is going back into that bloody awful house and nothing has changed!'

'Didn't his parents say they would move?' says Moony, her expression hard.

'Well, they did, but I don't believe them and neither does he!' Rose is struggling to keep her voice down. *Don't shout. Be calm.*

Moony gets to her feet and brushes shortbread crumbs from her tight black skirt.

'I told you before, Rose, we're not here to do exorcisms, we're here to solve crimes. We were helping Kentish Town police investigate possible malicious damage but that has stopped now and the family aren't complaining anymore. The way this whole thing exploded, I think it's much better for everyone concerned if we leave them be and move on.'

Like it's that easy. Step away, as if none of it ever happened.

'Oh, and move on to what?' she says, breath coming hard and fast. 'New careers maybe?'

Moony stops dead and then turns her head very slowly to look at Rose.

'I'm sorry?' she says, her voice much less certain than it was before. And is Rose imagining she has gone a little pink around the cheeks?

'When were you going to tell us, Sheila?' says Rose.

'Tell us what?' says Scarlett, bobbing up from where she had begun to pick up her cup and plate from the table.

Moony lets out a deep sigh and sits back down, about as willingly as if someone was pulling her from the other direction.

'I didn't want to say anything until I knew properly what was going on,' she says quietly.

'What's everyone talking about here?' says Scarlett. 'Because you're starting to scare me a bit.'

Moony takes a deep breath and rubs her face. 'Look, nothing is definite and Mortimer shouldn't have opened his mouth. I don't know how he even heard about this, but . . . well, there's a serious question mark over our future funding.'

'*What?*' says Scarlett, looking from Moony to Rose and then back to Moony again.

'It's why I've been absent a lot,' Moony continues. 'I didn't want to worry anyone when it might be that everything will work out.'

'We're not children,' says Rose tightly. 'We deserve to know if our jobs are in danger. Transfers take time to organize.'

'I know, I know,' says Moony. 'But I'm working so hard to try and find more funding. I don't think I could bear for all this to—' She coughs and blinks hard several times before continuing. 'What I'm saying is that I'll let you know for certain very soon, I promise.'

'What's the issue with the funding?' says Scarlett. 'I thought the bequest covered the shortfall in government money?'

'It does,' says Moony, 'or it did. But it has its limits. It's not a bottomless well of cash and some investments tied in with the estate haven't done as well as was hoped this year.'

Everyone is silent for a moment, then Rose gets up.

'I'm going home. Call me if you need me.'

She walks out of the office without looking back.

*

She's in her car when her phone buzzes with a text. It's from Scarlett.

Celeste Allingham's details, should you want them ... followed by an address.

37

Rose is too sore to drive so she gets a train to Winchester, dozing almost the whole way there, despite the double shot of caffeine she had in the office.

When she steps out of the white-fronted station building at around 3 p.m., it's cold but the sun is shining. She carefully takes a breath of the air, noticeably fresher out of London. Maybe a gentle walk will do her some good, she thinks, heading off in the direction of Celeste Allingham's house, which is about fifteen minutes from the station according to Google Maps.

The sky is a bright duck-egg blue and as Rose walks up leafy green streets, she fantasizes vaguely about moving out of London. Doing something completely different, maybe. But while she can imagine herself living in one of the pale stone buildings she passes, she can't picture exactly *what* she might be doing. Being a policewoman was all she ever wanted. It was supposed to be the home she never had. And it was, for a while. Now, she's not sure what it is.

As she walks, the houses seem to edge further back from the road and become grander, with high hedges guarding the privacy of those inside. There is a Tesco garage on the way, where she stops for some mints; her mouth feeling stale and dry.

Celeste Allingham's home stands at the top of a driveway behind elegant wrought-iron gates. A pale grey sign with cursive white writing says: *Caster Lodge: Artistic Retreats*, alongside website details and a phone number.

Rose has chosen not to ring in advance. She wants to be face to face with this woman. To see if she really will maintain that she can't remember a whole decade.

The gates are open and a lorry is delivering something around the side of the house so she walks up to the large, black front door and presses a buzzer marked *Reception.*

There's a pause and then a slightly breathless female voice says, 'Yes, can I help?'

'Hi,' says Rose, 'I'm here to see Ms Allingham.'

To her surprise, she isn't asked for any other information. The door opens from the inside with a loud click.

A short, stout woman with a pink face and messy streaked blonde hair smiles at her from the doorway as she walks up the drive.

'I'm just off myself, but she's expecting you! Go down to the drawing room where she's getting on with some things.'

Rose probably has long enough to set her right. But she doesn't. The woman hurries past her and onto the driveway, waving a hand as she departs.

Rose steps into a wide, high-ceilinged hallway that is painted the same light blue as the sky outside, with elegant white cornices like meringue around the tops of the walls. The floor is dark grey slate and a smell of orange and bergamot is coming from a large candle on a delicate iron table to her right.

As she walks down the corridor, hoping the drawing room will be obvious to find, the area opens up for a grand staircase. Above her head, a gigantic pair of angel wings in what looks like soft white material, are suspended. It takes a moment to work out that the material is actually thousands of the Styrofoam bubbles used in packaging. She's too busy staring up at the imposing artwork to notice someone poking their head out from a room at the other end of the corridor.

'Magnificent, isn't it?'

A woman with iron-grey bobbed hair and merry brown eyes

behind oversized dark-framed glasses is smiling at her, hands clasped in front of her body. She's tall, dressed in a long white silk blouse and slim-fitting black trousers. Silver ballet pumps are on her feet and a multitude of silver chains hang from her neck. She reminds Rose of a dancer as she moves towards her, hand outstretched, her body supple despite the fact that she must be well into her seventies.

'I must say I wasn't expecting you until much later, but I'm so glad you're here. Now, that wonderful piece you're looking at is the first part of the project we're going to discuss. Shall I get us some tea?'

'I'm so sorry,' says Rose at last, with a smile. 'I think there may have been some misunderstanding with your receptionist.'

'Oh, that's Jan, my assistant,' says the woman, her own smile faltering. 'What sort of misunderstanding?'

'You were obviously expecting someone,' says Rose, 'but it wasn't me. I mean,' she pauses and starts again, 'I didn't have an appointment or anything. I hope this isn't a bad time. First of all, am I talking to Ms Allingham?'

'Um . . . yes. But please call me Celeste!'

'Thank you,' says Rose. 'Celeste, my name is DC Rose Gifford. I'm with the Met in London and you spoke to my colleague, Scarlett Clarke, the other day? I'm sorry to barge in but I wanted five minutes of your time if you can spare it. It's in relation to some inquiries we're making right now.'

There's a beat, only for a moment, when Celeste seems to go very still but she recovers swiftly. 'Gosh,' she says. 'I remember Scarlett. What a nice young woman. Do come through. We're in chaos because we're getting all the studios redecorated. We normally have a full house but we're closing up for a couple of months. Lucky you caught me because I'm off to Provence next week. Anyway, come through.'

They walk into a large sitting room with antique yellow furniture. A mishmash of different artwork on the walls seems to cover every inch of the space in a jumble of colour and styles. Classical paintings are next to childlike splashes of colour, next to cartoon-style drawings.

'I know it's a bit much, but I do love it in here,' says Celeste, with a grin, gesturing for Rose to sit on one of the chairs. 'My late husband, God bless him, used to beg me to leave a bit of space on the walls. Said it gave him a headache, the cheeky bugger!' She lets out a laugh. 'But so many of our visitors have donated their work over the years, it feels like a celebration of all we do here.'

'It's wonderful,' says Rose, meaning it. 'You'd never get bored in here because there's so much to look at.'

Celeste claps her hands together in delight. 'Exactly!' she says. 'Now, do tell me how I can help you, darling.' Her eyes twinkle warmly. 'I think I told your colleague everything I could though.'

'I know,' says Rose, tilting her head apologetically. 'But we're still really interested in the period of time you lived in that property in Wyndham Terrace, you see. I wondered if you'd kept in touch with anyone from that time? Is there anyone else at all I could talk to?'

Celeste looks down at her wrinkled hands as though thinking very hard. 'The thing is,' she says, 'it was a bit of a lost era. I'm a little ashamed when I think about it now.'

That certainly hadn't been Scarlett's impression, thinks Rose.

'Well, as I said on the phone, we were all off our bloody heads half the time,' Celeste continues. 'I mean when I think about the drugs and booze!' She lets out a loud hoot. 'I'm surprised I'm still standing, frankly. And then—' she chews her lip, serious now '—I met my husband, Jonathon, and well, he was a QC, you see? I wasn't really in a hurry to keep up with all that crowd after that. He didn't really approve of my past.' She makes a comedy face of doom and Rose smiles.

'Can you remember the names of any other commune members though?'

'Oh golly,' says Celeste. 'Let me think. Well, there was a Harmony . . . and a Peter. Definitely a Peter. And a couple with a baby were there for ages but I'm buggered if I can remember anything else. I'm not even sure half the people there went by the names they were born with. I mean, at one point I think we even had a Moonbeam, would you believe?'

She looks lost in memory then peers at Rose with a wide grin.

'I'm so sorry,' she says. 'You must think I'm quite useless.' She pauses. 'Look, I know you have to be terribly secretive about these things, but am I allowed to ask what this is all about?'

Rose hesitates. 'We think there's a possible crime that took place then,' says Rose. 'That went unreported at the time.'

Celeste's eyes widen. 'Oh no!' she says. 'That's awful. You all keep mentioning a boy. It's not going to turn out to be some ghastly Yewtree thing, is it? Another story about 1970s sex with kiddies? Because I promise you nothing like that happened to my knowledge.' She looks appalled.

'No, nothing like that,' says Rose.

'I'm so sorry that you've come all this way for nothing,' says Celeste. 'I really can't help and I wish I could!' There's a vibrating sound from somewhere about her person. 'Oh.' She pauses and reaches for a phone that is next to her on the sofa. 'Excuse me a sec.'

She reads the message with a frown, then looks up again at Rose.

Rose forces a smile. 'I quite understand,' she says. 'I'll get out of your hair but first, on a personal note, can you tell me a little bit about what you do here? I've always wanted to learn to paint.' This is a lie but Celeste's face lights up with pure joy.

'Oh, you should do it!' she says. 'It's the most wonderful activity and in your job you could probably do with something to relieve stress.'

'I'm not going to argue with that!' says Rose. She's not quite ready to go yet. 'Can I be cheeky and ask for a look around? This is such a beautiful place and it must inspire your artists hugely. I think I might just book myself in when I get some leave. After you have your work done, I mean.'

Celeste pauses for second and then beams, rising to her feet.

'Of course!' she says. 'Seems the person I was expecting has had to cancel our meeting anyway, so I have time for a very quick tour.'

Celeste takes Rose around the rooms of the house, each of which is filled with paintings and sculpture. The walls in each room are painted in such rich colours, the effect is very calming. Rose can feel the beauty of the surroundings soothing her frazzled mind a little.

'What about outside,' says Rose, once finished. 'Can I have a peek there too?'

'Well,' says Celeste. 'As I say, we're about to get some work done but I guess we can have a quick look.'

They go outside to an area with a turquoise rectangle of pond covered in lily pads like something from a child's fairy tale. Comfortable chairs and tables are under an awning. A riot of flowers in different colours fill the air with scent and Rose finds herself thinking she actually *wouldn't* mind coming somewhere like this to unwind a bit. Maybe she should take herself off on a holiday. Once she finds somewhere to live and a new job, that is.

Celeste begins leading Rose in one direction but she can see a long building the other way.

'What's over there?' she says.

'And that's where the studios are,' says Celeste, a little hurriedly. 'But I can't really show them at the moment because they're in a state of disrepair. Let's go look at the orangery now.' Her voice is too bright, too eager.

'Can we not just peek in?' says Rose. Some instinct is driving her in that direction. 'I've never seen an artist's studio before.'

'I really don't think—'

But Celeste's words die as the door to the studio opens and an elderly woman appears. She has long grey hair and square glasses and looks confused. She's dressed a bit eccentrically in some sort of pink fleecy dress to her ankles that must surely be a nightgown.

She beckons Rose over with an impatient sort of wave and Rose begins to move towards her.

'Oh don't bother with her!' says Celeste. 'She'll chew your ear off for ages if you let her!'

She takes hold of Rose's elbow then removes her hand, flushing, when Rose looks pointedly at it.

'It's okay,' says Rose. 'I have time.'

Celeste has a helpless expression that makes Rose even more inclined to speak to the old lady.

'Can I show you my picture?' she says when Rose reaches her side. Her face seems innocent and childlike. She behaves as if they had already met.

'Not now, Rowan,' says Celeste, then to Rose's surprise, she turns a finger to her head in the universal but no longer acceptable gesture of madness. 'She is my longest-term visitor and she's not all there,' she says very quietly. 'Let me see my visitor out, Rowan, and then I'll help you, okay?'

But Rose finds her hand being taken by the woman, whose own hand feels incredibly soft and dry, like some sort of crepey material. She leads her into the big barn, where, sure enough, most of the room has been cleared out and there are boxes of tools and piles of wood ready for work to begin.

One easel remains in the centre of the room. A large canvas sits on it. The perfectly represented face of a young man looks out, painted in oil. He has dark hair that flops over one eye and intense green eyes that seem to hold her gaze.

'Oh,' says Celeste, 'that's wonderful, Rowan, but we really must—'

'Who are you?' says the woman called Rowan. 'You're quite lovely. I was once pretty too but it brought me nothing but trouble.'

'Um, I'm sorry to hear that,' says Rose uncertainly, 'but thank you! I like your painting. And to answer your question, I'm a police officer. I'm called Rose.'

Rowan lifts both hands up to cup Rose's face. Her shoulders drop at the same time as though the touch of Rose's skin is a great relief to her.

'I knew you'd come,' she says softly. Her eyes are awash with bright tears but she looks happy. 'I always said you would. It's about Vincent, isn't it? About what we did to my Vincent. I'm so glad you came. It's been so long, you see? I knew you would come one day.'

'Who's Vincent?' says Rose, leaning down so her face is on the same level as the other woman. 'Is he the person in this painting? And what did you do?'

There is a flash of movement and Rose looks up quickly. She's just in time to see the hammer about to smash into the side of her skull.

38

With a cry of shock, Rose throws herself out of the way, landing hard on the ground. Her damaged ribs flare in agony. She scuttles back like a reverse crab as Celeste comes at her again, face twisted with terror even though she's the one with the hammer. But Rowan launches herself at the other woman, trying to scratch her face. She's making an unearthly sound. It's a raw wail of pain that seems to come from something bigger than her elderly body could contain.

'No, Celeste!' she cries. 'You're not doing this to me again! I won't let you make me part of it! Not again! No! No! No!'

The fight instantly leaves Celeste's body at that and she drops the hammer. She starts to cry too, her mouth stretched wide and her arms wrapped around herself as though trying to hold something from leaking out.

Rose fumbles for her phone and calls 999.

'This is DC Rose Gifford of the Met Police. I need immediate assistance at . . .' For a moment she can't remember the name of the property, but to her great surprise, Celeste says, 'Caster Lodge, Bereweeke Road,' through her tears.

After this, Celeste says nothing at all until she's in the interview room at Kentish Town station. There was some debate, after the back-up had come screaming into the driveway, whether she should be questioned here in Winchester, or back in London.

But after a conversation with the SIO in London, a brisk and efficient woman called Sue Trainer, it was decided that she would be returned to the jurisdiction where the crime took place. Kentish Town have more resources than UCIT, so it is there she is taken. The murder squad are a different team to the one she met before and Rose is introduced to Trainer and DC Jimmy Omotayo, who allow her to watch the interview from their observation room. A kindly female PC gives her a cup of sweet tea and a packet of biscuits, commenting on how 'peaky' she looks.

Rose gratefully accepts both.

Celeste is stone-faced in the interview room. She's accompanied by the duty solicitor, her back ramrod straight and her hands neatly folded on the table in front of her.

Sue begins the questioning and Celeste holds up a hand to silence her.

'No,' she says, 'you don't need to ask questions. I'm going to give it all up. I won't repeat this. I want to make a statement.'

'Celeste . . .' the solicitor says hurriedly, 'maybe we need a little more time to put this on paper together?'

'No,' says Celeste. 'Let me speak. I want to get the words out and I don't want you to interrupt me or I'll never manage it. *Please.*'

'Go ahead whenever you're ready,' says Sue and sits back.

Celeste puts her head back and looks at the ceiling.

'It's going to be awfully hard to make you understand what it was like, you see,' she says. 'It was a different world. We were . . . well, we were so lucky. The *freedom* . . . of living in a different way from our parents before us. It was intoxicating. There was so much joy in that house.' She pauses for a moment and her expression is fierce, her eyes bright. '*I* created that community.' She thumps her chest as she says this. '*Me.* I created that explosion of creativity. The art, the music. And the sex.' She pauses, her expression wistful now. 'You see Rowan as a dried-up old husk like me, I expect,' she says, 'but when she came, well, she was so beautiful. The kind of ethereal beauty you don't see often. You want to paint it. Own it. I don't know, *make it your own*. We all wanted her. But she had this son, you see. Vincent. Ugh.' She gives a little shudder. 'I knew there was something off about him – a bad energy – the moment I met him. He had a certain cruelty. I know for a fact that he terrorized a couple who were living there in order to get the attic room. But at the time, it sort of amused me. What harm could he do? And Rowan wouldn't hear anything against him, not for a moment. Anyway, then my brother came to join us. Hugo.' Her composure cracks for the first time, her voice quavering. She takes a sip from a glass of water and resumes.

'And Hugo was entranced with Rowan too. We both were. And with each other. That was something you can't understand unless you have experienced that kind of bond with a person. We were one being. We shared everything.'

She pauses.

'Including Rowan?' says Sue.

Celeste's lip curls. 'Yes of course. As I say, we shared everything.'

Sue and Jimmy momentarily exchange loaded glances.

'Where is Hugo now?' says Sue.

'Gone. He died of AIDS in 1989,' says Celeste. She seems to have run out of steam and stares down at the table.

'Can I ask you about the events you referred to with my colleague now?' says Jimmy. 'You say you wanted to confess to murder.'

Celeste looks up at the camera in the corner of the room, as if she is looking for Rose, knowing she's there. She gives a small, cold smile. Rose has met a lot of bad people in her job, and the darkness that can lurk beneath a sophisticated exterior doesn't surprise her anymore. But it still feels uncomfortable to look it directly in the eye.

'Rowan insisted that we keep our relationship from Vincent,' says Celeste, 'and we did, on the whole. But on this one night, the party had broken up a little earlier than we expected and for once, there were only the four of us in the house. We'd dropped acid earlier together and although Rowan had been unwilling at first, we persuaded her that Vincent would sleep right through it. He wasn't even on the same floor.' She pauses and takes another sip of water. 'We didn't expect him to react the way he did.'

39

Vincent

For some reason that doesn't especially interest him, the house is quiet early tonight. They're possibly at a party somewhere else. Vincent is calm; focused about what he is going to do. Sure, Rowan will be upset but he will get in touch once she has had a chance to think on. Maybe she will agree to move on too.

The decision to up sticks and simply leave has been simmering for a while. But now he can't believe he hasn't done it sooner. He'll head to Leicester Square and look for a waitering job in one of the restaurants round there. If he has to sleep rough for a bit, so be it. It's summer and it will be better than being here.

He packs his sleeping bag, then a few items of clothing, toiletries, and some snacks into a rucksack and heads down the staircase onto the main landing. A sound makes him stop in his tracks.

It's his mother. She sounds slurry and upset and keeps saying, 'I think I'm a bit sick. Maybe I should go to sleep.'

Then, voices gently shushing her.

He creeps along the landing. It's either Celeste's room, or Hugo's. Maybe both, it's unclear. No surprise that's where she is. The usual hot rage pulses through him at the thought of Hugo and his mother. He should ignore whatever is going on in there and leave. She's made her choices. He turns to leave, then hears that she is weeping now, her words indistinguishable.

Swearing, he drops his rucksack on the dirty landing carpet and walks towards Hugo's door, hesitating for only a moment before shoving the door open with both hands.

The scene that greets him is so odd and confusing, he can't work out what is happening at first. So many white limbs, entangled, like a creature from the deep sea with pale tentacles.

When he begins to untangle it, he feels a wave of revulsion that almost makes him sick.

Celeste has her face buried between his mother's legs, the dirty soles of Rowan's feet facing him like those of a doll. It's horrific seeing Celeste properly naked. She's always wandering around with a bra and seeing her big white arse in the air makes him want to heave.

And Hugo . . .

He is squatting over his mother's face, his broad back and shoulders making it look as though he is squashing her like a bug. She has him in her mouth and is making little sounds, as is he, looking down at her, his big shaggy head bent and his hands clasping her face.

'What the fuck are you doing?' says Vincent in what sounds like a surprisingly neutral tone, considering the feelings pulsing through him. 'Stop it. You're total perverts. Leave her alone!'

Hugo turns his whole body free and meets Vincent's eyes with a gratifying amount of shock.

Celeste scurries off the bed with a little shriek and now she is laughing. Actually laughing. She sounds demented.

His mother looks at him with unfocused eyes and then starts to cry, before rolling off the bed and grabbing a dress that she holds in front of her body.

'I'm sorry, baby!' she wails. 'I didn't want you to see this!'

'Hey, man,' says Hugo, hands held up in front of him. 'You're too young to understand our scene. Just be cool and we'll talk about it in the morning, okay?'

But Vincent doesn't feel *cool*. He doesn't think he ever will again after the sight that has been burned onto his retinas. He wants to vomit.

If he had a gun, he'd kill Hugo now. One bullet in the centre of his forehead.

Instead he launches himself at the other man with a scream of pure hatred, managing to land a blow right in his eye. Reactions slowed by the drugs, Hugo yells in shock but is slow to push him off. Vincent begins to punch him over and over again in the face, his fist on fire with pain but it feels good.

And then a new agony explodes at the side of his head and the world turns to the brightest white.

40

'I had to do it,' says Celeste in a numb, monotonous voice, her eyes cloudy with the memory as it plays out in front of her. 'He wasn't as big as my brother but he had the advantage of surprise, of youth . . . of pure rage.'

'So what did you do exactly?' says Sue, leaning forwards.

Celeste heaves a sigh. 'There was this big iron doorstopper, you see,' says Celeste. 'Big heavy old thing shaped like a horse. Anyway, I whacked him on the side of the head with it, didn't I? I only wanted to make him *stop*. But it was obvious immediately that he was dead. Even in the state we were in, everyone could see that.'

She lifts her chin and looks at both police officers in turn, defiantly. 'There really was no point calling an ambulance. None at all.'

'But it was your duty to report this,' says Jimmy. 'Why didn't you alert the authorities to deal with this properly?'

'We didn't believe in *authorities*,' says Celeste scornfully. 'Don't you understand? So we dealt with it ourselves.'

'How exactly?' says Sue.

There is a long silence before Celeste begins to speak again.

'We had to get Rowan onside first,' she says, staring down at the table. 'She was hysterical. I thought she might actually choke on her tears at one point. But we explained to her that if we went to the police, she would appear in the press as the very worst mother in Britain. You know, for allowing her son to see her in a threesome. She understood that it was self-defence – we helped her see that. But we would have had to explain the circumstances. And let's face it, she was the mother in this scenario. Some would say she was the one who should have known better.'

There's a brief pause. Celeste takes a sip of water, hand trembling a little now.

'What did you do with his body?' says Jimmy.

She sighs. 'You won't ever understand this but we gave him a beautiful burial in the garden. Just the three of us. Hugo sang and played the guitar and I placed flowers I'd taken from a neighbour's garden and the heath all around the spot. It was actually a very lovely thing.'

'Will you be able to show us where exactly in the garden?' says Sue, clearly fighting to hide her distaste.

Celeste raises her face, her eyes cold.

'We didn't leave him there!' As if this was the most bizarre suggestion in this whole scenario. 'Rowan thinks that's where he is and that was for the best. But a neighbour's dog got into the garden one night and we saw that it . . .' she pauses '. . . well, we had to act quickly. We had to move it.'

The use of 'it' rather than 'him' stays with Rose.

Maybe it's a coping mechanism from someone who seems to display a staggering lack of remorse. Celeste claimed she'd always known they would come for her one day and had made her brother a promise on his deathbed that she would confess straight away should that happen, rather than attempting to 'drag it all out further'.

Rowan Tully is charged as an accessory to murder, but there is to be a meeting to ascertain whether she was going to be in any way fit to stand trial. It seems unlikely. Celeste has kept her close all these years, never quite trusting her to keep their secret, and the toll of the drugs and alcohol that dominated Rowan's life had meant she always needed that support.

This being a fifty-year-old crime scene, it's decided that the search can wait until the next morning.

Rose's mind is filled all night with the sounds of a spade digging into earth, the image of a body wrapped in a white blanket being pushed into the hole. Of flowers and singing and utter, utter wrongness.

41

They reconvene mid-morning at Kentish Town station. Sue Trainer, Jimmy Omotayo, Rose, Adam and members of the forensic team that will conduct the search at Wyndham Terrace. This includes the pathologist, a woman called Saoirse Benjamin, who Rose has heard of but never met before.

Scarlett had been hard at work already back at UCIT. This morning she's managed to track down the birth certificate and last known school records of one Vincent Tully, from Totnes, Devon. The secondary school he'd attended had been no help, even though it was still a working school. But she'd managed to find out where the largest intake of children had come from and then contacted that primary school. It was now a café called The Old Schoolroom but the owner had helpfully kept a bunch of historical photographs she'd found on the premises because she 'couldn't bear to throw all those little faces away'.

And so now, one of those little faces – that of a murdered boy – looks out from the image on the whiteboard.

Vincent is around ten here, in 1967, much younger than in Rowan's picture. He has dark wavy hair and pale, deep-set eyes that look rather mischievous. The side of his mouth is hitched as though he were about to say something to the round-faced child next to him, whose head is very slightly turned towards him. The patina of age from the blown-up black-and-white photo adds a certain distance, but all the same, Rose can't stop looking into those eyes.

Hello, Vincent.

'Thanks for coming, everyone,' says DS Trainer then, her voice sombre. 'Scarlett over at UCIT has done some sterling work for us in finding details including a picture of the child whose remains we expect to find at 42 Wyndham Terrace this morning. The Fuller family are vacating the property and it seems there has been a delay in them finding somewhere suitable, but I'm told they'll be gone by the time we're ready to head over there.' She pauses and looks at the picture, her expression grave.

'I said "child",' she continues, 'although we don't tend to think of fifteen-year-olds like Vincent Tully in quite that way, as the parent of a daughter that age myself, let's not forget that he was *not* an adult. He was very young when the woman in the cell along the corridor killed him, albeit in an act that wasn't premeditated, but was nonetheless disproportionate as an act of self-defence. Celeste Allingham, her deceased brother Hugo and Rowan Tully, Vincent's mother, then proceeded to hide what had happened, rather than giving him the dignity of a proper funeral and taking themselves off to the authorities to face the consequences.'

Everyone stares at the picture. The room is pin-drop silent for a few moments.

Rose feels a thickening in her throat. Despite all the damage and pain that has been caused in the years since that murder, she can't help thinking about the unfairness of it all. Who would want that angry teenage version of themselves to be trapped forever, unable to develop but unable to rest either? She certainly wouldn't have wanted that period of her life to have been preserved.

Vincent would have been a man in his early sixties now and no one can say what kind of person he would have turned into. Maybe not a nice one. But he never got the chance to find out and instead, simply became the worst essence of that angry boy.

'Now,' continues Trainer, 'I'm aware that there have been a lot of strange goings-on in that property, including a multiple murder in 2006. It's not for *me* to say whether or not there is a connection with what happened there in 1972.' Her gaze flicks to Rose and Adam, but not in a dismissive way, it feels to Rose. It simply doesn't need to be said right now. The here and now of Vincent's death is the issue, not what came after. 'But I think we can safely say that if we find what we expect to find in that bedroom, something very tragic and wrong will finally be brought out into the light where it belongs.' Another pause.

'Let's go, everyone.'

Rose gathers her things and prepares to go to 42 Wyndham Terrace for the last time.

42

Everyone is quiet on the short car journey to the house.

The sun comes out as Rose walks up Wyndham Terrace with Trainer and Adam. Her body feels heavier than usual and a muscle in her eye keeps twitching, a sure sign of exhaustion and stress. She looks up at the swatch of bright blue sky emerging from the clouds and it feels inappropriately cheerful when such a sombre task lies ahead. This, surely, is a task for leaden skies.

Even though it is her job to go there and see what's hidden in the attic, it feels more burdensome than it should for reasons she can't yet hold up to the light. But equally, nothing would stop her from being here. It's the least she can do now, for Vincent. To bear witness to the moment when he is free again.

There are a few gawpers hanging around the police cordon as Rose enters the house, which has been set up as a new crime scene. She feels greedy eyes roaming over her, working out who she is in the pecking order. These people who get a thrill from it . . . Do they like to brush up against horror, before going home and having a nice cup of tea and a biscuit?

The Fullers are staying in a hotel because there's no place for them here today. Rose wonders what's going through their minds. No doubt Anton has views on how it doesn't really matter if you have a bag of bones in your attic once it has all been given a good clean. Rose wishes she could have seen Gregory one more time. As terrible as this is, she feels it in her gut that the nightmare really will be over soon and wants to get that across to him in a way he will understand. It feels like something she could explain to him.

Inside the house two CSIs whose names Rose doesn't catch lead the way to the top of the building in an atmosphere that's muted and professional. There had been some discussion about whether a POLSA would be needed – a Police Search Adviser – who's sometimes called in to these kinds of cases. But Trainer has decided there is no need for the added expense when they know what they are going to find.

But *do* they, though, for sure? For the first time this morning, Rose experiences a thud of doubt. What if, after all this, there's nothing there? Could Celeste be lying? A fantasist? Entirely possible, although it's hard to imagine why anyone would make up something so monstrous.

Inside Gregory's bedroom, the CSIs go to the little green cupboard built into the eaves of the roof.

Catching her breath, Rose finally makes the connection.

That's exactly where she had been standing when she was thrown into the wall. Vincent wasn't trying to *hurt* her. He was simply trying to tell her something in the only, clumsy way possible.

The cupboard is opened up. It has evidently been used to hold old toys and board games and there's something poignant about watching the boxes – Monopoly, Kerplunk, Cluedo – being gently lifted out, along with a few teddy bears and a cushion shaped to look like a banana, now dull with dust and unuse.

One of the CSIs gets out a drill and removes the two doors of the cupboard. There is a panel of wood at the back and, just as Celeste told them, it hides a pile of bricks, stacked loosely to form a makeshift wall.

Painstakingly, the bricks are removed one by one and placed to the side.

Rose's chest tightens and her heart begins to beat faster until the dull thud seems to fill her ears. For a moment it is as though the whole room is one heart, pulsing and alive with blood.

The CSI peers inside and then turns back to the room.

'We've got something,' she says soberly.

The old-fashioned travel trunk is tricky to get out of the awkward space and it takes the CSIs some efforts to remove it. There is some discussion about the best way and then the consensus is that the only way is to put something underneath and lever it up until it can be lifted.

After all that, it looks surprisingly light when it's placed on the carpet in front of everyone. The dark wood is draped in dramatic cobwebs and covered in the remains of faded stickers. Rose can make out one that says, 'Sunny California' and another: 'Fly TWA'.

It's such a sad-looking place of rest that Rose feels a catch in her throat.

But that's the wrong term. It never really was a place of rest. Quite the opposite.

The CSI spends a few moments fiddling with the padlock, then breaks it off with a pair of pliers.

Rose holds her breath as the curved lid flips back and something that appears to be an item of clothing is held up.

'What is it?' says Adam.

'I think it's a football kit,' says the CSI. 'Wait, no . . . I can see . . . badges? Ah, it's a Scout shirt. There's a scarf too.' She holds up a faded dark green item, which still has the leather toggle attached.

Rose looks at Adam. He makes a silent 'oof' shape with his lips. So poignant that Vincent was buried with this childhood memento.

The CSI now removes what looks like a bunched-up old sheet and peers underneath.

She looks up and nods. 'Yes,' she says, 'human remains.'

But Rose already knew. She felt something she couldn't name passing her, with a cool breath against her cheek.

It's finally over, Vincent.

43

Hours later, Rose is sitting in a café, nursing a hot chocolate. She's by the window, where the remnants of fake snow from Christmas still stick like bobbly scars and a small fly buzzes and smashes against the glass at the top.

The recent bright spell has taken a distinct turn and cold rain lashes the window.

The café is quiet at this time in the afternoon, presumably having had all the mummies and kids in earlier. Now, a man in his early twenties is jabbing ferociously at a laptop, his expression almost angry. Rose can hear the tinny *tss-tss-tss* sound leaking from his headphones.

The door opens and she looks up, a wave of complicated feelings passing over her.

'All right, kiddo,' says Mack.

Maybe sensing Rose's vulnerable state of mind – he always was good at reading her – Mack spends a bit of time ordering at the counter before he comes over and stands at the table.

He's holding a tray with a cup of coffee and two muffins – one chocolate and one blueberry – which he places on the table.

'You can choose,' he says. 'Alternatively, I can start on one and then you can change your mind and demand a bit of that too, for tradition's sake.'

Rose surprises herself with the laugh but it causes her to wince again and rub her side.

'Ah,' says Mack, sitting down at the table. 'That answers my next question, which was going to be: "Are we having a hug or what?"'

Rose swallows. She hates it when tears threaten uncontrollably. She's a police officer, for God's sake. She's tough. She swallows again.

'Maybe not just now,' she says in a strangled voice.

'Been in the wars?' says Mack, lifting his cup of coffee and assessing her with his steady blue eyes.

'Had an argument with a wall,' she says, once she is in control of her voice again. It's so good to see her old colleague and friend. She takes a deep breath. 'Look, I'm sorry I haven't—'

But Mack is waving her concern away with his hand. 'Don't sweat it,' he says. 'I know what it's like in a new job. Knew you'd return my calls eventually.' He picks up the knife on the tray.

'I'm just happy to see you,' he continues, a shrewd eye taking in her exhausted pallor and bruised face. 'I hope you've been dealing with all that happened to you last year. You know, taking all the meagre resources on offer in that department.' He raises a knowing eyebrow and she smiles and averts her gaze to the window.

'Yeah, on it like a Scotch bonnet,' she says, thinking of Scarlett with a surprising pang of warmth. It's on her list, the counselling. Once she sorts everything else out. She knows she needs it.

'Now,' says Mack, 'why don't you tell me what has been going on down at Spooky Central, while I cut these muffins into two, so we can have a bit of both?'

So she does. She tells him all about the original, tenuous reason for attending Wyndham Terrace and about Heather Doyle, and Gregory. And Vincent Tully, the angry, vengeful presence trapped in that house for decades.

It is oddly easy to let all this spill out, including the super-natural stuff. Or maybe it's simply the relief of spending time with a dear friend who understands her as much as anyone ever has.

'One of the things we got from Celeste,' says Rose, taking a piece of blueberry muffin, 'who, by the way, was a truly horrible piece of work, was that Vincent hated living in that commune. He wasn't into the supposed "scene" of it. But can you imagine being a teenage boy and how confusing it must have been living somewhere everyone was getting off with each other? Including your own *mother*?'

Mack makes a face and pops the last piece of his muffin into his mouth.

'Imagine being stuck forever at fifteen,' he says. 'That's a kind of purgatory in itself, isn't it?'

'Yeah,' says Rose, 'no wonder he was so fucking angry.'

'But what exactly did he do to subsequent tenants?' says Mack. 'Apart from scaring the crap out of them, I mean?'

Rose looks down at the table, pressing a crumb on her plate with the tip of her finger, thinking.

'I think he had a grudge particularly against men,' says Rose. 'Celeste says he had it in for her brother the most. In her words, because: "Hugo was the sort of man who made other men jealous. He had that effect."' She shudders. 'So it sounds from what Gregory told us, that he would whisper things about what a bad person his dad was. And Heather too could well have had that going on. We can't know what happened in his past, but perhaps he had experiences that made him hate fathers, or a certain type of man?' She pauses. 'We'll never really know, sadly.'

'And this Heather,' says Mack. 'Have you heard anything further? Is she going to make it?'

'Seems so, yes,' says Rose. 'I had a call a bit after we'd been back to that property. It looks like they've been able to bring her out of the coma. She'll going straight back to prison, of course, as soon as she's well enough. But maybe she'll have some peace when she hears about this.' She pauses. 'I'm going to tell her myself, once she's been transferred to a London hospital, which is likely to be soon now she's awake.'

Mack looks thoughtful. He lets out a low whistle. 'Well, it's certainly not all gang stabbings and domestics for you anymore, is it?' he says. 'Are you glad you made the move?'

Rose feels her resolve wobble, then forces herself to meet Mack's gaze. 'That might be irrelevant,' she says. 'Seems the whole department is in jeopardy because of a funding crisis.'

Mack knits his bushy brows, his eyes concerned beneath them. 'What does that mean for you though?'

Rose shrugs and then smiles ruefully. She hesitates before speaking again, conscious that her voice sounds a little forced and high. 'I was wondering,' she says, 'whether Rowland would even consider having me back. I mean, we did make a good team, didn't we, even with the old witch not thinking much of me?'

Mack's expression tells her all she needs to know.

'Ah,' she says. 'I thought I'd be replaced. I just wasn't sure if it had happened yet.'

'I'm so sorry, kiddo,' says Mack and he really looks it. 'A new DC called Oliver – Ollie – nice lad, started three weeks ago.'

Rose can't bear the tragic look on his face any longer.

'It's okay!' she says with a fake laugh. 'I'll survive! It's not definite anyway. All a bit vague at the moment.'

'I think,' says Mack, 'from what I've heard about her since you left, that Sheila Moony is a really good copper. She cares about her team so talk to her. Don't do your Greta Garbo act.'

'Eh?' says Rose with a laugh.

'I vont to be alone,' he says, in a terrible accent. It might be German, but it's hard to tell.

Rose laughs. 'Whatever you're on about, I won't.' Keen to change the subject now she says, 'Tell me, how is Caitlin doing?'

Caitlin is Mack's teenage daughter who suffers from anxiety and was behind an accidental leak to the press in the Oakley case. He fills her in on the CBT sessions his daughter has been having and how much they have helped. They chat for a bit longer, then Mack has to get back to work.

As they both stand and move away from the table, he puts his arms around her very, very carefully and kisses the top of her head. She squeezes her eyes closed as a wave of emotion hits her. He's the closest thing to a dad she has ever had and she makes a promise to herself on the spot that she isn't going to leave it so long next time. She needs Mack to be in her life, however messed up and unconventional it might be. Now she has spoken fairly openly about her new job, maybe he can be a sounding board a little more often.

'Don't be a stranger,' he says as if reading her thoughts. 'Say after me: "No Greta Garbo."'

Rose laughs.

'Go on,' says Mack, 'say it.'

'No more Greta Garbo,' she says, swallowing the lump in her throat. 'Whoever she is.'

As she walks away, she thinks about Moony.

Talk to her. That's what Mack said. And that's exactly what she is going to do.

44

Moony's eyes widen when she finds Rose at her front door that evening.

She is wearing a stripy apron over her work clothes and has a streak of what looks like flour on her cheek.

'Rose!' she says. 'What are you doing here?'

'I want to talk to you,' says Rose.

'Adam filled me in on today,' says Moony. 'You can always sort your side of the report when you get back. You're on leave now, I believe? You certainly deserve it.'

'It can't wait,' says Rose.

Moony rakes her face with her eyes for a moment and then stands back to beckon her inside.

'I'm attempting to make some bread,' she says over her shoulder as they walk towards the kitchen. 'God bloody knows why. More of an arse-ache than it's worth if you ask me. Makes such a mess I don't know why anyone would bother.'

The kitchen surfaces seem to be covered in flour. In the background some kind of rock music is playing.

Moony claps her hands, sending a dusty shower of white scattering to the floor.

'Alexa!' she barks. 'Shut up.'

The music stops.

'Tea?' she says. 'Coffee? Gin?'

'Nothing for me, thanks,' says Rose, taking a seat at the table.

Moony comes over and sits down opposite her, a wary expression on her face.

'Have you come to tell me you want to transfer?' says Moony. 'Because it's far too early for that and I've actually got a potential donor lined up who looks promising.'

'I haven't come about that,' says Rose. 'I want you to tell me about my mother.'

Moony's eyes widen and she sits back in her seat.

'Well,' says Rose, crossing her legs. 'I called her that but she was my grandmother. Adele Gifford.'

'Yes,' says Moony after a moment, looking oddly wrong-footed. 'I knew that. But . . .' She hesitates, her expression betraying difficult emotions competing with each other. 'I did also know your actual mother.'

Rose's stomach swoops. 'You did?' she says. 'How come?' She hadn't meant to sound quite so squeaky.

Moony regards her carefully. 'Look,' she says, getting up. 'You might not want anything but I'm not sure I can handle this conversation without strong liquor. Join me?'

Rose nods, not trusting herself to speak. Moony spends a few minutes preparing gin and tonics. The effort she puts in – slicing lemons and crushing ice, running a lime around the rim of the glass – is either perfectionism or a desire to delay the conversation.

She places the glass in front of Rose, who takes a sip and has to admit it is delicious: crisp and citric with just the right amount of kick.

'Go right back,' says Rose, trying to arrange herself on the wooden chair so she is in the least pain. 'Tell me everything you know.'

Moony takes a long drink from her own glass, reducing the amount by a third in one go.

'That night you saw me at your house,' says Moony. 'You remember that?'

Of course she does. It was a seminal moment for Rose, the night a nice policewoman came to the house and let her wear her hat. It was only when she got taken on at UCIT that she discovered that policewoman – a PC at the time – had been Sheila Moony, her new boss.

'It wasn't the first time we were there,' says Moony. 'I was a very lowly member of a team that was looking into a man called Terrence Bigham. Have you heard that name?'

Rose feels a sort of thump in her chest. So she was right. 'Brian Mortimer told me,' she says. 'He also said . . .' she hesitates before speaking again '. . . about your husband too.'

Moony winces and takes another sip of her drink, smaller this time.

'I'm sorry,' says Rose. 'That must have been hard.'

'Yep,' says Moony, staring down at her glass. 'It was. But going right back . . . the first time I went to your house, you must have been very small. A disturbance was reported and we turned up to find a huge argument going on between Kelly Gifford and Adele Gifford.'

Rose swallows. 'Go on,' she says carefully.

'Kelly Gifford was throwing around accusations about her mother being a crook and she mentioned Bigham, who was on our radar.'

'What happened then?'

'We had to basically tell them to keep a lid on the noise but we made a note of it all. Tried to keep an eye on Kelly Gifford but she went right off our radar after that.'

'Where do you think she went?' says Rose.

Moony makes a face. 'We heard she was travelling. Our theory was that she knew she was in danger from Bigham so she tried to disappear.' She eyes Rose. 'We knew about you, of course.'

Rose forces herself to take a deep breath, prompting a knife of pain in her side. 'Why didn't she take me with her?' she says. As if it is simply one of many questions and not *the* question screaming in her mind.

'Probably to protect you,' says Moony. 'Figured you were safer where you were.'

There's silence for a moment while both women sip their drinks.

'She was sighted again about six years later, around the time our investigation was at its absolute peak, in London. But then she vanished off the face of the earth again.'

Rose's heart is beating uncomfortably hard. 'Did you question Bigham about it?' she says. 'And Adele?'

'Yep,' says Moony. 'But we never found anything suspicious. I think the general feeling was that she maybe came back to get a look at how you were doing and then used a fake identity to melt away again.'

Rose didn't remember finishing the drink. She stares into the empty glass. She can feel Moony's eyes on her. It's an uncomfortable sensation, making her want to flee so she can try to digest all this.

'I'm sorry,' says Moony. 'This is a lot to take in, I imagine.'

Rose nods. Then meets her gaze. 'I think what I really want to know is why you hired me, Sheila,' she says. 'Because it all feels a little bit crazy to me right now that I ended up working with you.'

Moony's expression softens. She reaches across the table as if she is going to touch Rose then seems to think again and places her palm flat on the table so her rings tap.

'I know it looks like an odd decision,' says Moony, her voice low.

'Certainly does,' says Rose. It's impossible to hide the rising emotion and she's conscious of speaking a little too loud. 'It looks a bit like it's tied up with a vendetta that has nothing to do with me at all. I was only a little girl. Is it because of your husband?'

Moony frowns and raises a hand to silence her. 'Whoa,' she says. 'Before you start going off in all sorts of mad directions here, let me reiterate what I said to you before. It was total coincidence that you ended up being on that case last year and it came up on the UCIT radar. I have no vested interest in having you come and work for me other than the fact that you seemed like a good policewoman with . . . as it turned out, certain skills. But it's not some fucked-up thing connected with all that. None of it was your story – not really.'

Rose is suddenly overwhelmed with exhaustion. She is so, so wrong about that. Every bit of it is her story.

'Look,' says Moony, softly now. 'I wish I had more for you. But your mother – your real mother – probably had good reasons for doing what she did.'

There's a long and uncomfortable pause. Rose doesn't trust herself to speak.

Moony shifts in her seat. 'Are you all right?' she says.

Rose nods, numbly.

'Do you want to stay here tonight?' Moony continues. 'I can make us some dinner and we'll watch telly. No need to even talk. It's just that . . . well you don't look all that great right now.'

Rose gets up slowly. 'No,' she says. She feels winded, literally, and has to take a moment to gather herself. 'I need to get back. But thank you for telling me the truth.'

Moony looks a little shamefaced and mumbles something about having wanted to tell her for ages but never finding the right moment.

At the front door, Rose wants to flee without any further discussion but as she goes to leave, Moony touches the sleeve of her coat.

'Rose,' she says. 'I hope you'll stay. I think we still have work to do and I think you have a lot to offer UCIT.'

Rose offers a sad smile. 'If UCIT survives,' she says.

'Yes,' says Moony, standing a little straighter. 'But I really am working on that.'

Rose turns. 'Goodnight, Sheila,' she says, walking slowly away.

45

Rose lies in bed that night staring up at the ceiling as car lights wash across it and the shadows turn from grey to black. There is no prospect of sleep.

Her mind has been churning with too many thoughts to process. The idea that her mother was alive for so much longer than she had believed is too big a thing to make sense of right now. That's something she's going to need to take out and look at from many different angles. Maybe it never will make sense.

She keeps circling back to that night. Not the one Moony knows about. The one seared onto her memory. The mysterious woman. The shouting. The sudden silence.

She never saw the woman leave, even though she had looked out of the bedroom window every time she heard a sound in the street.

Adele had been so strange after that night and drank more than ever.

Rose's body reacts to the shape in the bay window of the room before her mind does. She's out of the bed and holding the police baton, yelling, in one smooth move.

But it is only the hunched form of Adele, silently crying and wringing her hands, which are filthy again. Why are her hands so dirty?

Rose's heart is beating so hard she can barely catch her breath. 'What do you want?' she screams. 'What is it?'

Adele seems to melt away again with the force of her shouting.

As the night endlessly ticks by, she thinks of herself, smaller, looking through the bars of the stairs and feeling cold inside at the adult drama playing out behind closed doors.

She thinks of Gregory, sitting in the house where a murder had been hidden for so long that it ended up leading to more unnecessary deaths. She thinks of the pain buried within the walls of that house, destined to be played out again and again in a terrible loop of suffering and loss.

She thinks of Vincent. About a suitcase of bones that wouldn't be forgotten. The remains of a human life that never got to have any of the good things that may have been in his future. Remains that were literally right under her nose but she was too blind to see them.

Rose thinks about cowards who can't face up to the terrible things they've done.

Rose wonders why she keeps dreaming of dirt and graves.

She's not sure whether a few minutes have passed, or longer. But she pulls on clothes without paying much attention to what they are.

Almost on autopilot, she pushes her bare feet into her boots and goes outside. A thin, misty rain instantly chills her to the bone and she remembers that night recently when she found herself out there in her sleep.

Her subconscious mind is such a busy little bee, it seems. Maybe she needs to listen to it more often.

Rose cracks open the swollen door on the broken-down shed at the side of the garden, which she hasn't been in for at least fifteen years, that she can recall. She's not even sure she will find what she needs in here.

But luck is on her side for once.

She goes to the bottom of the garden and stands for a moment as icy rain mixes with the tears on her cheeks.

Then Rose Gifford lifts the spade and begins to dig.

Acknowledgements

I'm not sure readers know how much it means to authors when they get in touch to say they've enjoyed our books. It really is the biggest thrill and I want to thank every single one of you for your messages. Thanks also to the readers who have left such lovely reviews for book one in this series. I'm so happy that you love Rose as much as I do!

My crime writer and ex-policeman friend Neil Lancaster was an absolute star when writing this book, providing me with endless help on my many, many queries about police procedure, but also about geography for a crucial section of the book. Thanks too to (ex) DC Nigel Horner, newly retired. (I hope you are finally getting to do that travelling, Nigel!)

Emma Haughton, as ever, provides brilliant help on my most horrible early drafts (seriously . . . you wouldn't want to see them!) and if you haven't read her book *The Dark* yet, you're missing a treat.

Em Dekanor educated me in the highly serious business of jollof. I am looking forward very much to tasting it with her sometime soon.

My agent Stan gave me such brilliant editorial notes on the first 'proper' draft that it ended up being a relatively painless procedure getting it to the finish line. Thank you, Stan, as always for the great eye and also the shoulder when I'm having a wobble about it all.

I have been so blessed with the editors I have worked with over the years but I really feel I have hit the jackpot with Phoebe Morgan. She not only understands this process from the point of view of a publisher, but she really gets what it is like as a writer, because she is one too. (You should also check out *her* brilliant books!)

Thanks to copy editor Helena Newton and Susanna Pedder in publicity.

Colin Scott, you were as ever an absolute blast!

And finally, thanks to my husband Pete, who ends up so many bits of help over the writing process that I genuinely don't think I could do this without him.

I wrote the first draft of this during the height of the pandemic, when I would hear ambulances going past in my bit of London many times a day. I would also like to thank all the keyworkers who risked their lives to serve and care for the rest of us.

Making up stories when the world is melting down can seem like a pointless task. But it's my belief that we need fiction more than ever during these difficult times. It gives us that all-important escape from our everyday lives, allowing us to step inside the shoes of people totally removed from ourselves. And, selfishly, it was a lovely thing for me step into the world of Rose and the UCIT team again, while the real world was in turmoil around me. I hope you will enjoy reading this as much as I did writing it and I can't wait to show you what happens next.

Please keep getting in touch. I do so love to hear from you!

Caroline Green, London
December 2021

Twiter: @carolinesgreen
Instagram: carolinegreen70
Email: carolinegreenwriter@gmail.com

Even in your dreams you're not safe . . .
The nightmare is only just beginning . . .

When DC Rose Gifford is called to investigate the death of a young woman suffocated in her bed, she can't shake the feeling that there's more to the crime than meets the eye.

It looks like a straightforward crime scene – but the police can't find the killer. Enter DS Moony – an eccentric older detective who runs UCIT, a secret department of the Met set up to solve supernatural crimes. Moony wants Rose to help her out – but Rose doesn't believe in any of that.

Does she?

As the killer prepares to strike again, Rose must pick a side – before a second woman dies.